Gemma O'Donoghue was born in Essex, which is where she predominately spent her childhood, apart from a three-year sojourn in Dublin. She currently lives in Chelmsford with her husband, growing a collection of cacti and carnivorous plants. Writing has always been her passion and nothing is more enjoyable to her than the prospect of creating a new world at her computer.

In the Company *of* Shadows

G. O'Donoghue

In the Company *of* Shadows

Vanguard Press

A CIP catalogue record for this title is
available from the British Library.

ISBN 978-1-80016-686-8

Vanguard Press is an imprint of
Pegasus Elliot Mackenzie Publishers Ltd.
www.pegasuspublishers.com

First Published in 2023

Vanguard Press
Sheraton House Castle Park
Cambridge England

Printed & Bound in Great Britain

This book is dedicated with love to my husband, Craig, to my parents, Helen and Eddie, and to my brothers, Liam and Ciaran.

And to the loving memory of Auntie Mitts, who encouraged me in my early writing career and is gone but not forgotten.

Prologue

Longrider

"*H*umanity was Earth's greatest parasite," the presenter stated dramatically.

Her attractive features twisted into righteous anger, but the coffee table severing her legs somewhat detracted from that effect. I will adjust the settings later, I thought to myself. I never really watch HV programmes anyway because my hunting duties keep me in the field most days and I have little free time. And even now, on a rare pyjama day, the only interesting programme available is a documentary about their discovery. People must think I'm a woman with a Shade on my brain for the amount of time I devote to these creatures.

The presenter faded and scenes of destruction on Earth now filled my living room. The view panned over a city with hundred-floor skyscrapers and offices. Not a spot of greenery in sight.

"No other species sucked the life out of our host the way we did. Our swarm of billions annihilated our resources and our contaminated planet began to die. Fertile countryside gave way to an urban sprawl. The air became a choking dustbowl of noxious fumes. Oceans contaminated by waste haemorrhaged sea life onto the shore or to the seabed and over two-thirds of marine species were wiped out. And inland, the situation was no better. Many animals were overhunted. Others died because of the destruction of their habitats and those of their prey. And the combination of this resulted in a mass extinction, worse than that at the time of the dinosaurs.

"Only on the point of outright destruction did humanity acknowledge their mistakes and regret ignoring the warning signs. With Earth's resources nearly spent, there was not enough time to make amends, only enough time to think of an escape strategy. And with this aim in mind, leading astronomers scanned the skies for a viable exoplanet. Earth's greatest scientists, using high-powered telescopes, discovered a significant expanse of water and indications of plant life and most importantly oxygen, on a reachable planet. This planet was humanities' best chance of escape and was subsequently known as Diomedia.

"With the destination located, two space vessels were built and stored in separate, specifically designed locations on Earth, one in China and another in the United States. They were respectively christened *The Hopeful Voyager* and *The Traveller*. Every country in the world contributed to the production of the vessels and pooled money, materials and technological resources into their development. Each ship was made from fused silica for durability and reinforced by force fields to dispel smaller comets and asteroids, all essential to travel through the great expanse of space, further than any vessel in history. These ships were the pinnacle of modern technology and moved at three times light speed. Each ship contained ten thousand souls selected by lot with each country having a proportional representation in the lottery relative to their population size. Alongside them, another one thousand technicians were included to oversee maintenance work during the flight. The risks were great because at this point no manned exploration into deep space had successfully taken place. Nonetheless, mankind was desperate to escape certain death on Earth.

"With great optimism and hope, they vowed to learn from past mistakes and make their new home an Eden for future generations to come.

"In 2310, eighty years after the departure from Earth, *The Hopeful Voyager* started to slow as it neared Diomedia's solar system. The passengers became extremely restless, perhaps due to the glimpse of freedom after years of controlled living conditions. Understandably, their impending freedom created great expectations."

Suddenly the images of the spaceships dispersed and another woman appeared in the middle of my living room. She wore an old-fashioned bronze uniform, the kind they used to wear on board the ships, and her hair was pulled into a bun. This new woman announced herself as Amy Worth before beginning to recall her own experiences over soft idyllic music.

"There was anticipation in the air that spread until everyone was filled with an excited energy, including myself. Children eagerly pressed their noses up against the windows to get their first glimpse of our new

10

home. Through the misted glass we saw a super continent with water all around it and I remember thinking, water, unpolluted fresh water! It was amazing."

She vanished and was replaced by a sweeping scan of the desert landscape. Amy's voice continued. "Although we were so close, we'd had to wait because it wasn't safe to charge headlong into this unexplored area without first scouting the region. An initial reconnaissance group went down in a smaller vessel and scoped out the proposed landing destination. They did a lot of tests at ground level to confirm gases in the atmosphere weren't toxic and hospitable to human life; they tested soil quality; they ensured that no dangerous creatures loitered in wait to attack passengers as they disembarked. Of course, at that time we'd no idea about the Shade menace and no way to search for such creatures.

"Our droids looked further inland to find potential locations to settle in. They identified a formidable range of hills with a fresh water stream running from one of them as the most likely choice, later known as 'Mayton Hill': our future capital state. Other options were beside a huge lake north of the hills or further into the desert on a flat plain with plenty of local wildlife residing there. Beyond this the land was hostile and bare.

"Once all the tests were complete, and we were given the all-clear, *The Hopeful Voyager* descended. Our arrival on the new planet is simply known as 'Landing Day', and it is from this point all calendars on Diomedia are dated. A new planet and a new beginning.

"Once we landed, we wheeled out several pre-assembled temporary houses to create a mobile town; these buildings were fragile and intended to last a decade at most but useful until we could erect permanent housing. We also brought out our potted vegetation and the livestock that we reared on the ship. We kept them near the mobile houses because we weren't sure what kind of native animals lived here. And it was a good thing we brought them because Diomedia's creatures have a tough texture, a bit like eating sandy rubber.

"It was a simple life to begin with and a tremendous community spirit prevailed. Everyone's energy went into setting up the new states. And more hands would have definitely helped. But, unfortunately, there was no sign of the second ship, *The Traveller*. Our vessels lost contact during the voyage and it was never re-established and sadly, we have no way of

11

knowing their fate. It is speculated that the ship encountered technical failures, or was perhaps hit by an asteroid and some hope that it still journeys through space, and shall arrive safely one day… no one can know. Those poor souls…

"Apart from the shadow cast from the missing ship, everyone was busy building our new settlements and our new lives and we'd no suspicions of what was to come. It all started with the death of a boy named Charlie Lockwood…"

✱✱✱

"Pass me the ball!" a blond-haired child cried. He wiped a mop of hair out of his eyes, which immediately fell back in place once he moved his hand away.

"You've got to try a bit harder than that, Taylor." An older boy around ten years old shoved him over and ran off with the ball. Anyone could recognise his face. This was Charlie.

The blond child got up and blew a raspberry at him and kicked the ground moodily. The housedroid rolled up beside him, and its caterpillar tracks crunched to a halt while it waited patiently for Taylor to continue. He looked up. His brother waited up ahead, ball tucked under his arm and smiling benignly. Charlie coaxed Taylor with a promise to take it easier on him when they reached the field.

He ran to catch up.

When they reached their field, they made their way towards the goalposts, a couple of boulders naturally set about two metres apart. A few smaller creatures munched at the vegetation, ignoring the children.

The two boys halted abruptly.

Although the sun shone directly overhead, sharp narrow shadows coloured the ground like zebra stripes. The largest of these detached from a goalpost and floated upwards and then towards them until it was halfway across the field. Black-brown in colour, the haze was unusual and seemed alive. The holes in the mist appeared to shape a gaping maw, but as its dark form shrunk, the gaps disappeared; this was a Shade.

When the Shade reached one of the animals eating some dry shrubs, it hovered above it. The Shade flickered and twisted over the creature, almost touching the body before retreating away. It continued to float over the animal as it walked to another patch of shrubs.

Charlie went to investigate. Taylor remained, scared and obviously unwilling to go closer. Pulling at his brother's sleeve, Taylor motioned back the way they had come. Charlie slapped his hand away.

"I want to check it out. You can stay here if you want, baby!"

Taylor was visibly torn between staying with his brother and running away. After some internal deliberation, the former won out.

"I'll come with you... but be quick. I'm scared and I think it's looking at us?"

"Don't be stupid! Mist doesn't have eyes. It can't see anything," he chided his brother. "Droid six-zero-three, follow us."

Charlie slowly approached the Shade as Droid six-zero-three trailed him a metre behind. Taylor followed, a few paces back.

The Shade heaved and contracted. The movement grew more pronounced as the boys drew closer. It reached out with translucent arms that beckoned, called, and moved from its spot above the animal and towards the children.

✳✳✳

I spat out my coffee with laughter.

Another instance where the media anthropomorphised Shades — I have *yet* to see an accurate portrayal. It is not clear cut — it is not known whether they are sentient or mindless beings because they display instances of both. And having hunted these creatures for the best part of two decades, I should know. And they certainly do not act like ghostly paedophiles. Whoever created this documentary was definitely not a Hunter.

My interest in the programme waned, just not enough to switch it off. I heard the representation of a Shade takeover was decent.

✳✳✳

Slowly, the boys approached the Shade. Their arms lowered. Taylor's face blanched in fear. He looked at his brother, who appeared nothing but determined.

Without warning, the creature surged forward and slammed into Charlie's face. It gripped onto his neck and cheeks as Charlie stumbled back and fell over, then the creature seemed to be absorbed into the boy. Taylor's legs gave way and he dropped to the ground in terror. He closed his eyes and crawled away on his belly. A strange snarl came from his brother. Taylor kept his eyes shut. Droid six-zero-three was circling them both uselessly. It was not programmed for this situation. Taylor shouted at it to get their parents and it hurtled away and back to town to bring assistance.

Charlie was convulsing wildly. Blood poured profusely from his mouth. His jaw had elongated and broadened quickly. His lips curled, exposing teeth like razor-sharp needles. His hands curled and nails lengthened. The transformation took mere minutes.

Then Charlie stopped shaking. He abruptly sat up as if pulled and then knelt on his haunches, his back curved unnaturally. His breathing returned to normal as the bleeding subsided into a small trickle. He crouched in the grass, low and motionless.

"Charlie? Charlie? Are you okay?" Taylor asked tentatively.

No response.

"Charlie?"

Suddenly, his brother looked up.

***

Hours later, a search party reached the field. A white ball lay discarded by the stone goalpost, rolling back and forth in the wind.

The open field made the boys easy to spot. Their father broke into a run; even from a distance everyone could see the amount of blood on the ground. The others followed, drawing their guns in precaution.

Charlie crouched in the same hunched position, watching the new people. At his feet, Taylor lay sprawled across the ground, his body twisted and his throat torn.

When he reached them, their father slumped down and retched at the sight of his young son's broken body.

Charlie's face was hidden by a mask of blood. With a gaping maw, he lunged at his father. His new hunger was insatiable.

***

The images faded from the screen and the original presenter reappeared.

"All three bodies were returned to town and buried quietly. In their complete confusion, the search party decided to hide what happened and even the grief-stricken mother was not privy to the truth, that Charlie attacked his father and then was shot by the search party. Instead, they claimed their deaths were a tragic accident that occurred in the fields, they climbed and fell from some boulders, Taylor's and his father's partially eaten remains attributed to a scavenger.

"Inevitably truths will out, particularly unpleasant ones, and over the course of the next few months there were several strikingly similar murders. All victims had torn stomach cavities and evidence indicating partial consumption. The murderers lingered near the bodies after death, defending the kill like a predator and the majority killed due to their predilection for extreme violence against would-be captors. As learned to a regretful cost, it's unsafe to tackle them unarmed. Those captured were hospitalised for testing. Eventually, the original search party admitted everything to the police. Some blamed them for their silence and called for them to be exiled from the colony. However, their voices were few and this did not happen. After the Shades' discovery, authorities agreed it was impossible to foresee the threat because nothing resembled them on Earth and they were acquitted.

"The police exhumed Charlie's body. Autopsy results indicated his skeleton was severely distorted and did not resemble injuries sustained from a fall, as the search party originally told them. Also, despite the decay, they found evidence of human flesh in his stomach confirming the link between Charlie and the later murderers. Every person infected by a Shade shares the same distinctive traits of distorted jaw, mutated spine and strong nails like claws, sharp enough to easily pierce flesh. Inhabitants were informed of the symptoms and told to avoid those infected.

"Doctors continued their investigations and concluded the

transformations resulted from an unknown malady affecting the senses and skeleton, a new type of plague for a new planet. And frantically, they tried to find a cure. They combined samples of DNA with various drugs, used radiotherapy to target the altered cells and brain surgery to rid them of their violent streaks and return them to normal, all to no avail. Treating it remains a mystery to this day.

"A small minority of infected escaped from the settlements into the wilderness, their hunger drawing them to the farms and native herds beyond before their friends or family knew of their infection, and are occasionally spotted by farmers out in their fields or leaving behind the brutal murders of livestock. People felt afraid to venture outside the settlements alone or without a weapon in case they encountered a diseased individual. City walls were erected in an attempt to stop the infected returning and armed men stationed along them all hours of the day. Nonetheless, with a lack of understanding about how the disease originated, people still became infected and the murders kept occurring; the wall guards and police could not respond quickly enough to reported infected sightings.

"Nowhere was confirmed as a safe zone. No one wanted to leave their homes without a medical mask or a weapon. Many couldn't help but think of the Black Death in Medieval Europe; no one knew who would be struck next. It seemed like a divine curse. Some pioneers worried there was something doomed about their chosen location, so many decided to pack their possessions and settle by the substantial lake several miles further up the coast from the original settlement. It was separated from the ocean by a narrow strip of land; this city state is now known as 'Winsford Lake'. A smaller group of pioneers decided to relocate further inland to see if life was safer and cleaner near the mountains and named the city state 'Springhaven', restricting their contact to the other colonies ever since.

"For years, doctors tried to treat this mysterious illness. Extensive testing didn't find any viral or bacterial reason for the strange behaviour of the infected. However, they did discover an abnormality on all afflicted patients' brain scans — a curious shadow that fluxed across the brain. These shadows moved independently from scan to scan and most often settled over the frontal lobe, where they slowly ate away at the brain. These shadows seemed to be alive, turning, swirling and dispersing inside diseased skulls. Doctors could not make any sense of it; such a thing was unheard of in medical history, only loosely related to a parasite. They could not understand where the disease came from, how it entered the skull or how to extract it. Surgery proved ineffective because when a patient's skull was opened, they found only healthy brain, although with a portion eaten away as if cauterized. The blots on the scans resembled sun spots or shadows, so the doctors named it 'Umbras Cerebros' or as it is simply abbreviated, 'Umbras'.

"Typically, infected patients die in their beds after three years fighting the disease, their brain eaten through to a point where it caused respiration difficulties, heart irregularities and paralysis. But in death they are still highly contagious. During the first few minutes, post-mortem, a member of medical staff always became infected; as we know now, Shades leave the dead body to search for their next host in the immediate area. Contractors were commissioned to create specialised cells, in which everything inside could be frozen with a liquid nitrogen spray. Once it was safe to enter, the body could be removed to a safe location and incinerated, the Shade unable to leave the frozen body. Since this discovery, there have been no cases of the disease spreading from a patient to another host and it is now the accepted method in hospitals for the disposal of contaminated bodies.

"After a long spell of experimentation, a vet inadvertently made a medical breakthrough for Umbras when he witnessed the moment of contamination first hand."

A middle-aged man appeared in the centre of the room with his legs again disappearing behind the table. He held his glasses in one hand with the other thrust in his trouser pocket. He began.

"It started off as an unremarkable day, as these things tend to do, and at the time I was tending to a sick goat and didn't immediately notice the other animals' unusual behaviour. The farmer left to find out what spooked his goats and I didn't see him go. When I looked up from my work, I noticed the goats jostling at the far side of the field behind me and they strained against the fence like they were trying to escape. I searched for the farmer and eventually saw him at the edge of the field. A curious dark mist suddenly descended upon him swirling frantically trying to force entry. Then it entered his body and he fell, convulsing, to the floor. I couldn't believe it.

"Uncertain of the best course of action, I left the farm to find help — I wasn't really thinking clearly — and when I returned to the farm with a doctor and some armed men, we found the farmer devouring the sick goat. He was ripping into its flesh like a beast. We were horrified. He tried to charge us, but we tranquilised him and, when he was unconscious, I quickly inspected his body and noted he'd the same lengthened jaw and claw-like nails that affected those infected with Umbras. And his spine extended and his stance clearly altered, though he was sprawled upon the ground. A link formed in my mind.

"When we took him to the hospital, they ran usual tests for suspected Umbras infection and I managed to view the scans, which is not normally permitted, but I think the doctors were far too busy to notice my presence, and I saw a peculiar moving shadow across the farmer's brain and I enlightened them about the strange mist that attacked him before he became ill. I ventured my half-formed idea about the connection between the shadows or Shades, as they're now known, and the disease. Once the doctors confirmed it was indeed Umbras, they concluded the disease originated from these Shades."

At this point, the original presenter took over again. "Shades enter the body by forced inhalation via the nose, mouth and, in some rare cases, through the eyes and latch onto the victim's brain like a parasite. Doctors believe they are intercellular, endoparasites of unknown qualities; a free-moving parasite and not linked to any particular cell within a body. Umbras also lends the host increased physical durability, strength and speed. However, these advancements are outweighed as the parasite sucks the life out of the host; the longest recorded length of infection before death is just three and a half years.

"With a name and a cause for the disease, all that was left was to increase measures to stop infection, protect ourselves from the Shade menace and find a cure.

"Today, sixty-two years on from the Shade discovery, Mayton Hill is shaped by our need to prevent and protect against Shade attacks. The colony benefited from the rolling hills that overlook the coast. High walls surround the town with an even parapet running the length of it, even the farms, directly outside the town, have walls surrounding them to protect livestock. All wall guards are fully covered by specialised uniforms, armed with guns and gas masks to protect them from a substance as dangerous and as deadly as any toxic gas. They are our front line of defence. Every inhabitant must carry a gas mask on their person at all times, and children are taught in schools about the procedures for an attack and how to attach their masks properly.

"Winsford Lake, the second largest settlement, adopted a similar strategy. Guards patrol the walkways and on the very edges of the town, although their gas masks are different and allow citizens to spend a few minutes underwater in emergency situations. Shades avoid water and will not attack a person already immersed.

"As humanity adapted to live with the threat, we discovered that Shades are a valuable resource once we learnt how to utilise their power. Volcanologists studying the activity near the Droma vent observed Shades actively avoiding sulphur dioxide clouds and witnessed an instance where a creature was hit by a blast; it densified within seconds, turning into a tar-like fluid. They collected it and brought the sample to the hospitals for testing, and there, scientists discovered Shades' bodies are highly flammable in their condensed, liquid forms.

"But almost fifty times greater is their ability to burn whilst inside a creature; the animal's solid form amplifies a Shade's reactiveness and it is greater than any other fuel when set alight. This unusual discovery occurred when they first started to dispose of infected bodies via cremation. The original furnaces melted due to the extreme heat.

"Humans later learnt to utilise this fuel source and black energy is widely used to power homes, cars and towns, despite the difficulty and danger in acquiring it by registered Hunters. Black energy is a controversial subject, ever since it was first introduced, and activists constantly petition and protest against the way be-Shaded animals are burnt in an incinerator and have tried to end the practice, though they had little success in the courts. Also, to avoid targeting by activists, Shade Hunters remain anonymous for safety reasons…"

Shade hunting carries a lot of dangers and I do not need a programme to tell me about that fact. I switched the device off.

19

Part One

"It is on companionship, integrity and hope that we lay the foundations of our new world..."

- George Stanton, fifth captain of the *Hopeful Voyager*

1

Landmine

From my vantage point at the top of the valley, I observed the miles of rocky desert on either side. It's familiar territory and a favourite site for Hunters, even for a freelancer like me. Rain hasn't fallen here for months, possibly years. Above, the sky was clear and the sun nearly overhead. The ground so dry it crunches underfoot and dust floats around your boots — clouds of the stuff roll along the plains, expanding by the minute. Only the strongest, hardiest plants grow in this region, leafless, twiggy trees and shrubs, scattered in clumps across the landscape. About a kilometre in the distance, I watched a herd of gi' mont dragons traipsing towards a couple of scant trees. All eight were twice as tall as humans, and twice as long, too, their thick legs stomped on the ground, kicking up more dust, and their pale reptilian skin shimmered in the sunlight, herbivores but they could be aggressive if you got too close. There aren't many predatory animals on Diomedia and none with a taste for human flesh; apparently, we're toxic to them and they can sense it and usually give us a wide berth. Most animals are scaled here and frankly disgusting to eat unless you don't have another choice.

But I'm not a naturalist. I'm a Hunter. Though not of the gi' mont lizards below. My targets are other, more threatening, creatures with bodies so dark and ghostly they pass for shadows to the untrained eye. Droids can't help track them. Shades just avoid them and dart out of range. So, the task of acquiring them for ore falls on registered Hunters. As a freelancer with a proven reputation and Master Hunter status, my services are in demand by all the major black energy suppliers. Yesterday, I was commissioned by ShadeCo, the leader in the market, to help them achieve their monthly quota. ShadeCo also, happily enough, happens to be the company offering the biggest payment for Shade ore.

Midday is the best time to locate Shades because natural shadows are short, so their peculiarities are clear. I've been in the area for a while and it doesn't seem promising. I haven't seen any signs suggesting a Shade is nearby and my eyepiece is quiet.

Time to move, Butcher.

I re-entered my Jeep, put my equipment bag in the back and gestured for the engine to turn on and continued along the uneven ground. In the quiet valley, the engine roared and echoed. Each crunch and snap marked the plants that my vehicle left in its path. Dust whipped up behind the Jeep, obscuring the rear-view mirror.

After a time, I stopped again to assess the area.

A cluster of trees in the distance looked promising — the plants looped around in a doughnut shape with a muddy pool in the centre. The unusually long shadows darted off from the trees, left, right and centre. No animals around despite being the most habitable space for miles; animals typically have a special sense for these creatures and spook easily.

I parked near the circle of trees and didn't exit immediately, just waited. I folded my arms over the steering wheel and noticed my left one was tanned with dust because I'd leaned it on the windowsill during the drive. This stuff gets everywhere if you're not careful.

My eyepiece drew my attention to two medium density Shades. Judging from previous experience, they'd probably bring in seven hundred Diomedian Argents apiece inside a goat and maybe scrape fifty outside. One was attached to the largest tree in the oasis, the trunk three times as wide as the others. It seemed like an obvious choice because the shadow was larger and offered greater camouflage. The second Shade was ten metres to my left, flickering in the shadow of a boulder, like air in a scorching desert.

Before getting started, I checked my gas mask was fixed properly. The mask is by far a Hunter's most important piece of equipment. Shades cannot enter a body with a covered mouth, eyes, ears or nose. Keeping low and watchful, I carefully opened the door and crept around to the back of the vehicle. In the boot, I'd a goat lying prostrate, its legs bound together by string and the sedatives slowly wearing off. It bleated sleepily when it saw me. Instead, I lifted it up and carried it over my shoulders. An easy task for a guy my size.

Next, I moved towards the trees, cautiously entering through a gap. I walked to the centre and hopped over the waterlogged spaces. With one hand, I steadied the goat on my shoulders while the other held my rifle, pre-loaded with Shade-effective ammo. These bullets are designed to release a plume of sulphurous gas on impact, which merge with a Shade's cells, condensing and killing it in seconds. The weapon would be used as a last resort. The aim was to get one in the goat. There was a nice space to place the animal between a teardrop-shaped bog and a fallen tree. I lowered it down and untied the rope around its belly, all the while never taking my eyes from the shifting shadows. I pegged its rope to the ground and tied it to the collar around the goat's neck. Finally, I untied the string around its legs, nicked one of its legs with a knife so that it bled a little, and stepped back.

Almost immediately, the two Shades began to flicker and detach from their resting places. I noticed I was too close too late to get out of range. They would attack me instead of the goat if I moved quickly. They prefer intelligent beings perhaps because there is more brain to feast on — I never trained at a Hunting academy so I'm not sure on specifics. Drowsily, the goat rolled onto its belly and staggered upright. Giving it a hard push, I coaxed it forward. I raised my rifle and aimed at the closest Shade.

The bigger Shade drifted over like a swirling ball of black chaos and hovered near the animal. The fur on the goat's back bristled and fear immobilised it. It shouldn't be long now. I held my breath.

Moments passed. Nothing happened. My aim alternated between the two Shades.

Take the fucking bait!

Even without control of an animal's body, a Shade is dangerous and I'd the scars to prove it. Automatically, I touched the straps on my gas mask. They were secure.

Unexpectedly, a third Shade jumped forward. It surprised me. The Shade hadn't registered on the eyepiece, so it's a small one. It smacked the goat in the face and gripped its mouth to force it open. The Shade on its back vibrated furiously and attacked the other, as if it violated a code, the stake claimed on the first touch. It wrestled the intruder away from the goat's mouth. Most Hunters usually sit on the fence when it comes to Shades' intelligence. Sometimes they appear to talk to each other and move with purpose. And other times just plain stupid. I've seen a Shade attempt to possess itself and do loop-the-loops chasing its lower section. So it's hard to say either way.

The Shades continued to struggle above the afflicted goat, which fell to the ground, injured and terrified.

Meanwhile, the other watched almost interestedly, waiting. Then it surged forward, lengthening and entering the animal through its nose until nothing remained outside of the body. Only a trickle of blood indicated it had gone in.

The air filled with static and vibrated with energy. As the goat convulsed, the two Shades angrily scraped and tore at its fur, trying to force the other Shade out. It was too late. The transformation had begun. Foam streamed from the goat's mouth. I'd got the jackpot, now to collect the others.

I fired.

The gun shot rang out and the stock recoiled into my shoulder. When the shot smacked straight into one of the floating Shades, a gush of toxic air broke out of the bullet and engulfed it. Seconds later, the Shade splattered onto the ground as a tar-like substance.

The other Shade bolted as I approached. I dropped down to one knee and took aim at the retreating creature, then lowered my weapon. It'd be wasted. The bullets are effective at a distance of twenty metres or less and the Shade was already out of range. Within the industry, its well-established current hunting guns are outdated and an upgrade long overdue.

Leaping to my feet, I strode over to the goat and unravelled the rope around its chest. Crucial minutes passed since the entrance of the Shade and its convulsions started to ease. It bent its head back and stared at me while its legs shuddered independently. Straddling the goat, pinning it with my knees, I forced its legs together and wrapped them up with the rope. I knotted and double knotted it to ensure it was secure, but the goat's head was still free and it tried to take a chunk out of my arm. I punched it on the nose to subdue it and tied its jaw together with a belt.

Despite the bonds, the animal fought and shook and bounced off of the ground. I carried it with both hands to the Jeep. Climbing into the boot and then over the backseat, I locked the goat in a wire cage and padlocked the door. I shifted the cage onto the floor and wedged it behind the front and back seats. There was another cage on the backseat too holding a Shade-infected chicken I'd caught earlier. It pecked angrily at the bars as soon as I approached, but was safely held inside. Next to that was a bag containing a canister with a stopper. I took it out and returned to the tree circle.

The sludgy mess of the dead Shade had spread out and some started to seep into the mud. Stooping down, I opened the canister and placed it face down in the middle of the sludge and it began to suck up the liquid. When there was none left on the ground, the canister flipped itself upright and resealed itself.

Satisfied with my catch, I slung my gun over my shoulder and strode over to the Jeep. Another successful hunt complete! There wasn't anything to do now except return to Mayton and claim my money.

∗∗∗

"Is there a whole one inside this chicken? A whole Shade? It looks too small to contain one…" The young man crouched by the wire cage and poked his finger at the mesh. *Stupid.*

I was about to slap his hand away when he straightened up, amazement still showing on his smooth face. The collar of his technician's coat slipped down and he quickly readjusted it — clearly too big. I hadn't seen him before and doubted he'd been in the role long or he wouldn't be asking questions like that one. He's eager though — I'd give him that, if damn slow.

Hours had elapsed since I'd returned from the desert. These questions were getting irritating.

"How long have you worked here again?"

The youth glanced down at the heavy oak table next to him, embarrassed, and mumbled something I didn't catch. This table seemed out of place in a building otherwise cold and metallic. A large industrial scale sat on top of it with various screens bulging from the sides. Currently, all of them were blank. Inside the birdcage next to the scales, the chicken flapped its wings against the mesh, its clucks muffled by the tape wrapped around its beak. He checked his MID. This device is worn under the skin of the forearm and the images are entirely viewable. The skin around it looked pink so it must've been recently fitted, which would've placed him at sixteen, seventeen tops. He quickly read the screen. I glanced over his shoulder and saw that he was viewing the current price list, which indicated the amount of energy in each Shade per gram and the monetary worth.

"Could you please put the chicken onto the scales? Still in the cage, of course," he said, dividing his nervous gaze between the MID and me. "And you also need to fill in the H1-8 form — the one saying how much this animal weighed before the Shade infected it." This statement was nearly a question, as if he needed me to confirm. Inside the cage, the chicken clucked loudly — the tape had come unstuck.

After a short pause, he continued. "It says here all the cages have a standard issue weight and they can be deducted from the reading... but I still need to see the form."

Sighing in annoyance, I rooted through the pocket and emptied the contents onto the table. A grooved long-bladed knife clattered on the worktop, closely followed by a parking card.

"I've lost it." That was a lie. I hadn't bothered. His predecessor hadn't needed anything except the captured Shade, so I'd stopped completing the pointless H1-8 forms.

His face whitened. Deflated, the young man could not think of a way around the dilemma and let out a long breath of air. Apparently, his training hadn't covered this. He didn't know how to pay me without the information and I wasn't going to leave empty-handed, so it was an awkward situation.

When it was obvious he couldn't come up with a solution, I suggested, "I could fill in the form now?"

"I suppose," he mused and thought about it. "These forms are all electronically timed and dated when they're signed by the Hunter. And it'd look suspicious if it's signed a few minutes after you wrote it... unless... I wrote out a new one for you?"

"Fine by me," I shifted my weight onto my other foot. *This is going to take a while.*

This process was much smoother when Benji worked here. He was a grumpy bastard but very capable — and he understood the realities of hunting. And he knew that form completion isn't on most Hunters' minds — there were up to twenty-five forms that could be entered for each hunt but only five are actually mandatory, and they're a waste of everyone's bloody time. Benji knew that. In fact, the guy before him did too. In a few years, maybe the kid would relax once he's familiar with the job.

He sat down at the table and loaded a fresh form onto his MID.

"Surname?"

"Butcher."

"Forename?"

"Landmine."

A Hunter's alias is used instead of his real first name for privacy. The alias was a randomly generated phrase or word given to you once you passed the Hunter examinations. It's a precautionary measure introduced about thirty years ago because animal rights protestors target Hunters yet they're quite happy to use the energy generated from Shades. Hypocrites. Also, a couple of ShadeCo Hunters disappeared recently and it wasn't attributed to Umbras, so who knows what these activists are capable of?

He stopped typing and looked at me strangely. "What? I think I misheard you. Did you say Landmine?"

"Yeah."

"Okay…" There was a long pause. "How much would you say the chicken weighed before the take over?"

I decided to try my luck. "One kilo."

"One kilogram?" he repeated and didn't question it. "Could you kindly place the cage on the scales please? Thanks. Forty kilograms. Now I'll deduct the cage weight… It totals at thirty-seven kilograms and so that's five hundred and six Argents. Do you have your details with accounting?"

I nodded.

"I'll send these forms off and the money should be in your account soon. Have an excellent day, sir."

He held out his hand for me to take and waited uncomfortably for a few seconds before he realised it wouldn't be taken and let it drop.

"Hold up," I said. "We haven't finished. I've got a goat and a canister containing a Shade that needs valuating too."

When I finally left ShadeCo, the sun had lowered to the horizon and its beams cast long shadows across Mayton Hill. I felt exhausted. The last few hours of negotiations had been more draining than the hunt itself. After I'd signed off my hunt, they noticed they had mixed my details with another freelancer and needed me to complete a ton of forms before they'd allocate it to me instead. It should be sorted now. So all I wanted to do was go to bed for some well-earned sleep.

Mayton Hill, or Mayton to the residents, is spread across five hills with flat land in-between, and the largest hill towers over everything. Raising my gaze, I saw the tall circular fortress at the top. A single, steep stairway cut into the side of the hill wound up to it and the fortress was visible for miles around, far beyond the town walls and large enough to fit the majority of the population. It is an anti-Shade shelter for people to flee to in an attack. Most houses sit in the flat areas between hills and are one-storey domed structures with narrow awning windows, sturdy doors, and neutral-coloured walls to bounce off the sun's rays. The roads are broad and well-maintained, although all vehicles on the colony have sturdy wheels suitable for off-roading on the rocky desert ground. Learning from Earth, we recycle everything and Mayton's new president is passionate about our colony's cleanliness. When she came into office, she ordered a new line of maintenance droids to clean the streets and there are loads of bins throughout the town, each colour dedicated to particular materials.

On this planet, night brings hidden dangers. Authorities advise remaining indoors after dark, when the danger of Shade attacks increase because they're harder for the wall guards to spot. At night they're difficult to track and even my mask is unable to locate them efficiently. Though murders decreased recently due to heightened security, no one is ever completely safe. Even with the black energy industry booming, there seems to be an endless supply of Shades.

The streets were quiet.

At every step, the now-empty cages rattled and clanked against my leg and the sound rebounded along the street. Mayton was big enough that some people drove, unlike most other settlements, but my house was just a twenty-minute walk from the ShadeCo facility. It sat at the foot of the central hill, close to the steps leading up to the fortress and slightly removed from the other houses on the street. Apart from the extra space and unkempt garden around it, the house was unremarkable, average in size and design.

My MID unlocked the door automatically. I stepped through and entered the main living space that was part kitchen, part lounge. I'm not showy when it comes to furnishing, durability instead of luxury. The dining room chairs and settee were adequate just not so comfortable you could spend all day lounging on them. The bathroom to the side was the only private room. At the far end against the wall stood a wooden staircase leading up to my bedroom on the large, open mezzanine level. The bed was my greatest extravagance. It's a solid wooden frame with a foam mattress and soft down pillows, topped by a black and white throw covered in Celtic swirls. When I lie on it, I can look over the railing at the space below, able to see anyone trying to forcibly enter. Hanging over the chest of drawers beside the bed was a mangled toy duck, suspended on the wall by a length of twine around its body, tied to a hook. It's the *only* toy I've saved from childhood, somehow I couldn't bring myself to throw it away. Too many memories hidden in its old face.

The sparse dusk light filtered inside and formed pockets of darkness beneath the windows. I dropped the cages by the entrance and the door shut and locked behind me.

I addressed my hunger pangs with two rounds of cheese and pickle sandwiches, finished off with a pint of juice. Satisfied, I dragged my leaden feet up the steps to my bedroom, slumped onto the bed, and kicked off my heavy boots. It felt good to finally take them off after almost two days' hunting. I splayed my toes open. I couldn't be bothered to shower. Without undressing further, I lay back down and hoped for a dreamless sleep as I closed my eyes.

If you eat cheese before bed, it gives you nightmares.

The thought sprung into my head unbidden, and I tried to remember who'd told me the phrase. But it escaped me, revolving in my head until I fell asleep a few minutes later.

31

2

Longrider

I walked purposefully through the great vaulted corridors of ShadeCo's main office. My destination was the office of the current CEO, James 'Red' Martin. He personally arranged this meeting and his time was sacrosanct. In the twelve years I worked at ShadeCo, I have been there just twice. However, Red was more than my boss; he has been a family friend for years, my father's best friend in fact, and as a child I used to call him Uncle Red. He and my father worked on the same hunting team and one of my earliest memories was looking out of my bedroom window at their departing Jeep, wishing I could go with them; it was probably the source of my own desire to become a Hunter. When their group disbanded, Red's career soared within ShadeCo, although he never forgot his former teammates and used his influence to get them decent jobs within the company. So understandably, my father places him on a pedestal; the man can do no wrong in his eyes and he will never hear anything negative said against him. Despite our history, in the office, we needed to maintain a semblance of formality.

With every step, my camouflage bodysuit altered in hue to blend in with the walls and caused people in the hallways to do a double take at the floating head they were seemingly witnessing. I kept my canvas gas mask on even though I was inside a Shade-proof facility, whereas most workers remove them once they enter the foyer; these items combined with my unusual Mohican haircut jutting out of the top of the mask, separated me from the other, formally attired workers. This was a privacy matter, particularly as there were protestors smashing car windows in ShadeCo's parking lot today before they were scared away by the guards. There seems to be more activity of late. More than a few people glanced up from their desks as I passed by their office windows. It was fairly near the end of the working day, but not so close that workers were starting to go home or slacken their pace. The corridors were empty and my steps echoed alone across the marble floor. After a while, another's footfall joined in harmony with mine and increased until the individual walked around the corner.

Landmine Butcher.

He carried two empty cages and his broad shoulders lowered with fatigue. My first guess was he had just returned from the field, if the dust covering him was anything to go by. His dark hair shaggy and unkempt as usual and he was also wore his mask indoors. He wore a blue-and-white striped T-shirt that seemed to be a size too small and strained against his muscled arms and grey slacks. Several inches over six feet, he was nearly a foot taller than I but then Hunters come in all shapes, sizes and genders. As a freelancer, Landmine is not obliged to follow ShadeCo Hunter protocol as full-time Hunters do and comes and goes on a whim.

In my opinion, freelancers enter the profession for the money and do not respect Hunter traditions or values that have been with us almost as long as our time on Diomedia. They are not subject to regular hunting appraisals and I think their treatment of animals gave all Hunters a poor reputation in the first place and set the activists against us. ShadeCo animals are kept in the upmost comfort until they are used in the field, whereas freelancers tend to raise them in dire, constrained conditions difficult to moderate because inspectors give them a day's warning before they check anything. As a classically trained Hunter and coming from a hunting background, it's difficult to view freelancers with anything but scorn for dragging the profession through the mud.

Landmine nodded a greeting as he passed, which I curtly returned. I did not stop because I was pressed for time, apparently so was he.

Several minutes later, after travelling the length of the winding corridor and descending several flights of stairs, I arrived at a set of large double doors. They were locked. Normally, I was not permitted entry, but they temporarily increased my access rights. Beside the doors there was a recognition device. I removed my glove and placed my hand firmly on the pad and stated my pseudonym, "Longrider", in a clear voice. The unit lit up and scanned my hand. When I let my hand drop, it shot out a red beam and scanned my body too and then electronically repeated the name back. Shortly, the door slowly swung open and allowed me to proceed.

The restricted section of the building contained the executive staff offices. As such, the decor reflected the importance of the people who worked here; the walls and ceiling were white marble, veined with dark-green streaks, soothing plantasma flute music played softly from hidden speakers and catering droids weaved in and out of offices supplying drinks and sustenance. Security guards watched me carefully but let me pass without a hassle.

Following the corridor as it looped around, I passed a row of smaller offices before reaching a set of double doors with Red's name engraved in gold across them. I opened the doors and immediately stepped into his assistant's office. It was empty. She had left me a note on her desk saying she was called into another meeting but I could go in because he was expecting me.

The second set of doors was stiff. They took a lot of effort to shift and creaked painfully, as if shut for years and announced my entrance. As befitting his rank, his office was massive. The vaulted ceiling shot up to fourteen feet, the floor was a royal blue plush carpet that made you sink just a little with each step, and there were exotic flowering plants in each corner from the furthest explored regions of Diomedia. The CEO's solid oak desk was in the centre, positioned directly opposite the door, so he could easily see someone enter. At the moment, he was engrossed in his work and had not noticed me despite the outrageously loud creaking from the door hinges. On the far wall behind him stood floor-length windows displaying a bright sky and the sun sparkling over a calm sea. It was all a projection because most of ShadeCo was subterranean, but it gave the office a pleasant atmosphere.

I crossed the intervening space between the entrance and the visitor's chair. Red still did not look up. As I got closer, I saw through the translucent screen of his computer and observed Red focusing on his work, a deep V creasing his forehead as his eyes scanned the text in front of him. It was a while since I had last seen him and he appeared to carry extra weight, his suit strained over his barrel-chest, although this would be counteracted once he stood up because he easily reached two metres. A few strands of white cut through his rich dark auburn hair, which only slightly receded at the temples. Presently, he picked up the cigar and hung it from the corner of his mouth and left it there whilst he typed. I made a face. Medically speaking, they are no longer damaging to one's health, but they still stunk. I sat back in my chair and waited for him to finish what he was doing.

A few months ago, Red took me off my normal hunting schedule and temporarily assigned me to a highly confidential arms project, which aimed at developing a new range of hunting weaponry. He informed me it was the biggest project of its kind in the last decade and, as an experienced Master Hunter, my input was invaluable. Flattery apparently gets you everything because I agreed without even knowing all the details. I had been quite vocal about the inadequacy of current available weaponry; our guns were outdated, slow to handle due to their size, and far too heavy. It was time for change.

His gravelly voice finally boomed at me. "Good evening, Valya. I won't be long. Please help yourself to a sweet. They're quite refreshing." He passed me a bowl of lemon candies. I took one to be polite.

Typically, I did not allow the familiarity of using my real first name. But as we were alone, I let it pass. Nestled in his office in the heart of the building, I felt safe enough to remove my mask and rested it over the arm of the chair. It was boiling, as if the sun on the wall were real. A film of sweat covered my forehead and trickled down my face. I wiped it off with the back of my hand.

Finally, Red finished reviewing the document on the screen, placed his stylus on the table and turned his full attention to today's meeting. He took the cigar out of his mouth and tapped it on an ashtray.

"So…" He placed the cigar back in his mouth, which slightly muffled his words. "Tell me, how's the project going? Several contradictory reports have reached me and I'd like to know what's going on from you because I trust your judgement. After all this time, I'd hoped we have progressed," he added with a good-humoured smile.

As succinctly as I could, I explained the concepts and ideas the weapons team bandied about from the beginning to the current day, paying particular attention to describing the plans to reduce the size of the hunting rifles and the initial prototypes already created.

I stated, "I'm not keen on sending classified information via email so I've brought some blueprints with me with details about a few of the new guns and different types of ammunition capsules too."

Briefly, I rummaged through my backpack and produced an archaic tablet from my bag about the size of an A5 piece of paper and switched it on. Anything on MIDs could be copied. The tablet was more secure. I typed on the screen and when I found the documents required, I slid it forward on the table before him. His eyes lit up as he saw the contents of the first page. After scrolling ahead, he was visibly pleased with the information.

I continued. "Our technicians already created the first working prototypes for all of the weapons documented there and all of them are much smaller than usual weaponry, as per the spec, and those rounds have a much smaller calibre but contain the same amount of Shade-neutralising compound. It's just highly concentrated to allow us to create smaller weapons. Can you imagine? You can carry them around your waist and then bang!" I demonstrated with my two fingers and pretended to shoot him. "As easy as that! We've tested them out on the rifle range and have a few more sessions to go before we're finished with the range and after that, I'd like to take them onto the field to try them in action. For that, I need your permission..."

Red rested back in his chair and slapped the arms. He smiled widely. "Done and done. This is really something! I'm impressed, Valya, excellent work. You can tell the team that from me."

He placed his still-smouldering cigar onto the tray.

"If we can arm our Hunters with these lightweight weapons it'll increase our ore collection capabilities and make us the undisputed top producer of black energy. It'd secure our lead on the market beyond a doubt."

"It's definitely significant, but still, I'm not sure it'll increase our supplies by such a great extent, Red. When we planned and assembled the guns, our main concern was to ease the task of the Hunter. You know perfectly well how heavy the guns can be. It's a trial to carry them for long distances if your vehicle breaks down in the field. And you can't throw your weapons away with the Shades around, not without consequences."

"No, you don't want to come back with a razor smile. Umbras is a nasty affliction." He gave me a searching look. "I trust you haven't told anyone outside the project about this? Outside of the company, family or friends…"

I would never betray him or ShadeCo, and was offended he thought I might be corrupt. "Of course not!"

Red looked thoughtful and contemplative as he picked up the cigar again and took another drag. Giving him a glare, I decided to hold my tongue and occupy myself by snatching the tablet from the desk and placing it back in my bag, buckling the flap shut, then waiting for Red to continue. From the office next door, his PA had returned and her pleasant voice wafted over us as she talked to one of her assistants. Eventually, Red acknowledged his lack of tact.

"I'm sorry if I offended you, Valya, but it's my responsibility to remind you of your obligations to the company. As I'm sure you know, your contract forbids contribution to other suppliers, and that includes this project, and we can't afford to ruin this advantage. The blueprints are very promising and I'm interested in viewing the prototypes too. If I show them to the other board members, they'll be happy to give the go-ahead for field testing."

After this, he explained that rumours reached his ears that I had talked to other energy company representatives, and even if these rumours were false, it did not hurt to be careful. He said that ShadeCo could not afford to lose me as I was statistically their best Hunter and brought in a significant amount of Shade ore. *Again, flattery — but I'm not as easily appeased by it now*, I thought.

"Red, I'd never sell out. I thought you knew me better than that," I stated. My lips curled in distaste at the thought of such disloyalty.

Enough of this.

The meeting had finished and I wanted to leave before he insulted me further. Besides, I might say something I would regret later. I stood up, swung my bag over my shoulder, and reaffixed my mask.

"Bye, Red. A bit of advice, get your facts straight before you start accusing anyone else!"

Red looked at me in shock. Probably he was unused to being spoken to in that manner. I maintained a quick pace and barely acknowledged his PA, who was leaning against the door frame that divided the two offices. As I passed, she informed Red his next appointment with a group of,

'Springhavian yokels', was due to start in five minutes, and they were waiting in the reception area above.

Red's sigh echoed around the high ceilings as he mused aloud. "There's no rest for the wicked."

Damn right! I shut the door behind me with calculated amount of force, enough to show my annoyance yet not enough to rattle in the frame. It was probably construed as moody but satisfying nonetheless.

***

In hindsight, perhaps I acted a tad rashly... sometimes Red can be downright rude and you just have to show him you'll not tolerate it. How he became an executive, I'll never know…

Actually, I could not understand why he accepted the position as CEO of ShadeCo. Three of his predecessors met with untimely and suspicious deaths and it would be enough to put anyone off, even the most ambitious. I resolved to get another member of the team to meet him next time; I get the feeling he still sees me as a moon-eyed little girl in awe of his hunting prowess.

At any rate, I had another reason for being in this part of ShadeCo HQ — to speak to my father. It was a couple of weeks since I saw him and before I was allocated on this project we spoke several times a week, and I thought I should be the dutiful daughter and rectify the situation. I veered towards the staircase and further into the depths of the building to the generator rooms where he normally worked.

***

Whenever I enter the generator rooms, the immensity of the space always strikes me, and this occasion was no different. Twenty metres above my head were arched ceilings reinforced by metal girders shouldering the weight of the building above, strong enough to withstand the impact of a bomb. Much of the ground space was taken up by the three massive generators that whirred and vibrated with activity and the combined noise was deafening; most technicians wore specialised earpieces to protect themselves against the constant clamour. My mask muffled some of the sound, so it was bearable. Platforms were attached to the generators to allow technicians access to the mechanisms and railings ran along the length to ensure no one got too close to be sucked inside. Droids took on the more dangerous work and repaired the inside mechanics.

I walked alongside the middle generator and spotted my father testing the temperature levels; I recognised him from the rigid stance that stemmed from his bad back. Otherwise, it was difficult to tell the difference between them because they all wore identical fluorescent, yellow-jacketed uniforms. He stood on the platform connected to a generator with his back turned and absorbed in his task, so he did not notice me approach. He certainly could not hear me above the commotion.

"Father!" I shouted up. "Father!"

In a burst of inspiration, I took out a light, empty cartridge from my pocket and hurled it at the back of his head.

It worked and he turned around in surprise, massaging his neck and glancing over the banister. He looked much younger than his fifty-eight years. His angular face had kept the wrinkles at bay and his hair was still pale blond, the same colour as my own.

"Valya! What a pleasant surprise!"

Gah! "Don't use that name! It's Longrider when we're in here or anywhere public," I reminded him and checked if there was anyone close enough to eavesdrop. No one was nearby, fortunately,

"I'm sorry, Muffin. It just slipped out. How are you anyway?"

He's doing this on purpose now. That nickname is not acceptable in any situation!

"Old habits," he apologised as he shut the control panel. He descended the steps and asked, "Let's go somewhere quieter where we can talk."

I readily agreed. The *hum* from the generators was not conducive to a decent conversation and I followed him to the staff room. Peeping into the recognition panel, Father waited until it flashed green and the door slid sideways to let us through. It shut and locked firmly behind us. Apart from the extensive soundproofing, the staff room was basic by anyone's standards. On the far wall stood a long line of recently upholstered chairs; their bland green design was probably not even fashionable twenty years ago. They served as a practicality more than anything else. A couple of low coffee tables stood in front of the seats and were self-cleaning, so they were immaculate, however, the same could not be said for the coarse carpet covered in dark stains from drink and food spillages. My father wandered over to the kitchen area and started to prepare two mugs of coffee. Apparently, catering droids did not come under the budget for this department.

I punched the seat cushion a few times to soften it up and sat down. I removed my mask and placed it on the chair beside me. Then I readjusted my hair by pressing my hands together on either side of the spikes and pushing upwards until I reached the tips. I started at the front and repeated the action to the back of my head until I was sure all of my hair was in place.

While he prepared the drinks, he called over his shoulder. "Sorry in advance for the coffee, we don't have very refined tastes here. We're just simple folk. Are you still enjoying your time as an office worker?" he joked, already knowing my answer. He leant against the counter while he waited for the water to boil. "How is the project going?"

"You know I can't properly discuss the details. It's confidential, though I will say it's running according to schedule." After a pause, I continued, "And I've considered resigning as a Hunter and working here permanently…"

He guffawed. "People will sooner grow gills and migrate to the ocean. You were set on becoming a Hunter since you were five years old."

"I know." Even then I'd had a singular focus. I was obsessed with the guns locked away in my parents' bedroom.

With steady hands, he carried the drinks over to the seating area and stooped slowly to place my mug of milky coffee on the table. His skin looked inflamed around his MID. I found that unusual because they only do that a short while after they are implanted. He sat down stiffly, keeping hold of his mug so he would not have to reach for it later.

"What's wrong with your MID?"

"Oh." He looked down at his arm. "My last one started to play up so I'd a new one fitted."

"Is that why it was impossible to get hold of you a few weeks ago?"

For some inexplicable reason, he did not meet my gaze. "Yes. It wasn't working properly."

"It said you were at home, but when I went there, the house was empty."

"Well, it's working now so no harm done." He smiled, avoiding the question.

"What about the other time you went off grid? You know earlier in the year when you disappeared for a whole week. I nearly reported you as a missing person."

He laughed. "I told you that I went on a fishing trip."

"I thought you said you went on holiday to Winsford."

"Yeah, a fishing trip to Winsford."

A lie. The only thing you catch in that lake is a disease. Also a week is excessive. Winsford isn't far from Mayton and he could easily have reached me via MID. I decided to let it drop though, even if I didn't understand it. No point in arguing.

"Right. If you say so… well, I met Red earlier to discuss the project and he seemed a little distracted. Have you spoken to him recently? Are you planning anything for the twentieth anniversary of Sibilius Mount? It's coming up soon."

"Is it really…" He trailed off. All the good humour drained out of him and I immediately regretted mentioning it. He stared morosely at the steaming mug of coffee in his hands.

He hardly ever spoke about Sibilius Mount. I researched the incident during my Hunter training and only found vague details. The surviving Hunters were reluctant to recount their experiences. What I did discover was Sibilius Mount is the only recorded attack on several Hunter groups by a unified force of Shades. The particularly disturbing aspect to this attack was it suggested these creatures possess a higher form of intelligence than previously believed. Red lost two of his team that day and several other Hunter teams were entirely wiped out. They were lucky to escape. My father *never* talked about the specifics.

Eventually he emerged from his thoughts and chose to answer my previous question. "Not recently. Only at his parties and even then he's acting the host and flitting between conversations. I don't suppose he's much free time any more and neither do I really, especially with your mother's illness. But whenever we do catch up, it's just like old times. Red is still Red: straight thinking, blunt and to the point and funny as hell!"

Intuitively, I decided against confiding in him about our exchange because I was not sure what side he would take. When it came to his former teammates, he refused to hear anything negative. Nonetheless, I wondered who had spread the rumours.

He mused, "I owe him a lot. He gave me a job at the end of my hunting career when I'd no idea what to do next. That's one of his greatest qualities — he never forgets a friend and rewards loyalty lavishly. Frosty is even his personal assistant."

Frosty, dubbed such because of her surname 'Frost', was the only female member of Red's former team. From what I gleamed from Father's stories, she was his right-hand woman, always taking care of the organisational tasks. She chose their missions and filled in the relevant paperwork too, an ideal choice for a PA role because she had been doing logistics for years anyway and Red trusted her implicitly.

Father took an early sip of the hot coffee. It burnt his tongue and he spluttered into his hand. We were quiet for a time. I stirred my coffee and added sweetener to make it palatable.

Finally, as I knew he expected me to show some daughterly concern, I asked, "How is she?" I didn't need to say her name.

His smile returned. "She's much better now. Her chest isn't paining her as much with the new medication. The doctors reckon she's on the mend but they'll need to monitor her and they're keeping her in the hospital for now. You should go see her. I know it's asking a lot but I'm sure she'd be happy to see you. She is your mother after all."

"Maybe," I answered evasively.

In times of serious illness, disagreements should be pushed aside to avoid any regrets — in theory. In practice, I found it difficult to forget the past and reluctant to visit. Our personalities clash viciously, and I never bonded with her as a daughter should. For her part, she never saw me as anything other than an accessory or an annoyance. Father has always been the intermediary. I could confide almost anything to him.

With a swirl of the dregs in my cup, I finished my drink in one gulp. I picked up my mask and put it on, careful not to disrupt my hair too much; the mask seals around my hair, so Shades cannot enter through the gap.

We both rose to say goodbye. As there was no one in the room, he pulled me into a bear hug and squeezed tightly. Releasing me from his grip, he allowed me to leave while he cleared up our mugs. The door released and I was again hit by the overwhelming racket of the generator room.

***

On autopilot, I returned to my apartment, my mind whirring about Father's strange behaviour with his MID and unexplained absences. He's acted weird for months now. So out of character from the predictable man I knew him to be. Could he be having an affair? If that was true, it wouldn't bother me particularly. Yet it seemed unlikely. He was devoted to my witch of a mother. Whatever it was, he clearly didn't want me to find out. Very odd.

Climbing the steps up to the entrance, I pressed my MID onto the recognition device beside the door then typed a corresponding pin onto the pad. The door lock released and slid open with a soft swoosh. As I entered the lobby, the droid concierge reactivated at the sound of my footfalls and issued a greeting. Without lingering, I ascended a flight of stairs to my apartment. Along one side, there was a succession of wide windows which offered a serene aspect of the gardens, where the flowers and plants were flourishing and the mix of colours made them a pleasure to view. A team of service droids maintained these gardens and residents funded the upkeep.

My apartment is moderate. It consists of four rooms, all roughly the same size with wooden flooring throughout apart from the master bedroom. In there, I allowed myself the luxury of a deep red carpet. All of the rooms had active paint on them and I set it to a beach landscape, which made them appear larger than they actually were.

I hung up my bag on the coat hook by the door and removed my boots and placed them on the shoe rack. After this, I strolled through the hall and casually peered inside the rooms to check that nothing changed since the morning. All clear. Directly, I went to my office at the end of the corridor, which occasionally doubles up as a guest bedroom. One of the walls is painted black and covered with hundreds of white tally scores. Softly glowing beside the window was my MID-effective desk; this has a reactive surface where MID images are projected onto the desktop. It allows me to have increased typing ability and an easier view of the system pages.

I sat down and pulled my chair closer to the desk, switching on the

43

device. The surface was suddenly filled with words and images from the last document that I had been editing.

"Home," I ordered. The image changed to the home setting and at the top right hand of the screen, there was a small triangular ShadeCo symbol, indicating that the device was actively connected to the company's database. Access to these files was limited and I had to be at HQ to view the entire database. Several messages appeared on the vertical scroll bar on the left. Glancing at the names, I noted three were junk messages and automatically deleted them. Another was from a ShadeCo developer who was working on the project with me. I ignored this message for now and scrolled down further. The most recent was from Red, which I opened.

19:58 1 May 72

Good evening Longrider,

To follow up on our earlier conversation, I have received necessary approvals from the board and notified your project manager that you require the prototype weapons for preliminary field testing and they are available to you for as much time as you deem necessary. However, please allow me to reiterate that I urge you to ensure the information remains in strictest confidence, particularly whilst you possess the weapons. Do not let any persons outside of the project view them, either accidentally or intentionally. My concern may seem excessive, but I encountered a myriad of problems concerning project leaks recently and, therefore, steering towards the side of caution where possible.

When you have completed your tests, please compile a report of your findings and include any recommendations you might have as to their improvement. Send the document to me personally.

I look forward to reading your results in due course.

Kind regards,

James Martin
CEO and Chairman

"Do not let anyone outside of the project view them." I slapped my hands down on the table. It shuddered. "He must think I'm an idiot!" I shouted at the writing on the desk.

Very rapidly, my urge to work disappeared and I pushed back from the table. My MID assumed I wanted to respond and had begun composing a message with my last two exclamations.

"Delete!" I yelled at the desk in a panic. It reverted to Red's original message.

After re-reading the message, I observed that it did not warrant a response apart from affirming that the message had been read. A couple of weeks should suffice to do the required tests and the prospect of returning to the field again was a pleasant one. Tomorrow morning, I resolved, I would take them onto the range again and finalise the tests required there and then I could move onto the field.

On the left side of the screen, I noticed a new task icon appear. Out of curiosity, I clicked on the symbol. It was linked to the calendar and highlighted a date a couple of days ahead. The reminder simply read, *Trainee class.*

Groaning inwardly, I rested my head against the desk.

I forgot all about that.

The gun project took up so much time I had not attended to my other duties.

ShadeCo Hunters are obliged to deliver guest lectures to trainees twice a year minimum, though frequently four or five times, and these lessons superseded all other tasks including the weapons project. I had explicit instructions on this and this lesson had been scheduled for weeks. I could not drop out now. Fortunately, I had prepared the material already because I delivered a similar lecture to the previous year's candidates, all I needed to do was tweak it and contact their usual lecturer to confirm.

The project will have to wait, I thought as I retrieved the lecture file.

I worked on it until I was bored of typing. I saved the file, intending to finish it tomorrow.

3

Longrider

As I approached the steps to the academy, I groaned inwardly at the sight of a cluster of activists and wondered if my choice of hunting attire was a good idea. They waited around the entrance and carried their usual placards with anti-ShadeCo sentiment, accusations of mistreatment of animals, Shades and even humans. All of it entirely fabricated. They waved their placards threateningly at me and tried to bar my way. One protestor even shoved me. I pushed him right back and he fell over. They dispersed enough to let me inside the building. Security at the door prevented them from following.

They're getting more aggressive.

I strode down the hall towards the lecture hall smoothing up my hair. There is nothing worse than a wonky Mohawk.

Let's get this over with.

I knocked once on the door.

"She's early," the professor exclaimed from inside the room. I heard a scraping of chairs and desks before she yelled, "Come in!"

Attempting to appear casual, I strolled into the lecture hall with my hands thrust in my pockets. I nodded at the lecturer, Professor Nasif, and stopped in the space at the front of the class, taking my hands out of my pockets and resting them on my hips. Only eight students remained, whittled down from the original class of sixty. I scrutinised them, getting their measure. They all seemed very young. Taking a few steps backward, I leaned on the desktop and crossed my legs, one boot over the other then folded my arms. Each movement was deliberate and precise.

"Good morning, trainees. As some of you might already know, my name is Longrider and I've officially worked as a Hunter for ShadeCo for the last twelve years — ShadeCo will also eventually be your employer for a minimum of two if you complete the training. For identity reasons that you should be aware of by now, I shan't remove my mask, so if you can't hear me — well, I suggest you lean closer and listen harder."

I knew what they were thinking and aware of what I look like. It is true that I have a slight built, yet that hides a wiry strength. After all, you do not attain Master Hunter status if you are a weakling; completing a thousand captures is no mean feat.

"I can see by your superior expressions you think you know it all already and I can't teach you anything. Well, if you go into the field with that attitude, you certainly won't be coming back! Death rates are high for newly qualified Hunters and to me you seem hardly more than children. Until you've been on your first solo hunt, you won't know what it's like. Reading can only teach you so much because the main aspect of being a Hunter is the practical side."

A couple of boys in the back row were talking among themselves and sniggering. I bounded up the stairs and stood over them.

"Listen, you prepubescent shits, my schedule is pretty busy at the moment. There are other tasks that I could be doing right now, but I've come here to assist you with your training. And if you think you know everything already then you're free to leave and I'll talk to the other pupils here who have at least a modicum of respect." I gestured at the doorway and waited.

Out of the corner of my eye, I noticed the two girls in the front row turn around and grin at me and nod approvingly. The boys did not stir and remained sheepishly in their seats.

"No? Good. Now shut up and listen."

I marched back to the front and continued. "I'm here to teach you survival skills and they aren't ones you can learn from any book, so please turn off your devices and mute your MIDs. There are some abilities that can't be taught and only acquired from experience and necessity. You may encounter times when your equipment is faulty and only have your mind and objects in the field to get you through. That is the sign of a real Hunter — the ability to adapt to your situation using everything available. To carry on going, even when it seems hopeless."

A pupil in the front row blurted out, "How did you get through the Dust Ground without a mask or weapons?"

Silence. Professor Nasif, who'd been gently rocking in her seat, bolted upright and glared at him to be quiet.

He ventured, "Everyone knows that it's a black spot for Hunter deaths."

"There were a number of factors in my favour that day — the main reason was an abundance of plants called whitemoss. These plants can be woven into makeshift masks because the stems and leaves are too dense for Shades to penetrate and they're still porous enough to let air enter; this is not common knowledge, it's just something my father taught me. And I still had one weapon. I always keep my kukri sword with me smeared with damsel-weed. It affects Shades' composition when you slice through it as the severed section densifies and shrinks it; two or three swipes dispel them. Also, there was a torrential downpour and Shades seek dry areas when this happens and don't stay in the open for long, even if they've started to attack beforehand. So, I was lucky."

Even before I finished, another pupil raised his hand. I nodded in his direction.

"Have you seen anyone taken over by a Shade?"

A morbid curiosity took hold of the class. They sat forward in their seats. Though the effects of a Shade takeover were explained in their textbooks, few people alive had seen the process happen in real life. Those with Umbras cannot speak, partly due to the extreme jaw modification and partly due to the fact the Shade latched onto the brain, altering the individual's personality.

"No. The question is irrelevant. Your training alone will give you enough awareness to know what's happening if you see it."

A pretty blonde girl in the front row blurted out, "Why do you use goats as your preferred method of bait instead of chickens, which are recommended to trainees?"

This must be Red's niece. They have the same baby blue eyes and even though she was sitting, I could tell she is tall too. He frequently talks about her and her natural ability. More disconcerting, he claimed I am her idol and she studied all my hunts. I am not sure how I felt about that. Being a role model is a lot of pressure. Until now I had not met the girl.

"Qualified ShadeCo Hunters use goats because it's a matter of size, only a freelancer uses chickens or anything else they can get their hands on. ShadeCo requires the use of larger animals to allow for higher-density Shades to enter the host and increase its density further. As it's a parasite, the host has to be big enough to hold it and as a rule of thumb, the smaller the animal, the smaller the Shade. So, if you are hunting larger Shades you'll have to bring along a larger animal to capture—"

She interjected. "Why do they do that? Aren't larger animals harder to control? Wouldn't it be better to have several smaller captures rather just a few big ones?"

With a sigh, I replied, "If you hunt with one at a time and move after each capture, they're fine. You just need to contain the animal within the first few minutes of takeover and move to another hunt site. Shade activity attracts other Shades and so no matter what size creature you use, if you try to get more than one infected animal in one go then you're putting yourself at risk. In my experience, Shades seem to be able to sense the presence of other Shades and they can be dangerous even if you're wearing a mask."

She challenged me again, though it seemed in excitement rather anything else. "But what if you used three chickens and get the captures and then return to HQ and get some more?"

"By that token, you could go back and get more goats. Your manuals tell you to use chickens because they're easier to handle post-takeover as you'll be slower than a qualified Hunter. These manuals are also written for trainees. Basically, it's the easy method. When you're qualified, if you don't want to spend every waking moment in the field, you need to increase the animal's mass not the number of animals. Using multiple animals is inefficient timewise, consumes space in your vehicle, and most importantly, is dangerous. So if we can get back on track..."

No more than five minutes passed before another trainee asked, "Where do you get your guns from?"

"Guns... I can't remember a lecture without someone mentioning them at least once. When your training is complete and you receive a licence, ShadeCo provides you with two free weapons of your choosing per year. If you want more, you'll have to pay for them yourself. Fortunately, ShadeCo provides Hunters with unlimited ammo... I'm not sure if it's true with Hayward Bros as they are smaller than us and most

Hunters usually move to ShadeCo if they can — you'll have to ask one of their employees. As for the guns, I'd recommend one from the K Gun Series. Currently, these are the lightest weapons available, although that's not saying much. They can carry nine rounds and are the most powerful at close range."

The lecture continued in this way for the better part of an hour. Occasionally, I discussed survival tactics but their questions flowed and I went off on tangents for most of the session. When only a few minutes remained before the end, I announced I'd answer one more question. I looked around the room and gestured towards the girl beside the blonde, another stunner suited for modelling rather than hunting. Her hand was raised tentatively in the air.

"Have you ever felt the job was too difficult, or felt you were in the wrong career?"

I mused for a while then answered. "No. There are times when I feel I need a holiday, as do most people, but afterwards I've always wanted to return to hunting. Once your training has finished it's a very satisfying job and if you're skilled then the rewards are substantial. But if you're not one hundred per cent certain then you should reconsider. It's dangerous and there is no room for mistakes, especially as you'll be on your own. Hunters don't work in groups any more and you have to rely on yourself."

I turned to the lecturer. "Professor, I'll send you a summary of everything I intended to discuss today. Unfortunately, we've not had time to cover the majority of it... maybe you can discuss it with them in another session?"

"Yes, that won't be a problem. It's been a pleasure having you here, and I hope you'll be back soon." She walked over to me shook my hand. Although I'm of average height, I towered over Professor Nasif, who barely reached five feet.

As I walked out, I already considered the lecture; nowhere near my finest. I allowed them to ask too many questions and got distracted. The previous classes were too nervous to ask me much. It was a learning curve. Next time, no questions until the end.

4

Landmine

A second visit to the ShadeCo head office in as many days isn't my idea of a good time.

The kid hadn't processed my capture details correctly at all and it hadn't registered in the database. Without a recorded hunt, I wouldn't be paid for the Shades, plus I'd given them free ore, and there was sweet fuck all that I could do about it. And the density of the Shade I caught today was nowhere near as large as the earlier hoard. Once the company took their share, I'd take home a third of the value of what I should have made on the first hunt.

ShadeCo bastards!

And to add icing to this spicy little cake, my aunt called me earlier with nothing except complaints on her agenda. The usual stuff. I wasn't doing enough for Marie, ignoring my family, responsibilities and never being around. This wasn't exactly true. I pay her hospital fees. I send her food and visit her, occasionally. It wasn't my fault my dad's will gave the estate to a distant relative rather than his own kids. That money might as well be on Earth for the use it was doing me. My aunt is just one of those people who enjoy moaning. And as I was already in a shit mood, her penetrating voice had the same effect on me as punching a bear, and I erupted.

I mulled over the argument as I climbed up the last set of stairs leading back to ShadeCo's foyer from the records office. When I saw the swarming mass of workers waiting to get out at the end of the work day, I groaned. The main exit had two sets of doors that permitted a few employees to go through like a barge lock. They had to wait for the first door to close before the other was released.

51

This system couldn't cope with the amount of people leaving at the end of the day and there was a significant backlog. There wasn't an obvious queue and workers jostled to get out and get home. I waded through, parting the crowd with my size to quickly reach the front.

When the door opened, people pushed me from behind and we swarmed inside. My arms were glued to my sides and workers were squeezed uncomfortably beside me on every side. Twenty workers crammed in a space for twelve. The first door slowly revolved back and gave a soft puff as it secured. The second door opened and we were hit by a wave of warm air. The workers fanned out into the car park. I inhaled and my nostrils were filled with the latex smell of the gas mask. My MID started to vibrate and my aunt's pinched face covered my forearm. I ignored it and eventually the call rang off.

Fuck it. I need a drink.

∗∗∗

Dionysian Dreams is one of two bars in easy stumbling distance from my house, which made it an ideal watering hole. And it lived up to its namesake with lax rules about practically everything, which suited me just fine. Tonight it was heaving, but a few drinks down my neck and I wouldn't notice it. Already, three rows of punters queued at the bar waiting to be served by the rainbow-uniformed staff, who worked flat out to get through their orders.

Droids whizzed overhead with trays of drinks, delivering them to various groups at the tables and on the dance floor. The bar had attempted a classic feel with Grecian pillars, semi-naked statues, and mosaicked floors. Clasped hands formed the entrance to the dance floor. It worked if you ignored the heavy drumbeat, people bouncing around on the dance floor and continually changing lights turning dancers and statues green, blue, violet and pink on repeat. Cages hung above the dance floor holding several dancers wearing little more than multi-coloured loincloths. Someone threw a bottle. It hit the side of one of the cages and bounced back, spraying its contents on the people below before disappearing into the crowd.

I wound past a table full of girls celebrating their friend's eighteenth birthday. All wearing barely-there dresses revealing as much thigh and boob as a man could want. They were a noisy bunch even with the music and a few of them seemed familiar — particularly the young curvy girl in the tight green dress with fantabulous tits. Her eyes caught mine and she gave me a wide smile. I winked at her then at a couple of the others too before continuing to the bar. *Attractive bunch.*

I recognised a couple of lads standing beside a tall table. They waved me over, but I gestured that I was getting a drink. Then I spotted the girl in the tight dress again, who continued to look at me with unmasked interest. I gave her a quick grin before turning back to keep my place in the queue.

***

Two hours elapsed before the woman I'd eyed up earlier ambushed me by a urinal in the communal toilets. Apparently she knew me. I'd danced with her a few weeks back then walked her home and acted the perfect gentleman. Can't say I remembered. It didn't sound like me. But when she offers you a job in the toilets, it's not something to question. The relaxed policy towards sex was the main reason why Dionysian Dreams is so popular. As long as you didn't do anything in the main area, the staff didn't mind what went on in the toilets or private rooms.

"You're absolutely gorgeous," she purred as she ran a hand over my chest.

"You're not bad yourself." I leant forward and she tilted her head back expectantly. I planned a rough kiss on her lips, which seemed to drive her wild because she grabbed my neck and pulled me closer. She drew away and coaxed me into a cubicle with her.

A while later, after we'd finished, I opened the door slightly and checked if the coast was clear. My caution didn't matter because the girl barged past me anyway to wash her hands at the sink, heedless of other people.

Her eyes met mine in the mirror. "I'm going to the dance floor. I'll see you there?"

As I needed a slash again, I gave a noncommittal answer and stayed put.

In all honesty, I didn't have any intention to speak to her again. She's too young, really. At thirty-two I'm almost old enough to be her dad. Not bad as a one-off, but too immature to have a casual thing with. So when I returned to the main area, I wound my way past the crowds of people towards the exit and through the anti-Shade measures.

Outside in the brisk night air, the breeze nipped at the bare skin on my arms. I felt drunker than I thought I'd been and in an excellent mood. It was still early. I decided to go to another bar a few blocks away and ambled down the streets, taking my time. While I walked, I thrust my hands into my pockets and gazed up at the sky, beautifully clear and the stars shone like millions of tiny pinpoints. The larger of our two moons was full tonight, the other a half and together they provided enough natural light to walk by.

After a while, I reached the second, more subdued bar. No garish lights lit the building or booming bass here. The only light that streamed out of the ground floor windows came from between steel shutters. Huge letters above the doorway stated 'The Mayton Castle' against a teal background, which was the only thing setting it apart from a large house. Most people go to Dionysian Dreams on a Thursday night rather than the Castle. This bar isn't really a place to go to impress, more of a place to get quietly drunk and have a chat.

Two powered-down droids were stationed both sides of the door and didn't budge as I walked past. Anti-Shade measures hit me as I entered. A blast of cold air smacked me, ruffling my clothes and hair. Taking a few steps forward, I opened the second set of doors to get out of the gust. Once inside and in relative safety, I removed my gas mask and looped the straps around my belt. I patted my shirt and trousers to remove the dust that landed during my short walk, but the boots were a lost cause, so I left them as they were.

The bar boasted the best whisky collection in Diomedia, the oldest of which they claimed was distilled on Earth. On the far side of the room was an area sectioned off by a frosted glass wall and in this section, the bar offered oxygen pipes. This hobby had declined in popularity recently. I settled in the first section. The barkeep wiped away a beer ring from the counter with a cloth. I gave him my order and pulled up a stool.

The regulars were here. My friend, Chris, sat at the far end of the bar nursing a pint of the home-brewed perry the Castle offers. His considerable gut curved around the bar, though he wasn't particularly close to it. Next to him was Louis, a ShadeCo analyst. His goggles were propped on the crown of his bald head. He always wore medical gloves and wiped the rim of his glass with his thumb after every sip. Sitting two seats down from me was an unusual-looking woman I'd never seen before. The sides of her head were shaved, and her platinum-blonde hair tied back severely at the base of her skull, enhancing her angular features. She swished her drink around in the glass casually then turned towards me, her brow furrowed, her almond-shaped eyes narrowed like someone examining a rare species of animal. She looked away and downed her drink. I noticed a striking scar running parallel to the line of her chin, and wondered how she'd gotten it.

She shot me another sidelong glance and said, "Do I know you from somewhere?"

"I don't think so." I looked down at the glass in my hand. "Do you want a drink?"

After a brief pause, she replied, "Why not. Another won't hurt. I'll have a brandy, please."

The barman overheard her and immediately filled her glass with an amber spirit. She took it neat. I looked on approvingly. For a short time we sat in silence, sipping our drinks. I wondered if I knew her. But I couldn't remember a jot.

"Valya," she said eventually. "And you are?"

"Michael." I reached over and shook her hand.

Still nothing.

"So, Michael, why are you here and not at Dionysian Dreams? Isn't that the place to be on a Thursday?"

"I've just come from there. But it's rammed. I couldn't think properly."

"It's not really my favourite place either — it's full of barely legals, drinking their weight in poor-quality alcohol and dancing until they pass out or find someone to fuck in the toilets. There is a time and a place for all that and I think I'm past it." Her voice had a slight slur to it, which suggested that she'd been here for a while. I downed my drink and didn't answer. She'd better not be a mind reader or this conversation would quickly come to an end.

She continued. "Really, really, not my sort of place — even when I was kid. I guess that's a bit boring, but, I've never enjoyed the whole

55

dressing-up thing."

"You're still young."

"I'm thirty. Admittedly that is relatively young, though old enough to allow yourself to feel like a cantankerous bitch. At any rate, my palate certainly appreciates decent quality brandy. The stuff they sell in Dreams could double up as syrup to smother on food... why do some people possess the ability to destroy your mood in seconds, with just a single barb?"

"Just talented that way, I guess."

"Not you." She smiled down at her glass and sighed. "Someone else. I went to visit her in hospital earlier. You shouldn't really talk badly about someone who is seriously ill, although she tests that beyond reason... long story short, this woman is and always has been a prima donna. She puts on the suffering martyr act whenever the nurses are in the room and fawns as if I was the most precious thing she'd ever seen, but when they leave, she reverts back to her normal vindictive self." She growled at her glass and was silent for a moment, then turned back towards me. "Sorry... I'll shut up. You don't want to hear all this."

I shrugged and took a sip of my drink. "Funnily enough, I can understand your view..."

"Really?"

"Yes. Everyone knows someone like that."

She nodded and downed the rest of her drink. "Can I ask you why you've got a biohazard symbol tattooed on your arm?"

"I liked the design. It's related to my job a bit."

"What do you do?" Her pale eyes were unsettling, just a few shades darker than the whites of her eyes and surrounded by a dark blue ring not unlike a husky's. She seemed to be able to tell what I did just by the way I moved and talked. Maybe she was a police officer.

"Chemical engineer." My lie came out as smoothly as I was capable of after a few drinks.

She scoffed. "Really?" Her eyebrows rose questioningly. "You don't really fit the mould. You look as if you spend most of your time working out rather that slaving away in an office. I thought chemical engineers were much..."

"Scrawnier?"

"Yeah, right, scrawnier."

"What do you do?"

"I can't reveal that. If I did, I'd have to kill you." Her eyes flashed and her lips slid into an ironic half-smile.

Before I could reply, the music abruptly stopped. The bouncer droids activated and darted into the bar. Metal shutters slammed down over the doors and windows, sealing us inside. The harsh emergency lights came on and the staff stopped serving. Everyone stopped speaking.

A female voice announced from the speaker, "At 28:05, the Watch identified a Shade located at the west gate. We strongly advise remaining indoors until we confirm the Shade threat is neutralised. Please ensure you follow proper safety procedures. Confirm your mask is entirely intact and covering your eyes, mouth and nose at all times, and please do not go outside unless absolutely necessary. If you must do so, ensure you are not travelling on your own. Stay in groups of three or more and keep together. Be vigilant. Transmission over."

As a freelancer, I didn't have to participate in Shade hunts in the city. That was pure company Hunter territory and I only really help out if I've nothing else to do. And definitely not this pissed.

Valya scoffed and slapped her palms down on the counter.

A couple of guys complained loudly and had a slurred argument with the bar staff because they wanted to remove the shutters, who pointedly refused. The bouncer droids hovered closer. The drunks raised their hands defensively and backed away from the bar. They sat back down in their booth and didn't kick up any more fuss.

"Shades are getting active again, it's the third sighting this week. Either that or someone on the Watch is falling asleep on duty," Chris volunteered.

One of the barmen poured another round of fiery blast punch cocktails. "I tell you," he said as he leaned in closer, "maybe these Hunters aren't doing their job properly. That's what they pay them for. They should be killing all the nearby Shades."

Valya jolted upright and snapped. "Hunters aren't meant to just be killing off Shades. They capture them for fuel and there is meant to be a balance in that. If there are no Shades, then there's no energy and that would be it for us, kaput! Diomedia isn't like Earth. We don't annihilate a species just because it's inconvenient for us!"

"Whoa! No disrespect by it… I was just saying that Hunters are trained to hunt Shades, so they should defend Mayton by killing as many as they can." The barman dropped his gaze and wiped a drop of juice that had spilled onto the counter.

"I understand what you mean," another punter added to Valya as she picked up her drinks. "Without black energy the city wouldn't run." With her two pence said, the woman wandered back to her friends in the booth nearest the window, clutching the bottles close to her chest.

Valya frowned at her glass and muttered something under her breath that sounded a bit like 'ignorant'. Then she turned to me again and said, with a sigh and a shrug, "I did warn you I was in a foul mood."

I didn't know what to say so I mirrored her shrug and watched the monitor behind the bar. It was showing a news story concerning a missing woman and child. A nice picture of the pair in happier times appeared, both attractive Latinos and apparently from Springhaven, which is odd as usually anything about that settlement didn't make Mayton news. It showed a clip of them being approached by two men and injected with something and easily manoeuvred into a plain black jeep, similar to the ShadeCo ones, and they haven't been seen since. I didn't fancy their chances. I wondered if the activists had a hand in it.

A short while later, I asked Valya, "Do you want another drink?"

But the stool was empty. She'd disappeared.

5

Longrider

𝒯he gunshot ricocheted around the range and faded slowly. High concrete walls on every side trapped the sound like being inside an empty dam. Amblers would not want to accidentally wander into the firing line, even if shooters enjoy the challenge of a moving target.

Every Wednesday and Friday, the range was closed to the public; to get in you needed to be a Hunter or hold a trainee licence or be in a position of authority, such as the police or fire department. This allowed professionals freedom to practice without the distraction of amateurs and, on these days, many easier targets were pushed out of the way and lined up against the sides, while the distant ones, like the one I aimed at, were given greater focus.

I readjusted my aim and let off two shots in rapid succession. These shots were followed by two thumps as they found their mark, a human-shaped dummy with a target clipped onto its chest. The dummy spun on impact and revolved slowly until it faced me again. At eight hundred metres away, without a sniper sight, I thought they were adequate, particularly as I was up late last night and felt a bit worse for wear.

The speaker above me sounded a shrill whistle, informing the marshals it was safe to approach the target. This also warned me to hold fire. I lowered my mid-range rifle and turned the weapon's safety catch on, then pointed it at the floor as an added precaution. This was not a Shade effective weapon and its bullets could kill a human.

A droid with a high visibility orange central unit hovered out of the shooting area and zipped across the field. As it reached the dummy, it slowed and checked it over. It revolved around the dummy and tooted three times, indicating I hit the bullseye. It then unfolded a new sheet of paper and replaced the torn one, tugging gently to ensure that it was secure. It then darted back and hovered over the safety, once again out of the firing line.

Apart from the staff watching in the wings, my party was alone on the veranda. Tobias, my old mentor, along with Red himself. Tobias and I planned to meet up here for a quick catch up before he saw his current student and it was pure coincidence Red was in the area after an official visit to this year's trainees. Handily, the training academy is connected to the range. Red lifted up his goggles and rested them on his forehead, pulling down his respirator so he could talk freely.

"Wow! That was excellent! It's always a pleasure watching you shoot," he said sincerely, his clear blue eyes sparkling.

"Thanks, Red. It comes with the territory. I need to be able to defend myself because no one else is going to cover me."

"I agree. Solo hunting," he sighed. "To be honest, I've never understood the trend. It made the profession far more dangerous than it used to be. And less efficient. In a team, you'd always watch each other's backs. And there were fewer deaths, if you exclude the Sibilus Mount tragedy..." He seemed contemplative for a moment. "They were good times, weren't they, Tobias?"

"They were," Tobias said briefly. He was not a man of many words and those he said were pronounced slowly and languorously. In spite of having slow speech, his reflexes were fast and he was an excellent Hunter in his prime.

"Group hunts are outdated, Red. You've been out of the game too long. When you work alone you spend less time in the field and every hour outside of the settlement walls, the risk to life increases exponentially. Besides, our weapons are better than back in your day."

Red was right about the safety aspect, but it was not something I permitted myself to dwell on. Changes to the profession came about in part because of instances in which greedy individuals fled with their group's capture and weapons. These were double-edged treacheries because they not only robbed their companions of their livelihood, they endangered their lives too by leaving them less well-defended in the field, and the legal system does not provide much support for victims. It is a sad fact Hunters cannot trust one another any more.

Even with groups, it has always been dangerous. Accidents and deaths in the field happened before the switch. I believe this is mainly due to the lack of government rules around freelancers and their actions on the field are unmonitored. Company Hunters like myself are obliged to have bi-monthly performance reviews to keep standards high. Sloppiness causes mishaps. Shades are unpredictable.

"Would you like a go?" I passed Red the rifle.

His eyes lit up excitedly like a child handling a new toy. "I thought you'd never ask!" he said gleefully. "Prepare to be amazed!"

He took out his glasses from the case in his pocket and put them on. He checked that the weapon was loaded, altered the sights by looking down the barrel, then lay down on his stomach.

I was confused that he had changed the weapon's setting. *Those sights were definitely set correctly.* I switched my eyepieces to the telescopic mode to see where his shots landed. We gave him space to fire. There is nothing more distracting than someone breathing down your neck while you are trying to concentrate.

"The ability to shoot never leaves you. Just like riding a bike. Once learned, the technique is always stored in the back of your memory for later use. For times like this."

Steadying his arm and focusing his aim, he lined up the target in the crosshairs. He inhaled and pulled the trigger three times in rapid succession.

He exhaled and glanced up at me, clearly confident he found his mark even before the runner droid confirmed it.

It was true his shots hit, just not the dummy I was looking at. Instead he hit another target two hundred metres farther back in the range. I whistled in awe. The shots must have been near a thousand metres. He got up stiffly, massaging his lower back as he gently handed me the rifle.

"When did you last pick up a gun, old man?"

"Not for years. I'm a bit out of practise," he apologised. "So I didn't want to overdo it."

I scoffed. "Of course you didn't. If you wanted a competition then you should've said. I was just practising earlier and my last shots just warm ups."

He grinned and checked his MID. "I've a meeting in fifteen minutes and Frosty will be wondering where I am, so I'll have to regretfully decline. Another time, Longrider, though this isn't backing down for good. I'm up for the challenge when we can schedule proper time for it. And perhaps Harald can join us next as well? That way I can beat him too."

"My father was a better shot than you back in the day."

Tobias agreed.

"That's not true! I was always the sharpest shooter. I could teach you a thing or too—"

I ignored the comment and cut in. "Get out of here, Red. You're going to be late."

He gave us both a low, theatrical bow before spinning around and striding towards the exit. His aides, who had appeared at the entrance, approached him immediately to brief him about his next meeting.

Tobias picked up the weapon and grinned. "My turn now."

***

After about an hour of shooting practice, Tobias and I decided to go for a stroll through the academy's campus for old time's sake. I intended to return to the main HQ later to collect the prototypes and return alone to the range but it was a beautiful, crisp day, so I would take my time doing so.

The academy consisted of two main buildings, excluding the shooting range, one being the dormitory and the other containing the lecture halls; the latter building was connected to the range by a single brick bridge running between the second floors. It was run similarly to a military school and, reflecting this, behind the academy were acres of mud, dust, wires and assault courses for the physical training sessions. For two years students were broken down and built up again, fierce and resilient to anything the field could throw at them. The training was tough.

Tobias and I found ourselves on the bridge and we looked over the balustrade. Below us, the students stood to attention, lined up in one row of three and another of four on the paved quad below. All wore matching khaki uniforms: a tank top, trousers, and durable black boots. Standard issue exercising attire that must always be worn, it was the same as when I here. Two men stood in front of the trainees with their arms folded behind their backs. They were the fitness instructors who will push the students to their top physical condition. The drills forced trainees to increase their strength, stamina and speed, skills just as necessary in the field as the ability to use a weapon.

From one of the academy buildings, Red's niece darted out. She was late and knew it. Taking her place nervously in the front row, she tried to be as inconspicuous as possible.

Immediately, the older of the two trainers chastised her for her tardiness. His voice carried clearly and I recognised him from my own student years.

"So you will be joining us then? I hope we're not interfering with your social schedule?"

"Sorry, sir! It won't happen again, sir!" she declared.

"It better not, missy, otherwise you'll be cleaning latrines for the next month!" he bellowed and then addressed the whole group. "This morning, we'll start with an eight-mile run followed by a circuit of the assault course. Any questions? Good! Seventy-two Team! Right turn! Forward!"

The trainees started to march rhythmically, left foot forward, right foot forward, left, right, left, right, left. The first trainer ordered them to run in formation. They picked up their feet and increased their pace. At the same time, he ran alongside them, abusing them equally and indiscriminately, while the second trainer jogged a few paces behind to push the trainees at the back.

"Idle maggots! That is not a *run*. That is a leisurely stroll! We are not going to one of your grandma's tea parties. Now move it! Double time!"

Tobias turned to me and rolled his eyes.

I commented, "Well, I don't miss this. That guy used to be my trainer too, a Mr Sinclair. He was horrible, no one liked him. When we ran, he used to punish us if we sped up and bumped into the recruit in front, or if we lagged behind and made the formation appear sloppy."

"He fancies himself a military man," observed Tobias.

"You got that right. He used to remind us that he descended from an illustrious military family and he ran his training sessions like an army drill. He's a soldier without a war and can never achieve what his ancestors could on Earth. Pathetic, really."

"You say it like it's a bad thing, Longrider. Diomedia is safer than

Earth, even with the Shades. At least we are not trying to kill each other."

"That is true. So far…"

Sinclair was also a great advocate of military songs and insisted they increased morale and motivation. All trainees had to chant along because if they did not then he would push them harder. I felt a pang of nostalgia when they started up a song that went to the olden tune of 'Glory! Glory! Hallelujah!' They joined in with the chorus while he sung the verses:

He was just a rookie Hunter
On a vast and barren plain.
With a Hunter's rifle
But not a bullet to his name.
One knife in his pocket
And bottled prize to claim.
And he ain't gonna' hunt no more!

GORY, GORY, WHAT A HORRIBLE WAY TO DIE!
GORY, GORY, WHAT A HORRIBLE WAY TO DIE!
THE SHADE CAME AND TOOK HIM STRAIGHT THROUGH THE EYE
AND HE AIN'T GONNA' HUNT NO MORE!

His mask was broken on his face,
And it was not the brand to blame.
Earlier he fell over
And broke it on the terrain.
Though he tried to struggle,
Through the eye crack it came
And he ain't gonna' hunt no more!

GORY, GORY, WHAT A HORRIBLE WAY TO DIE!
GORY, GORY, WHAT A HORRIBLE WAY TO DIE!
THE SHADE CAME AND TOOK HIM STRAIGHT THROUGH THE EYE
AND HE AIN'T GONNA' HUNT NO MORE!

Your senses will be numb
With a Shade upon the brain.
Your life goes out as it goes in,
And your world is corrupted by pain.
If you go unprepared
It'll happen to you the same
And you ain't gonna' hunt no more!

Tobias and I watched the students until their figures shrunk to pinpricks in the distance and their voices faded away.

I smiled to myself.

The shape of hunting would be transformed by the new gun series. It will make hunting easier and likely save lives on the field, possibly some of the trainees below. Not for the first time, I was glad of my involvement in the project.

6

Landmine

*W*ellwood Lodge. Always so welcoming, the grounds and buildings so well maintained and staff unswervingly friendly and helpful. My sister, Marie, has been treated here with the utmost care for nearly three decades. Yet, despite the pleasantness, it didn't change the fact that it's a hospital and she's unlikely to ever leave now. I hate this fucking place.

I entered the main building and strode up to the solitary desk directly opposite the entrance. A young receptionist startled at the scrape of the door and quickly switched off her MID. A medical mask covered her mouth and nose to prevent the spread of disease but her eyes were wide and friendly. She asked me to sign in using the computer tablet resting on the right-hand side of the table and then supplied me with a guest pass for identification purposes.

A polite notice on the table warned of a sickness bug circulating amongst the patients and staff. I sprayed my hands with purposefully placed antibacterial gel and rubbed them together.

Another set of doors led through to the interior of the building. I walked down a long windowless hallway, brightly lit by artificial tube lights. I saw a familiar doctor heading towards me and was fully prepared to continue when he stopped directly in my path.

"Mr Butcher, may I have a word with you please? I understand you're here to see Marie?"

"That's right. What's the problem?"

Normally I leave medical decisions concerning Marie to my aunt. She lives in the area and is readily available if she has to come in. I just pay the bills.

"They're private medical matters and I don't want to discuss them out here in the hallway. Please accompany me to my office, it's not far." He pointed towards the way he'd just come. "Then you can decide whether to continue your visit today, or if you'd prefer to return later in the week."

What's happened now? My stomach lurched.

I followed. He led me up some steps and we continued along another corridor and walked to the office at the end. I glanced down briefly at the bag in my hand containing chocolates and grapes and wondered if I'd return home with them uneaten. The doctor lifted his forearm and his MID was scanned. The door slid open. Once we entered the room, I took a seat.

The doctor sat in his high-backed chair and leant forward confidentially. "Mr Butcher, there's been an incident with your sister today and I'd like you to be aware of the situation before deciding whether or not to continue your visit." He explained. "A few months ago, we spoke to your aunt about introducing another drug to control her anxiety with fewer side effects, in particular drugs that won't affect her liver. And at the same time, we're reducing the use of her current medication, brezac, which she's been on for several years now. Regrettably she developed an addiction to the drug and even with a graduated withdrawal she's constantly tense and startles at the slightest thing."

He took off his glasses and let them hang by his chest. "About an hour ago, at breakfast, one of the other patients accidentally spilt tea on her lap in the dining room and she attacked him. The nurses on duty tell me she was physically restrained, sedated and taken to her room. And they've had her under constant surveillance since so she won't be a danger to herself. But she isn't communicative and barely responds to their presence. She isn't aware of your intended visit and wouldn't be further distressed if she didn't see you today. So I'd recommend returning later this week when we've stabilised her and when she's more lucid."

Here he paused and stared intently at me, waiting for my response.

"Thank you but I'll stay." If I left now, I'd not return for weeks, if not months.

"Well, if you're certain, though I don't advise it… it can be distressing seeing a loved one in such a condition."

"No, I'll definitely stay."

"If you're sure… if you need the nurses' assistance at any time, they're on duty outside her door. And please don't try to move her into the common room. She might get distressed by the other patients."

I stood up and automatically the doctor rose too. He stepped forward and shook my hand.

"Thanks for letting me know."

It irritated me that my aunt hadn't told me about any of this. Frankly, I was shocked by Marie's dependence on the drugs. I knew she'd been on them for years, and the dosage increased since her violent relapse at fifteen at a ShadeCo summer party. We weren't sure what set it off, perhaps the crowds or a particular person at the party, she never said and never spoke of it. After that she never returned to normal and had stayed at the hospital ever since. But all the same, it's hard hearing.

∗∗∗

When I entered her bedroom, she sat slumped in a wheelchair by her bed. A line of drool dripped from the edge of her lips and threatened to fall onto her lap. Thick brown hair hung in waves around her shoulders and its health and shine contrasted with her pale face. She looked skinny; her arms stood out like matchsticks below the puffy sleeves and her collarbone jutted out. A luminous orange bracelet around her wrist distinguished her as a patient and it contained a chip inside that could be scanned to immediately view her medical profile.

After I placed the bag of presents on the chest of drawers, I sat down on the bed beside her and felt a lump in my throat and instantly regretted my decision to stay. She turned her head drowsily towards me but didn't say anything.

"Rie?"

No response. The hanging line of drool finally dropped onto her dress, leaving a wet patch on one of the pleats.

"That's an ugly dress. Did Aunt Maple give it to you?"

I hadn't spoken to my aunt since our last argument and I'd be damned if I'd be the first to apologise. She knows my job's too demanding to be a full-time carer. Marie didn't have anywhere else to go. At least the medical professionals here give her the attention she needs.

Marie's reply was slurred, containing more groans than words.

This usually provokes a reaction. I rummaged through my bag.

"Would you like a chocolate?"

As I hoped, she outstretched her hand to receive a sweet. Her expression was neutral and only when it was in her mouth did she give me a smile. A brief one, no more than a second, and then it was gone. Then her lips drooped down into the line as before.

We sat in silence and I looked at her for further changes. Bruises on her shins, purple over green and yellow but they weren't suspicious because her coordination's poor and she falls over frequently. She's definitely thinner though. Responsively, I passed her another chocolate, which she snatched from my hand.

I shouldn't leave it so long between visits. I need to make it a habit to see her at least once a month...

It's a familiar promise. One I continually break and, truthfully, never intend to keep. This place disgusts me and no matter how many times I visit, I can't shake off the suffocating, crawling feeling these walls brings on. Only a spell on the field can bring me peace, that barren wasteland without a soul for miles. Much better than this confinement. My visits here are never long.

7

Landmine

The day was a scorcher. Unrelenting. My mouth felt dry and cracked and I'd an overwhelming urge to jump fully clothed into the nearby waterhole to cool off. It was very tempting indeed.

The goat's ear flicked at a persistent fly. It kicked at the ground and reached down to eat some brittle plants. They crunched loudly in its mouth. I'd tethered it so it couldn't go far. Not that it would have. The goat continued to munch on the plants and its tail swished happily with the tether slack on the ground. This watering hole must be heaven for it: enough food to eat for days, a ready water supply, enough tree cover to offer shade from the heat of the day, and soft ground to lie on.

The water's surface rippled with life, although shallow and couldn't have reached two metres at its deepest point. Tiny insects darted above it. A couple of metre-long lizards lay on their bellies by the water's edge while they drank and basked in the sun. They were herbivores and ignored me and the goat. Another hairless creature scampered out of the vegetation by the bank towards the dry ground and scratched at the earth and made a hollow for itself. The only unnatural element in the scene was my Jeep, partially obscured by a bush on the far bank, and empty except for a few supplies and a few guns. A breeze rustled the leaves and swayed the shrivelled and deboned head hanging from the Jeep's rear-view mirror as a kind of talisman. The guy that sold it to me claimed it came from a man who'd succumbed to Umbras. I wasn't sure if it was genuine. But it looked interesting anyway.

Where are the Shades?

The animal life here is enough to draw them in. But these creatures are relaxed — not a good sign. They are always edgy when a Shade is nearby. It doesn't make sense. Several hours had already passed on this hunt and I hadn't encountered anything close to a Shade.

With a thump, I sat beneath a wide-trunked tree. These trees were a rarity in the desert. The usual ones are spindly and short.

I was certain there'd be one here. *Maybe my equipment is malfunctioning?* I dismissed the idea. I'd tested it only a month ago and everything was in order. This was merely a blip. It happens.

Exhaling deeply, I quickly pulled up my gas mask and took a swig of whisky from my flask, involuntarily shuddering at the bitterness. Strong stuff, better than anything sold in the shops. My empty stomach gurgled as the liquid entered, reminding me it was a while since I'd eaten anything, not since I visited Rie.

My eyelids felt heavy in this heat. I hadn't slept well recently. Slowly my head sank, and I rested my chin on my chest.

Then I jolted upright. Sleep could wait.

I stretched my arms then placed my hands palm down on my knees and sat forward. After a while, I felt my eyelids gain weight again.

A low rumble wrenched me out of my daze.

The sound grew until it roared, resonating across the hills and the desert behind me. It startled the two lizards and they slunk into the water and took cover beneath the surface until only their noses were visible. Other smaller creatures scattered too. The goat remained unaffected and kept eating the undergrowth heedlessly. Pebbles beside my boot rattled up and down. Possibly the noise was something natural like an earth tremor or a boulder rolling downhill. There were a lot of mountains in this area. It might also be manmade by another Hunter nearby.

Now alert, I altered my mask's eyepieces to telescopic settings. Far in the distance, there was a monstrous vehicle hurtling across the plain at considerable speed, disregarding anything in its path. Heavy-duty wheels squashed plants and animal life effortlessly. Blacked-out windows hid the inside. The owner obviously wanted to remain anonymous. It must have been customised, judging from the armoured body. I couldn't think what purpose this would serve on a planet where no wars had ever taken place. In the early afternoon sunlight, the armoured plating glinted wickedly. A huge dust cloud followed in its wake and floated up twenty metres into the air.

It was closing quickly.

There wasn't enough time to get to my Jeep and collect the rest of my arsenal before the vehicle arrived, so I decided to scarper and hope they'd just pass by. The tree behind me was the obvious choice. Despite the lack of low branches, I managed to get a foothold, stealthily climb up and conceal myself in the thick foliage at the top.

Up here, I had a restricted view of the waterhole below. On the flipside, anyone looking up wouldn't be able to see me through the leaves. Using one hand, I made a small hole in the foliage and created a better viewing space. I switched off the telescopic mode on my eyepiece and clutched the hilt of knife at my side.

Even though I couldn't see it, the thunderous roar of the engine, indicated it was now very near.

It came into my field of vision and grumbled to a halt by the lake's edge.

My goat, with a clear lack of self-preservation, ignored this intrusion and kept eating. There was definitely something wrong with this animal's sense of survival. When I glanced down, I observed that I could land on the roof of the car if I jumped out of the tree, though there was no logical reason for that action for now.

Five large figures emerged from the vehicle. All were tall and broad-shouldered with lumpy potato-like heads and hair shaved almost to the skin. I immediately thought of Umbras and then pushed the thought from my head. The Umbras infected were feral and not capable of intelligent thought. Their clothes seemed strange, a mixture of padded coats and cargo trousers combined with trekking boots that made them seem bigger than they actually were. Appropriate for cold weather but not here. All were armed with guns and knives and one even casually held a double-barrelled pulse blaster. There wasn't a Shade-hunting weapon in sight, which ruled out the possibility they were Hunters. An accented voice called out from inside the vehicle and the others turned around and grunted in reply. His voice was muffled but the meaning became obvious when three of them started to plod towards my half-hidden Jeep.

When they reached it, they moved aside the bush to check inside and inspect my spare weapons, one of which was on loan from ShadeCo. One of them lifted it up and yelled out, "ShadeCo!"

"Carry on," the man inside the vehicle shouted.

With surprising speed, they slashed all four of my tyres and the spare one in the boot, moving mechanically. As they desecrated my vehicle, I felt a mixture of confusion and anger and gritted my teeth while I watched. The gun slung across my shoulder and one at my belt were loaded with Shade-effective ammo, which is useless against humans. I was outnumbered and out-armed. I groaned inwardly because they were stealing expensive equipment. *What an idiot for leaving them in there! Should've had the fucking foresight... I knew the activists were more violent lately. Should've been more careful...*

The driver's door of the vehicle swung open and a blond-haired man got out and started speaking what sounded like Spanish or Italian. A short lag and the translator in my ear explained what he'd said. They were not only taking my guns and equipment, but my whisky! The disrespectful assholes!

I studied the new man more carefully. This man appeared more sophisticated than the others, who seemed like cronies. His mask was unusual, black with pinhole eyepieces with raised intricate tribal artwork across it. Judging from the way he ordered the others about, he was probably in charge of this crew. But I considered them all bastards equally and intended to take revenge when the advantage was mine.

The goat bleated. I shifted position to see what was happening. The other two men slowly approached the animal with outstretched arms. It trotted up to the end of its tether to greet these new people, probably with the expectation of being fed. *Stupid animal.* At the last moment, they swerved and circled around the netting until they faced each other, then bent down and slashed through the cords on the floor. The net was used to snag a Shade and pin it down — a secondary option because the main point was to get it in the goat. *Great, more equipment ruined.* The net retracted until it shrunk into a couple of heaps on the floor, when it was out of the way, they were free to walk over to the animal. One of the men lifted the goat in a deft movement and slung it over his shoulder. A few more steps and they disappeared from my line of vision. They reappeared as they approached their oversized vehicle.

They filed back inside and the last man slammed the doors shut. Just before the engine turned on, I could've sworn I heard the goat cry as it realised too late that it was with unfamiliar people. I almost felt bad for it.

The vehicle growled back to life, thick smoke emitted from the exhaust before it shot off, careered into the undergrowth, tearing the plants apart and then darting off into the desert.

When it had shrunk on the horizon and the sound had faded into the constant whistling of the wind through the desert, I descended. Half sliding, half dropping down the tree, I jumped the last two metres to the ground and rolled forward to buffer the fall.

The oasis was destroyed. Deep tyre prints marked the moist soil, which rapidly trailed off as the ground became hard and rocky. Torn branches and leaves lay either side of the tracks. Scraps of metal and tyre from my Jeep were scattered around the area, some floated in the water.

I strode over to my drooping Jeep to assess the damage.

I didn't need to bend down to see that they slashed all of the tyres beyond repair and would fall away if I attempted to drive it. Surprisingly, they hadn't touched the chassis or seats. Then I inspected the engine. I tapped the bonnet. From the outside it looked intact but as it released, I was hit with a face full of steam.

Recoiling, I shook my head. The eyepieces on my mask misted with hot air and I couldn't see. Taking out a rag from my pocket, I rubbed them clear, and then checked inside the bonnet again.

Shit. I sighed.

This amount of damage was irreparable out in the field. I needed to get the vehicle back to Mayton. Doubtfully, I glanced at the Jeep. I couldn't push it. It was at least a day's walk from where I stood without the Jeep.

Signal strengths are unreliable out here, dust storms and magnetic fields interfere with it. My MID was out of range. Nothing for it. I'd have to leave the Jeep here and return later to tow it away.

With an action decided, I rechecked the vehicle to see if there was anything worth taking. They took all my spare ammo. I'd four rounds of Shade-effective ammo in the gun slung over my shoulder and twenty in the one on my belt. It should be enough, judging by the lack of Shades recently. I snatched up an empty backpack lying on the backseat as it would be useful to carry anything I might forage on the way. From food, my thoughts turned to water. My limited supply was worrying, especially as this was the only waterhole for miles. With some regret, I emptied my flask and went to the edge to fill it with water and dropped in a purifying tablet to make it drinkable. If I rationed it, the water should last a day — enough for the walk.

Finally, I went over to where the goat had been. The nets were heaped on the ground and, although sliced up, they could be mended. I tested the netting with the tip of my boot. One side flew into the air at the pressure and tried to ensnare my foot as it landed. *The trap still works then.* Deactivating the net, I picked both pieces up and shoved them into my backpack along with the flask.

It was important to conserve energy where possible, and my other possessions weren't worth taking or light enough to carry easily. With a brief glance back, I began my trek to Mayton.

✳✳✳

A few hours later, soaked in sweat and skin reddening like an Irishman in moonlight, I arrived at the base of a mountain. I stopped and wiped the back of my neck with my hand. I raised my gaze to the alcove about twenty metres up. The air was moist here. And I could swear I heard running water… that decided it. I started to climb.

I've got a wide reach and can access ledges and crevices that most others can't. Even so, the footholds were uneven and slippery, so I took my time.

After a while, I hoisted myself over the top and onto my stomach. The area was larger than I had thought from ground level. My instincts had been correct; I was rewarded for my efforts with a small waterfall and basin and a refreshing breeze. I ambled over to the basin. Here, the area air felt dense with water spray. There wouldn't be any Shades nearby as they couldn't tolerate this level of humidity.

As I knelt down at the water's edge, I removed my mask and splashed my face and neck to cool down. Fresh earthy smells hit my nose, along with a musty odour from algae coating the rocks. With cupped hands, I collected some water and drank it down, so quickly that the cool liquid hurt my head. I pinched the bridge of my nose until the feeling eased. When I had my fill, I reattached my mask. It was highly unlikely a Shade was present here, though it didn't mean there definitely wasn't.

After this, I scrambled over some larger rocks and eventually sat down on a flat stone, hidden behind a boulder and in the shadows. From this position, I had a side view as the waterfall crashed into the basin. The water swirled on entry and sent ripples across the surface. Spray flew into the air at the base and I found my T-shirt quickly soaked. At least it was better than sweat. I assumed the water in the basin disappeared underground and resurfaced nearer the sea because the desert was scorched for miles. I removed my boots, rolled up my trouser legs and plunged my feet into the cold water. My leg muscles tensed but it felt invigorating all the same.

Though it was pleasant and, in other circumstances, I could've spent a considerable amount of time here, I had to get back.

I tried my luck and attempted a call on my MID. It cut off halfway and refused to connect again.

Reluctantly, I lifted my feet from the water and put my boots on. Before I descended, I knelt by the edge of the recess and observed the area below. Not too far away, I spotted a small black Jeep obscured by camouflage netting and through the webbing I recognised the distinctive triangular ShadeCo symbol. It was a standard rented vehicle from the company. There wasn't any sign of anyone else. After quickly descending, I went to the Jeep and waited a while. They were with ShadeCo, and as they were my sometimes employer, perhaps the driver would give me a lift.

I checked the nearby area and couldn't see anyone, so went back to the Jeep and waited.

An hour passed and nobody came. I'd given them a chance and waited long enough. This Jeep was fair game. I'd send out another vehicle for the driver later.

In my pocket, I'd an emergency kit for situations like this. It was a small case containing a screwdriver, a wire cutter, a can opener and a home-made lock picking kit. I always kept this box on me. Using the screwdriver, I removed the plastic panel underneath the steering unit to access the mechanics inside. After testing the switches, I overrode the controls to use it manually. With a grumble, the engine started and the controls on the dashboard lit up. I replaced the panel and made sure it was fixed in place. I tested the wheel and it moved with a little applied pressure.

Excellent!

I took off the brake and accelerated forward. The Jeep shot from static to fifty miles an hour in a matter of seconds, even on this uneven terrain, and in no time I was hurtling back to Mayton.

8

Longrider

𝒫art of why the field tests are so helpful is the ability to test the weapons with added environmental factors. Any tests in a shooting range are not fully reliable because simulation can never accurately depict all elements.

I released my twentieth shot of the day. The recoil jolted against my arm and shoulder. For such a small weapon, it certainly packed a punch.

The bullet hit the target board just wide of the bullseye and the new smudge of colour merely added to the others and was rapidly becoming quite a rainbow. I replaced the ammo with paint capsules to show clearly where the shots had hit. This would be evidence for the lab to analyse.

Being out in the field meant I needed a conventional weapon with me too; two weapons with Shade-effective bullets were in the holsters under my arms. I still did not feel confident enough to only bring prototypes out with me. Nonetheless, I was definitely improving. The last shot landed closer to the centre than the previous ones.

In a very short period of time, it became evident the new weapons were temperamental and required alterations. These details would be included in my report to Red. I wondered what father would make of the new guns. He used to be a Master Hunter too, and his opinion would have been useful right now. Actually, any other Hunter's opinion would be welcome.

Running my free hand over my hair, I brushed the spiky tips against my palm and stared hard at the target, determined to hit the centre with the final bullet.

I held the weapon with both arms outstretched and my finger on the trigger. At the point of shooting, I heard something unusual. A noise akin to gunfire. Or a car's exhaust backfiring.

Is something wrong?

I ran flat out up the slope towards my vehicle.

It might be nothing.

The Jeep was hidden by camo-netting. It should be fine. My muscles ached, stiff with the steep climb but I pushed through and over the apex. It was gone! All that remained was the netting discarded in a pile and some arcing tyre tracks on the dusty ground.

I did not have words to properly articulate my frustration, so let out a series of yells and kicked at the dirt.

I regained my composure and returned the paint-filled gun to my leg holster. I switched my eyepiece to the telescopic sight and observed my Jeep obscured by a cloud of dust and unquestionably hurtling in the direction of Mayton. It was too far away for specifics. The thief was a man with dark hair but the seat obscured most of his body. He must be stupid. A ShadeCo Jeep is easily traceable and practically impossible to sell. The more pressing matter was the boot's contents. All the other prototypes were in there — all meant to be kept top secret.

I punched the boulder beside me. It was not practical, but the pain felt semi-cathartic and gave me something to focus on.

Forcing myself to think rationally, I looked at the situation objectively. The main issue was the loss of the weapons. I needed to find them as quickly as possible before the loss became public knowledge. If it got out, my reputation would be in tatters despite my hunting record. My position in the company would be put into jeopardy as well. The secondary issue was the loss of the Jeep. If I could find the Jeep, it should lead me to the weapons. I had the registration number with me at least.

My MID automatically displayed my coordinates. I switched onto the call function and selected the Desert Emergency Service or DES; this service is run and financed by each city state to support those in the field. An operator, human by day and droid by night, was available at all hours for Hunters and others who encountered anything from injuries to vehicle malfunctions. Normally, the operator coordinated a car from the respective supplier's headquarters to rescue the worker, along with a medic or a mechanic — or both, if necessary. At least that was the aim. In practice, connectivity on the field is notoriously bad and there are great swaths of areas where it is impossible to contact anyone. Luckily, I managed to connect.

I gave the operator detailed instructions of my coordinates. In turn, she informed me that a rescue vehicle would be sent out within the hour and ordered me to stay where I was. Before ending the call, I gave her details about the thief and asked her to send word to the police to detain him if possible. I obviously omitted the information about the weapons.

After this, I scouted the area for Shades. When I was satisfied it was secure, I sat down cross-legged on the ground. There was little to do except wait patiently for the rescue vehicle to arrive.

✱✱✱

In the desert, no one can hear you sigh… clock watching is dull and my threshold for boredom is low.

Each second lengthened.

Time seemed to stand still.

Even the lizard in front of me was moving in uber slow motion, placing each foot carefully and wavering several moments before raising another one. I drummed my fingers against my knee. For variety, I leaned back against the boulder behind me and rolled my head from side to side until my neck clicked satisfyingly. I looked to my left, where a swirling dust cloud had just cropped up. I noted the nearby boulders as potential cover if the storm worsened.

On the plus side, the wait provided ample opportunity to consider what to do with the thief when I found him. Initially, I wanted to cut off his pilfering fingers with secateurs so he would never steal again and pluck out his eyes for good measure… but with each minute that passed, my anger subsided. My plans became less severe, until I finally resolved only to give him a good pummelling and a stern lecture to make him repent his thieving ways. However, if he had done anything to the guns, the punishment would increase accordingly.

To ease the boredom, I took one of the remaining prototypes out of its holster and examined it. The months of hard work had paid off. The barrel was long in comparison to the rest of the weapon. Part of my report recommended shortening it to increase accuracy, even if doing so would result in a reduced firing range. I felt it was a fair compromise. Hunters are trained in close-quarter combat and these weapons were designed solely for their needs. The current weapons had a limited range anyway. The main issue would be getting the project manager to agree.

Lining up the sights, I took aim at a small lizard and pretended to fire. *Bang!*

A few hours elapsed before my MID flashed indicating a call was coming through. I pressed receive and a cheerful voice chimed, "Hello! Am I speaking to Longrider?"

I replied in the affirmative.

He continued. "Hopefully your wait was fun, but there's fuck all to do here, so wanna get going? I'm just calling to let you know I'm nearby and I'm driving around and I can't see you, could you—"

Interrupting, I said, "In that case, stop where you are, beep the horn and I'll come to you."

He chortled. "Yes, ma'am!" A couple of loud toots wafted from the desert, followed by another set.

I hung up and stiffly got to my feet, stretching my protesting muscles.

In between the beeps I heard a sudden noise, a cross between a dog's panting and a growl. My mask identified a human form behind me. I tensed and spun around to face the rapidly approaching footsteps.

My hand automatically went to my knife. I un-sheaved it and steadied my position.

She emerged behind one of the larger boulders and rapidly closed the gap; her rags streamed behind her like a comet's tail. Her huge red maw was wide in anticipation and her arms were outstretched in a strange welcome. She must have been infected for a while because her jaw was severely distorted.

In the background, the driver kept sounding the horn.

When she was almost on me, I swung the knife and stabbed into the soft flesh of her armpit. The momentum wedged it in further as she collided with me. We fell together. On landing, my knife moved deeper, up to the hilt. She struggled and snapped at my face. I shoved her over and pinned her down with my legs and left hand, while I held the hilt of my knife in the other. I twisted the weapon, though the flesh protested and sucked against it. With a great deal of effort, I managed to pull the knife out. Blood gushed out of the wound, around the blade, spurting all over my clothes; it did not seem possible that someone could have so much blood inside them. Beneath me, her movements slowed until she finally shuddered and relaxed and fell still.

I felt a momentary sadness. Once the Shade takes hold, the person is effectively dead. There is nothing left of the person's mind. Umbras is incurable.

To the clamour of the Jeep's continued beeps, I stood up and lifted the knife to the light; underneath the blood the weapon had a decent coating of damsel-weed.

Now, it was time to wait. I asked the driver to hold on a little longer via my MID.

Sure enough, rising like a smoke flume out of her open mouth, the glutted Shade left the woman's ruined body, searching for another host. It would not have that chance. As soon as it fully emerged, I swiped at it, severing it cleanly in two. The Shade shivered visibly in the air and fell to the ground. I tore off a strip of the woman's top and scooped some of the condensed Shade in the middle, crossed over and tied the four corners of the material to contain part of the gloop. *Hopefully it won't seep through.* The ore has value even outside of a host.

I grabbed the woman's leg and walked towards the Jeep, dragging her behind me and holding the knot of shirt tightly to ensure the Shade did not spill. By now, the dust cloud had drifted on and the field clear once again.

As I got closer, I was surprised to see the driver without goggles on, particularly as there were definitely Shades in the area. Where there is one infected, there is usually another. It was an open-top vehicle, too.

"Hello!" he called out, leaning over the side and waving at me. His grey overalls were incredibly scruffy, splattered with oil, grease and other stains. He beamed at me and his eyes crinkled with good humour, while the bottom half of his face was hidden by a respirator. His goggles sat back on the crown of his head, spiking up the hair around it. I was overwhelmed by the stupidity of this in the field and I fought the urge to snap at him, instead, I gestured to him to lower his goggles. He caught on quickly and dropped them over his eyes. I shook my head incredulously. No sense at all!

At the same time, his eyes darted to my bloody clothes and widened at the woman behind me. "What happened? Are you hurt? Is she hurt?"

"She *had* Umbras," I explained simply, emphasis on the past tense. "And no, I'm not hurt, although she tried her best to rip out my throat."

"How did she get out here? I thought all infected people are admitted into hospital."

"Well… some escape. She's not the first person I've seen out here and I doubt she'll be the last. You never know when someone might become infected and it's impossible to hospitalise everyone before the change occurs, especially if they're alone when it happened. Sometimes they escape."

I lifted her over the side of the vehicle into the backseat, next to his toolkit. As she was quite heavy, she landed awkwardly. I leaned over to straighten her up and strapped her in place. When I noticed the grimy state of the seat, I hesitated to get in and then glanced down at my bloody jumpsuit. I leapt in and thanked him for picking me up.

"That's no problem. It's my job! Where's your car?"

Good question — I have no idea.

"It was stolen by some asshole who took it while I was distracted. I believe I told the emergency contact about the situation. I just need a lift back to Mayton."

With obvious unease, he checked over his shoulder at the body in the back. "I was told that there's a Hunter stranded out in the Farnan region in need of a mechanic. I came prepared." His toolkit was in the backseat, next to the sprawled-out body, bursting with wrenches, spanners, a socket set, and other assorted equipment.

"My only car problem is the lack of one. It's quite a long walk back to town and time isn't a luxury I have at the moment." I drummed my fingers on the arm rest to make the point. I noticed his gaze kept drifting towards the back of the vehicle. "The Shade is dead. The woman's dead. She's not going to reanimate and attack you while you're driving. Don't worry about that. Shades don't reanimate corpses."

"Right," he groaned. "Still, she is unsettling." He took off the brakes and we began to make our way back to Mayton. He kept nervously checking the rear-view mirror every few seconds. It was some time before he initiated further conversation.

"Have you got any idea who stole your Jeep?"

"No. That's something I'm going to investigate."

Khoi, as he later introduced himself, was far more at ease when he had something to concentrate on. He drove the car nonchalantly, with one arm draped over the open window and the other gripping the steering wheel. We narrowly dodged a boulder here, bounced over a dune there, and crunched over parched weeds everywhere. The toolkit and corpse both clattered around in the back and I wondered if both would fly forward if we hit a particularly harsh bump. I folded my arms and gently stroked the top of my knife's hilt, now back in its sheaf at my belt.

Miles whizzed past. In the distance, the underdeveloped dirt track transformed into the main road, complete with tarmac, signposts and proper road markings.

We were gaining rapidly. Then there was a sudden smoothness as we hit decent road and the shaking stopped.

Raising my gaze, I observed Mayton Hill stretched over its emerald hills with the silver-and-white domes of citizens' homes scattered across them. ShadeCo itself was located at the far end of town and from my perspective the building was hidden by Aydin's Leap's broad apex, the second-largest hill. A twenty-foot wall runs the length of the town and acts as the first defence against the Shade menace. When we got closer, we would be able to see the wardens and droids who patrol it.

The single parking lot rapidly approaching to our right paled in comparison to the grand view ahead. The pyramid ShadeCo symbol announced that the lone building there was an official ShadeCo depot; it was considerably smaller than the one connected to the city wall and the main road. The building was painted a hideous duck-egg blue and topped by a slate roof glazed with a layer of field dust. Gates flanked either side of the building, one for entry and one for exit. Sturdy fences with an arcing length of electronic wire at the top prevented thieves from breaking in, and huge floodlights on all four corners of the structure served as beacons for drivers on the main road. There were a few cars in the lot, though the drivers themselves were nowhere in sight. Perhaps they were inside the centre, waiting for the next shuttle.

As we drew nearer, the vehicles became more distinct. One was a security van with a florescent-yellow strip running along the doors and a black ShadeCo symbol emblazoned on the side. The other four vehicles were standard hireable black Jeeps. We had scores of these at the company HQ and the differences between them were hardly perceptible. My stolen Jeep was one of these and it might well be here.

"Stop here please!" I directed Khoi.

We screeched to a halt beside the lot. When the vehicle slowed enough, I sprang over the side and strode over to the gates, scanning my MID at the recognition unit. The unit flashed green and the gates slid open. As soon as the gap was wide enough, I squeezed through and entered the yard. Immediately the heat radiating from the concrete floor struck me, even the air wavered with warmth.

With purposeful steps, I approached the Jeeps and systematically checked their IDs. No luck with the first one or second, but the third was mine. The same ID. The wrapper from what would have been my lunch lay open on the dashboard and a half-eaten bagel lay on its side beside it. Clearly the thief had not liked my meal choice. My water bottle lay on the passenger seat and now entirely emptied of its contents. *I wonder if everything is the same.*

Still waiting outside the lot, Khoi called from the Jeep. "Should I park up?"

"Yes, come in. I need to check something. I'm not sure how long it'll take," I shouted back, then unlocked the vehicle and opened the door.

A wet patch soaked the driver's seat and I did not want to speculate why. Also, the panel underneath the steering wheel was ajar and had been interfered with. I clambered over the passenger seat into the back, and then peered over the backseats and into the boot. Empty. The weapons and ammo were gone. Panic rose in my chest. With a great effort of will, I forced it down and tried to think rationally.

Holding onto a faint hope, I went onto my hands and knees and checked under the seats. Nothing there except lint and mud and dust. I straightened up.

Khoi's voice carried over the lot. "You okay?" He rose out of his seat and motioned as if he was going to join me.

I slipped out of the vehicle and raised my hand in a halting motion. "I'm fine! Just stay where you are!"

How could I have been so stupid as to leave them in the car! I'm going to get into so much shit!

The thief had to be a ShadeCo employee or linked to the company in some way otherwise he would not have returned the vehicle here or even been able to enter without breaking in. I wondered whether he had the audacity to talk to the guard in the hut. I went to the security building and knocked on the door, startling the solitary guard, who spilt coffee on his lap. In a soundless curse, he wiped at his stained trousers before answering the door.

In a waft of cold air, the guard emerged. He stared at me irritably.

I went straight to the point. "See that black Jeep over there?" I indicated with my index finger. "Who returned it?"

His small eyes narrowed further as he concentrated for a moment. "A guy brought it back a little while ago, maybe an hour or two. He didn't have a user code and I thought it's odd because how could he use the vehicle in the first place? When I asked for identification, he showed me his pass and it was valid, so I let it go. I haven't had anyone check it over yet, maintenance isn't due for another half hour."

"What was his name?"

The guard shrugged his shoulders. "I can't remember. Something Butcher."

"Don't you monitor activity here?"

"We've got surveillance. I can check the recorded entry list if you bear with me…" He scrolled through his MID until he came to the record sheet. "Oh, the car was actually returned by a Longrider Ericksen… could have sworn he said Butcher. Well, that was the person registered on the user code anyway."

Butcher was not an uncommon surname. However, the thief being deep in the field suggested it was a Hunter and I only knew one with that name. Even so, I questioned him further. "What did he look like?"

"Tall. Well-built. Looked as if he could kick the shit outta' you if you look at him the wrong way. I never saw his face because he wore a black gas mask and never took it off. Oh, and he had tattoos too." He looked apologetic that he could not recall further details and wiped the sweat from his brow.

That definitely confirms it! But why steal my Jeep? Has information about the guns leaked? How did this happen? Only a handful of people knew I intended to bring them out today. Who told him?

The guard's information was of great assistance so I did not tarry longer than required. I thanked him and explained an edited version of the events, entirely omitting the information about the lost weapons. No one needed to know about that. The guard voiced his negative opinion of Butcher leaving a woman alone and defenceless in the wilderness, disregarding the fact that I am a *Hunter*. It was one of the curses of having a slight frame. People assume vulnerability. It was an incorrect assumption.

I cut him off with a quick goodbye and sprinted back to the rescue car, hopping over the open window into my seat. Khoi sat listening to music and tapped his hands in time to the beat on the steering wheel.

"I'm finished here. We can return to town now… thanks for waiting."

"No probs," he said, removing the brakes and allowing the vehicle to slowly roll forward towards the gate. When the Jeep's bumper was about a foot away, the guard activated the release from inside the building and we watched it slide open.

"So, will you let me to see your face since I saved you? I have a feeling you're pretty under there," the mechanic joked.

I raised a questioning eyebrow. "Think all you want, I'm not taking my mask off. You can keep your speculating to yourself."

"All right, touchy," he chuckled. "I know how guarded Hunters are about their identity. It's not surprising considering the number of attacks on staff and vehicles recently — even in HQ parking lot. I've worked in ShadeCo long enough to know that much."

Folding my arms, I replied stiffly, "Good Hunters are." I pointedly shifted in my seat and faced the towards the side window for the remainder of the journey.

I'll look on the company files. They'll hold his details and then I can resolve this matter. Maybe he doesn't realise what he possesses or at least hasn't done anything with it yet.

9

Landmine

$\mathcal{I}$ browsed through another manufacturer's stock. Nothing similar to what I looked for. Irritated, I switched off the screen. Finding that pirate vehicle's source was harder than I'd first thought. For one thing, I couldn't find a vehicle with even a remotely similar spec. Even mod garages doing customisation work didn't offer anything like armour plating or gun mounts. Probably privately made and easy to find if you knew where to look and I hadn't a clue… I slapped my palms on the desk in frustration.

A message popped up on my MID. The retrieval truck had collected my Jeep and was now on the way to the mechanics. Hopefully, the damage would be fixable and I wouldn't have to fork out for another one. Money was the word of the month. With the wasted hunt and the quarterly bill from Marie's hospital due too, I really didn't need another surprise cost right now. Hunters permanently working at the Big Three certainly have an advantage in this area. The firms regularly pay out for damages sustained to vehicles on the field. But the drawback was a fixed salary and monthly supply quota, while freelancers are paid in full for the value of the supplied ore.

The catch now is that until my vehicle is fixed, I can't hunt, and if I can't hunt, then I can't pay for repairs. What a bloody mess.

Another unknown was the box beside me. I drummed my fingers on the plastic lid. This container held a couple of guns along with several clips of Shade-effective ammo and there were two more empty shapes cut in the velvet at the bottom to hold another two weapons.

Initially, I'd simply wanted to return the Jeep and its contents, yet the guns caught my attention. They were different to any I'd used before. I carefully picked up a gun with a gloved hand and examined it.

Compact. I tossed it from one hand to another. Light too. It'd be easy to carry a few without feeling the weight. Typically, Shade-effective guns are too heavy to carry more than two at once, and then you had all your other weapons to carry too, but I could have carried six or seven of these without feeling a thing. I planned to keep a hold of them and return them to ShadeCo once I'd analysed them. Maybe...

My housedroid hovered behind me and it bumped into my shoulder to puncture my thoughts. I waved the droid away but it stayed put.

"We have a visitor at the door, Michael." The monitor on the droid's body displayed the area directly outside my front door. I saw two lads about nine or ten playing on their lawn with flying battle bots, ramming them into each other with as much force as they could generate, sending bolts and sparks into the air before they crash-landed in the road.

There was no one actually at my door.

As I turned away, the droid hovered over again, more persistent, but its monitor was still empty. Maybe the kids played too close to the external sensors.

I strode over to the door and swiftly swung it open with the intention of scaring them. My arms were raised like a bear ready to attack.

Instead, a figure rushed at me and kicked me squarely in the stomach.

Reeling backwards, I staggered away from my assailant.

The attacker darted forward and hit me on my nose. Unfortunately, I'd taken off my gas mask at home, so I'd nothing to buffer the blow. It stung.

I raised my fists in a classic defensive fighting pose.

For the first time, I noticed despite the genderless mask and the unisex body suit, she was clearly a woman. This threw a spanner in the works. It didn't seem fair to return the punches. She was willowy and looked as if she'd crumple at the first hit. The clothes were plain with a small ShadeCo symbol at the breast, though the canvas gas mask was familiar. She was a Hunter. Long-something or other. I needed to restrain her...

I deflected another sudden kick with the side of my forearm, knocking her off balance, and she bounced back to regain it.

Growing confident, she circled and gradually moved closer with one fist raised to eye level, the other drawn back to her body suggesting that she was trained in a form of martial arts. She jabbed. I dodged. Although I am an avid boxer, it still didn't seem right to attack fully.

I tried to talk her round. "What's your fucking problem?"

She lowered her fists slightly. "What's my problem?" she repeated incredulously and threw another punch.

I caught her wrist with the side of hand and deflected it away from my body. She darted out of range and the settee now stood between us.

"My problem is with you, Butcher! Stealing my vehicle and leaving me stranded!" accused her muffled voice. It sounded familiar.

She darted around the couch, while I stood my ground. Another blow was directed at my face and I blocked again by grabbing hold of her wrist and turning it down. But that was a bluff because her real attack brought her knee into my groin.

Fuck it! I'll make an exception.

Winded and feeling a deep ache in my stomach, I shoved her away. From the force of the push, she stumbled and tripped over a low table, breaking it and landing on her ass with a thud on the wooden floor.

It was only a brief pause.

She rolled onto her feet quickly, this time with a handgun clenched in her fist. It was aimed at my chest.

I looked from the gun to her to the gun again. She was out of reach. If I lunged for it, she'd see it coming and might fire. It also might be a bluff.

I raised my hands and unclenched my fingers.

She's a Shade Hunter. Not an assassin.

And I took a step nearer.

"Don't move!" she ordered. The gun didn't waver.

Just a little more…

I took another step.

If she was going to shoot she'd have done it by now.

There was some movement to my right. Abruptly, the housedroid planted itself between us offering a tray of drinks, of all things.

The woman pulled the trigger. The droid's central unit shattered and it dropped to the ground like deadweight. The tray clanged on the ground and the glasses shattered into fragments and the drinks and ice cubes spilt over her boots.

Her aim reverted to me.

"Explain yourself!" she demanded.

It was one thing to shoot a droid, murder was quite another. I was sure the gun was there to prove a point only. "To be honest, I don't know what you're talking about."

"The Jeep and the weapons," she stated curtly.

The items weren't really hers anyway, just property of ShadeCo. "I needed the Jeep and I didn't care who it belonged to. Nothing personal, it was left there unguarded and I took my opportunity. Maybe next time, be more careful on the field."

"Don't tell *me* how to do *my* job," she spat and added in the same tone as a curse, "*Freelancer!* If that was the case then why did you take my gun too, eh? You were watching me, stalking me! And waited until I was suitably occupied and took the guns. Who sent you? How much did they pay you, hmm? How much? A thousand? Two? Well? Answer!"

"I told you. I needed the Jeep. I don't care about your guns—"

"Bullshit! You're a liar! And a disgrace to the Hunter profession!" Even though her mouth was muffled, the anger in her voice was clear. The emotion didn't appear to affect her aim. The gun wasn't wavering. Not even a little. Still, probably just for show...

"The weapons seemed interesting, so I wanted to examine them. They're for hunting?"

She didn't answer my question. Instead, slowly, she backed towards my desk, keeping her gaze on me and slightly lowering the gun. Clearly she'd noticed the weapons and ammo on the table and was going to reclaim them.

Suddenly, she tilted her head and aimed at me again. "Who else have you told about these?"

"No one."

She stopped and stared at me fixedly.

"No one."

At length, she said, "It better stay that way."

After this, the silence stretched time. Each second ticked off on the antique clock on the wall, a collectible from Earth. I couldn't think of anything to say to her so I stayed silent.

Eventually, she replaced the gun in its holster and sighed.

"And I thought you were a decent guy. I guess my judgement was impaired that night… it goes to show first impressions can be misleading. Even a murderer can be charismatic when they want to be, the infected aside. You're a disappointment."

She folded her arms and she said smugly, "You could be prosecuted for this. Police are cracking down on attacks in the field and are making arrests left, right and centre. Also, senior management at ShadeCo wouldn't respond well to this threat to security and information, and if they found out you'd be shamed and ousted from the profession. Every black energy company will shun you, from the small players to the giants like ShadeCo and Hayward Bros. Just a thought."

Vindictive bitch, this one. I smirked to myself. That was okay though, as I had my own ammunition.

"What's so funny?"

"You can't threaten me."

"Why not? You don't think I'll do it? You have grossly underestimated me then, Butcher!"

"It goes both ways. I could be difficult too. How would they react if I revealed you'd left the guns around for anyone to take? It's your word against mine. And how would it look for you? Careless maybe, neglectful… d'you reckon you'd be assigned a project like it again?"

The last detail was a guess. Yet it seemed to hit home because her shoulders tensed, either in annoyance or anger, I couldn't tell. Her knuckles whitened. Her hand rested on the container and turned halfway towards me. Finally she sighed, "What a cluster… we seem to have reached an impasse."

Relaxing slightly, I agreed. "It's a bit of a clusterfuck…"

"It is indeed."

She stared at me fixedly. The mask's face was blank. It was impossible to tell what she was thinking at this point. We both held enough ammunition to ruin each other.

"There's a lot at stake here." She repeated that she was angry with me for stealing the weapons. "But I'm…" she paused and drummed her nails on the lid of the container, "…willing to overlook your thievery if you choose to forget the weapons in this box."

She tapped the lid again with added meaning.

"That's it? Pretty simple if you ask me, what with the fighting, the gun and the destroyed droid."

"Well, what would you suggest then? The other options aren't suitable."

"No, no, no, it's fine with me. It solves our problem painlessly, it's just simple that's all." In need of refreshment, I sidled towards the kitchen area to the drink cabinet. After the eventful past few days, I felt that we could probably both use a stiff drink, not juice like the droid had offered. I'd deal with that mess later. "Do you want to seal our deal with a drink?"

She glanced again at the box and seemed doubtful. I half-expected her to refuse and was surprised when she asked, "What do you have?"

"Spirits? Beer? Wine? I've got a lot... considering, so it's your choice."

"Considering what?"

"That I live on my own."

"Oh. I'll have brandy then if you have it."

She followed me into the kitchen and picked up a stool. It was high. She planted her feet on the bar around the middle of the table because her legs were too short to reach the floor. Even so, I knew what she was capable of, so I poured the drinks side on to avoid turning my back to her.

"Why didn't you tell me you were a Hunter too? You said you were a chemical engineer."

The question threw me and the best I could manage was, "Eh?" I handed her a glass.

She repeated the question, pronouncing the words a little more slowly.

The woman from the bar...

"I don't generally tell people unless they know me well. Not with the stigma attached. Can't be dealing with the campaigner crap. And to be fair, you didn't tell me either."

The gas mask's dead eyes stared at me.

"Mmm," she mused, swirling the drink in her glass and warming it in her hands. "It's not just the property destruction by ignorant activists, the threats on the field, or the stupid questions people ask, it's the total lack of understanding about the nature of Shades. People don't consider Shades dangerous any more or how necessary they are to society. Without black energy, the planet would shut down and there needs to be a balance between capturing Shades and not overhunting them. It's ridiculous how some civilians treat them. To most people, Shades are a mild irritation and Umbras a disease only caught by unlucky individuals in the wrong place at the wrong time. Do you know that the DES officer who collected me from the field wasn't even wearing goggles? Honestly, we're in the middle of the damn desert and there was nothing covering his eyes! How foolish! People are getting far too relaxed."

I chuckled and finished the brandy in one, savouring the burn.

Opposite, she rolled up her mask to her nose so she could drink. The down-turned mouth and angular jaw were familiar. We clinked our glasses together and she quickly downed the liquid as well. She coughed involuntarily. The moonshine might be a bit strong, but she apparently thought she could handle another before returning home, as she reached her glass out for more.

Reaching over, I grabbed the neck of the bottle with one hand and brought it to the table. As I prepared the next round, I pointed out, "It'll be easier if you take off your mask." And handed the glass back with a few fingers of brandy.

We downed them as quickly as the round before.

She agreed to take of her mask on the proviso that I shut the door first. It was still wide open after our fight. Swiftly, I strode over and entered a code to lock it.

Perhaps the strong booze was already kicking in? Maybe it took the edge off her anger and reserve? Maybe she just wanted to offload? The aim of this was to avoid repercussions and I'd let her talk, if she needed it. She undid the fastening at the back and then pulled the canvas mask over her head and placed it on the table beside her. She smoothed up her shockingly blonde hair, checking that it was still held in place and then she looked at me directly.

"Natural or fake?"

"Butcher! You don't ask a woman that sort of question. It's rude and intrusive..." She smiled wryly. "However, for the record, Scandinavian heritage will out. It's natural, when I was a child my hair was practically white."

I nodded and poured another round.

The liquor sat fine with me, but it might not be her thing. Some people can't hold it and I was much bigger than her, pretty sure I could fit my hands around her waist. A few hours had elapsed already, although our pace slackened after the initial three drinks. I asked if I could get her something else.

"No. 'Tis is fine." Her voice had a definite slur to it. "You know, this situation's bizarre. A short while ago, I intended to beat you up and now I'm accepting your hospitality as if it's an ordinary thing." She barked in laughter. "Damn! What a day, what a week. Y'know? For a 'lancer, you're all right, even if you *did* take the fucking car."

She raised herself up slightly, reached over and punched my arm playfully.

We started to talk shop and shared different techniques. She seemed surprised to find out I'd never had formal training at an academy before I'd taken the Hunter exams. Apparently, it's very unusual, but then I'd never really discussed training with another Hunter and I've been registered for nearly fifteen years. She'd gone the typical route of having a sponsor, signing up to one of energy companies' training programmes, along with mentors and training schedules and lectures.

Strangely though, I found I enjoyed her company. Almost as if the attack hadn't happened. Almost. I could still feel the left side of my face throbbing where she'd hit me.

***

Another couple of hours passed. The rounds flowed freely. She didn't seem to be leaving any time soon and was burbling on, talking for both of us. The bottle was empty. I called the droid to bring over another until I remembered that she destroyed it, and snatched the bottle from the counter myself.

As I handed her another drink, she asked, "Should we make another toast?"

"To what?"

"Perhaps 'n *entente*? Or hunting? Or something?"

"To our agreement," I grinned at her and lifted my glass.

"To our agreement," repeated Valya, lifting her glass, tapped mine and downed her drink.

We slammed our glasses on the table.

"Another?"

10

Longrider

Still at Butcher's.

Didn't intend to be here so long.

The room's spinning crazily. I don't think I can get home. Like this. Maybe I'll wait it off...

Butcher's face is rotating in front of me. Left, right and... diagonal? The features are blurry. His movements are jolting. Not sure if that is deliberate. Is he messing with me?

Oh damn.

I shook my head to clear my vision. It didn't work. The spinning seemed to speed up if anything.

Thinking about it. I've revealed too much. He's a near stranger. Though he's an unkempt-sort-of-handsome. Usually like 'em slicker. How strange. So, I'd let my guard down.

Now, the greatest part of me screamed nausea.

"Gonna' be sick..."

Accordingly, I fell sideways out of my seat. And flumped to the floor. I landed awkwardly on my arm. It jerked into my stomach. I couldn't hold back. Acidic vomit poured out. Clear and hot. Onto the wooden flooring.

I heaved again and let out another gush.

When I'd finished, I turned my head away. The mess smelt bitter. Not my finest moment.

Quite comfortable here, really...

11

Landmine

*E*ven in my hazy state, I could tell she'd just thrown up. Then the unpleasant smell wafted up and reached my nose to confirm it. I groaned. With the droid gone, I'd have to clean that up.

Honestly though, I wasn't surprised. We'd emptied the bottle between us and I'd considered opening a new one, but that thought fled quickly. She wasn't in any state for anything except sleep and maybe something incredibly greasy to combat the hangover when she woke up.

Lightweight...

The room spun slightly and worsened as I moved. Holding onto the worktop, I wobbled around the table to where she lay curled on the floor and prodded her with my toe. She let out a single snore and shifted onto her back. I couldn't leave her there like that. If she were sick again, she'd probably choke. When I picked her up, she was limp and pliable. I carried her over to the settee and lowered her down on her side. Her breath was toxic and I guessed that she'd go again at some point, so I propped her head up with a pillow for good measure. After this, I staggered to the kitchen and retrieved a bucket that I positioned beside her head.

Valya's gonna' feel like shit tomorrow.

That was a satisfying thought. I could feel my face throbbing from the blow earlier and my cheek was starting to swell, closing my right eye.

Once I took care of her, I returned to the kitchen to deal with the puddle seeping into the slats of the wooden floor. It was difficult to think clearly. Resting my hand on a chair for support, I stared at it while the bitter smell fully assaulted my nostrils and noted — noodles?

I'll deal with that later.

Better sleep it off.

Unsteadily, I swayed to the kitchen sink and turned on the tap and drunk directly from it. I wiped my mouth with the back of my hand. Then I staggered back to the lounge, slumped down on the nearest armchair and kicked off my boots.

I closed my eyes, knowing there'd be a hangover waiting for me when I awoke, although nowhere near as bad as Valya's.

The last few days had been pretty peculiar. And I'd a strong feeling that my life would somehow be different in future. Just why was hard to say yet. The mental connection with someone was a new experience and I was having difficulty processing it. I didn't know her very well but we had an understanding. An agreement. The attack might've been a good thing.

A short while later, I nodded off too. The sleep was dreamless.

Interlude One

Longrider
Twenty-Seven Years Before

Snores echoed from the end of the tiled hallway even though it was past midday, and the corridor was dark. All the blinds were closed and most of the doors shut and locked against intruders. The house plants had taken on a sinister form and the leaves seemed to coil like tentacles and curled in the shadows. In the partial light, the little girl looked down its length and the hallway appeared to stretch further as she watched. She squeezed the handle of her toy cart behind her; it was empty and required cargo. She stood steadfast and fixed her face into a determined frown and toddled towards the only ajar door, her parents' bedroom at the end of the passage.

Passing glass tables, wilting potted plants and discarded toys, she was not deterred, even when a cleaning droid knocked into her cart when it exited one of the locked bedrooms.

When she was at the doorway, she evaluated the room through the narrow slit between the door and the frame. It was gloomy and she could barely make out anything. She gently pushed the door further, to let in more light, and silently ventured inside. The air was stale — an unwashed body mingled with unwashed clothes in an enclosed space; the latter lay in a pile by the foot of the bed. The lump under the covers indicated one occupant and there was a crinkled sheet on the other side of the bed. Her dad had long since gone to work and the breakfast he had prepared for her was long finished.

She wheeled her cart to the door frame so the door didn't swing shut accidentally and seal her in. Quietly, she snuck into the room on tentative tiptoes, careful to avoid unnecessary noise. The thick carpet squeezed between her toes, a pleasant sensation at odds with the worry she felt as she approached the prone figure. Drawing up alongside the bed, she beheld the comatose form of her mother, who was half emerged from the covers with one arm dangling lifelessly over the edge and the other flopped over a glass. Her hair was draped over her face like a platinum curtain — the same colour as the girl's, though the woman's had dark roots. Her jade-silk nightdress was rolled up to reveal a pink, fleshy thigh, smattered with freckles that disappeared into the covers at her knee.

Nearing the headrest of the bed, the girl examined her mother's face for immediate signs of awakening. Her eyelids were closed while her lips were slightly parted and her breathing was deep and heavy and gently stirred the strands of hair at each inhalation and exhalation. Watchfully, she took a step nearer the bed. The girl softly prodded her cheek with an index finger and then again with greater force, leaving a nail mark when she moved her hand away. But her mother didn't stir.

The girl smiled to herself and wiped her own greasy tresses over and behind her ear then backed away slowly.

Still on tiptoe, she crept over to the closet and glanced over her shoulder.

Her mother hadn't budged.

Gradually and cautiously, moving inch by inch, she opened the door. A creak sounded from the hinges.

It seemed deafening to the girl.

She spun around, certain that she'd be caught in the act. But her mother was dead to the world.

Her heart raced in anticipation as she turned back to the closet.

Inside, the closet was typical. All the clothes hung from a rail running from one side to the other, there was a shelf with hidden contents. She wasn't interested in that. What she wanted was accessible. On the floor lay a multitude of unordered shoes stacked over each other which formed a barrier to the leather trunk she wanted. There was a sticker on the top right hand of the case, which had squiggles on it along with the letters, 'A' and 'Y', two letters that were also in the girl's name. She clambered over the shoes, squashing several pairs out of shape and eventually standing on a pair of boots. With small, deft hands, she undid the trunk's clasps and pushed up the lid.

In the padded centre of the trunk, there was an enormous gun, almost the same size as she was, even the barrel was wider than her arm. It was sleek, streamlined and impressive, and the canister at its core glowed with an aluminous light.

Using both hands, she reached down and pulled at the stock. It was heavy. Her muscles shivered with the strain, but she managed to lift it over the side. However, she could not hold the gun further and it fell down with a dull thud. She skipped backwards to avoid it crushing her toes. At the same time, the gun flattened several more shoes, including her mother's favourite killer heels.

Spinning around, the girl saw that her mother was still asleep. Her chest rose and fell evenly.

The girl exhaled in relief.

Now, more concerned with speed than caution, she grabbed the stock with both hands and dragged the gun behind her towards the cart in the doorway. The carpet purred and parted as the gun passed over it, leaving an obvious trail from the closet to the hallway. She kept her eyes forward and struggled on. At any moment, she expected to be grasped by her mother's hands.

When she eventually reached her cart, she lowered the weapon onto the ground and gave her arms a break. It really was very heavy. Then summoning all of her three-year-old strength, she picked up the gun again and dumped it onto the cart, which rolled forward a few paces after it was given its load. The wheels were sturdy and it easily took the gun's weight. She walked around to the front of the cart and picked up the handle.

After the initial burst of strength to get the cart in motion, it felt far easier to move the gun, especially with a tiled floor outside, the wheels glided over it.

Her mission was a success.

With excited glee, she skipped down the hallway towards the main room at the front of the house and from there, to her den. As the hall spread outwards and upwards into the large main room, her pace increased until she ran as fast as her legs and her cargo would allow. The plastic of the cart started to crack and bend under the weight of the gun but fortunately she didn't have far to go.

She pulled up beside the dining room table and allowed the cart to roll to a stop. The table was covered entirely by a chequered tablecloth, with tassels along the edging that stretched to the floor, so the table legs and the space underneath were entirely hidden.

This was her lair.

Here she could pretend to be whatever or whoever she wanted to be. Some days she was a wolf. Yesterday she was a pilot. Today she was a Hunter, just like her dad.

She lifted up a corner of the cloth and moved aside one of the chairs to create an entrance. Next, she wheeled the cart inside before dropping the edge behind her. Her hands appeared beneath the cloth and pulled the chair back into its original position. The tablecloth was thick enough to hide her den, yet porous enough to let some light through, so she was not in pitch black. A bowl of fruit containing a bunch of bananas propped up against one of the table legs and beside this was a half-litre bottle of water with a long straw protruding from the top. Sprawled across the tiles was a dirty, grey toy lizard, so well-loved his face was partly chewed away, an eye was missing and the tongue long gone. The girl bent down and picked him up by his head and plopped him out of the way.

In the limited space, she tipped up the cart and dropped the gun to the floor with a clatter. She sat down next to the weapon and tapped some of the switches around the glowing canister. After a short time she hit the right combination, and it fell out onto her lap. Lifting it up, she gazed at the swirling green mist inside. She watched it revolve like it was alive in the confines of the canister.

Outside, she heard her name called.

It was her mother and she sounded mad.

Even with the tablecloth barrier, she could tell that her voice was high-pitched in anger. The girl stayed as quiet as possible until the footsteps padded past her hiding place. She reached for the canister instead of her toy, clutching it to her chest.

The voice muttered under her breath, and then called out. "Fine! If you don't want to eat, that's fine. But I'm going to take a bath now, so you'll have to wait until I'm done." Then she added warningly, "And you better not disturb me." Which echoed around the high walls along with her footsteps.

The girl waited until she was certain her mother had left before she placed the canister down and resumed playing with the gun.

She prodded the trigger and applied more pressure until it gave a satisfying click. It was unloaded. Nothing came out of the barrel except a rush of air. She did it again to the same effect.

One of the lair's sides flapped up.

Her mother's face was there. It glistened from her wash and one wet cowlick had escaped its towel-turban and curled on her wide forehead.

"What are you doing with that?" Her eyes widened when she saw what was in her daughter's hands.

Without thinking, the girl threw the canister at her mother's face, smacking straight into her nose. She squealed in pain as the girl scrambled out the opposite side of the den. She ran blindly, her little legs pumping as hard as they could and went headlong into the kneeling figure by the front door. She threw her arms around her father, hoping he'd be her saviour, allowing him to pick her up.

"Hey there, Muffin! What've you been up to?" He lifted her easily and straightened up, his rifle strap hung precariously from his shoulder. Shifting her to one arm, he adjusted the strap and moved it closer to his collar.

"Look what your daughter has been playing with!" Her mother held the unloaded gun accusatorily at them. There was a cut across her nose. "And she threw the canister at me too!" She glared at the girl. "Valya, you've been a very naughty girl!"

His pale eyes widened in surprise when he saw the weapon; it was one of his hunting guns. He looked down at Valya in his arms, the cheery tone gone from his voice. "How did you get that? I thought it was safely tucked away in our closet."

"I found it," the girl said to his chest then glanced up nervously. "I wanted to be a Hunter like you." She hid her head in his chest again.

His frown melted slightly. "Guns are dangerous, Muffin. They're not toys. Promise me that you'll never touch it again without me around, is that clear? Valya! Look at me."

"That's right." His wife agreed. The girl's eyes were wide and she spared a quick glance at her mother, then turned back to her father and nodded her head in understanding.

"Now apologise to your mother."

The girl obeyed.

"Good." He turned to his wife. "But how did she get this? How'd she know that it was in the closet?"

"She's a conniving little imp and waited until I was asleep to creep in and steal it." Her mother folded her arms and looked as furious as it was possible to look wearing only a towelling robe.

"Do you really think a three-year-old, works like that?"

He placed her on the ground and her mother swooped down and planted a slap on her arm. The girl didn't cry out. She rubbed the spot where it landed and stared at the ground while her mother chastised her. "Don't you *ever* do that again! What would've happened if the canister burst open and I breathed it in, hmmm? Do you hear me? Never again you stupid little girl!"

"Calm down, dear, she gets it. She said she's sorry and won't do it again." He strode over to his wife and held her shoulders and rubbed them softly.

"Why are you home so early?" She pouted and ran her hand down his chest.

"Red decided he didn't need us until later on, so I can stay here for a couple of hours if you want." He kissed her tenderly on the bridge of her nose, where the canister had left a scratch and she titled her head back to allow him to do so.

Remembering Valya was still there, her mother told her, "Why don't you play with your toys or something? Stay in here and out of mischief and try not to be a nuisance to the droid."

Her father added more kindly, "Mummy and I need to talk. I'll be back out to play with you soon." Then he picked up the canister and gun and led her mother out of the room.

Valya found herself alone once again.

Landmine
Twenty-Seven Years Before

Some traditions keep for generations, even if they don't entirely stay the same and the original meaning becoming long-lost with time and changing attitudes. There was no exception on Diomedia. The Winter Festival tradition is still celebrated, although the religious associations were gone and only the lasting commercial semblance remained. It was one of the customs that survived the transition from Earth.

At dusk at the Winter Festival of forty-five, a prosperous family took their seats around the oval dining room table that was laden with an abundance of food and more than they could eat in one sitting. The centrepiece was a roasted bird twice as big as a human head, mounted on a stand above the other dishes. Surrounding it was an assortment of trays containing potatoes, greens, native root vegetables, and most importantly, little fried sausages.

The tall, trim man at the head of the table stood up so he could have a better angle for cutting the bird into wafer-thin slices. His suit was expensive and the fitted cut at the waist and shoulders suggested it was bespoke. His sleeves were rolled up to his elbows to avoid staining from the bird's juices. The table's glass surface was marked with blobs of gravy and red sauce, and the nano-perceptive table surface had already cleaned itself twice even though the meal had scarcely begun. Several travelling vegetables strayed from their food pyramids and rolled down onto the table. The adults' glasses contained a seasoned wine and their faces were rosy, everyone contently waiting for the feast to commence.

Once all the dishes were served and everyone's glasses were filled, the three house droids hovered over to the corners of the room, then switched onto standby.

It was a rare occasion for the family to gather together like this and

Michael, the youngest and just five years old, naturally had to show off to his audience.

"Ouch! Mum! Make him stop!"

"Michael. Edward. Butcher! Stop hitting your sister, or I'll take away your truck and you won't see it for a week!" his mum scolded, her eyes narrowed in her round face. The use of his full name indicated her anger. Obediently, he lowered the toy and laid it on his lap. His mother gave an approving nod. But when she looked away, he gave his sister a sidelong glare. At two years older than him, she was his natural enemy.

Marie squealed as she found herself at the receiving end of yet another whack. "Mike, she told you to stop, so stop, stupid! You're so irritating!" She punched him in the shoulder.

"Both of you! That's enough!" their mother shouted.

She glared at them until they both lowered their gazes to their plates and both mumbled an unfelt apology.

Michael turned the truck over in his hands and looked down at the toy. He was glad of his choice; it had thought-sensitive controls and could reach speeds of up to twenty mph, which is no mean feat for something that's only fifteen centimetres long. His other presents had to wait. The children were permitted to open one gift before dinner. Marie received a holographic image maker with badges to attach the hologram to once it'd been created. Each member of the family had circular pins on their party hats and bespoke holograms projected a foot above the wearer's head.

"Pass me the tatties, please, Miriam," asked his uncle, a stout man with crimson jowls, several years older than his brother, Michael's father. He shifted in his seat and winked at Michael. "Your mum makes the best tatties that I've ever tasted."

"Joe, don't be silly, of course they're not! And don't they always say that ugly women make good roast potatoes?" They both laughed as she passed off his compliment, yet she was clearly delighted anyway. It wasn't often she had the opportunity to cook for the family, because usually the servants and droids oversaw menial household tasks. Today most of the servants had taken the day off, so she had a chance to show off her culinary skills without interference.

As their laugher subsided, the voices of the old couple seated at the other end of the table filled the silence, and the others listened patiently to their reminiscence about the first Winter Festival on the planet. The old woman said, "The first Winter Festival was not nearly as comfortable as this. Everyone was crammed into a hall, if you could call it that. More like a massive marquee. Because it took place before all of the permanent buildings were complete." She paused involuntarily to catch her breath and took a sip of wine before continuing. "It was frightfully cold. The wind whipped up the door flaps. Do you remember, Wallie?"

"Yes I do, dear." He was arched over his plate, the bony spine highlighted by the white shirt. A long sliver of meat dangled from his fork and slowly approached his mouth.

"I was only twenty-three, ah, so young! I hadn't met Wallie, I was dating a chap called Topper at the time. My father, bless him, was in charge of the catering and I tell you, we didn't have all this luxurious food. He had to make do with what was available. Food was still rationed because we didn't know what was safe to eat at that point, some of the animals here can give you nasty stomach cramps." She paused for breath and sipped a little water. "We only had a drop of gravy, and most of the dinner was bread and a little meat. But it tasted wonderful because, though it was simple, it showed how far we'd come. There was such a feeling of hope... I can't even begin to describe how it felt..."

Michael's father called across the table. "That mood is present today, Mother. Everyone's reliant on everyone else, as much as always, and ensures no one goes without. Everyone has enough to eat. Has shelter. Has electricity in their houses, at least for part of the day. And I have great plans for ShadeCo. Over the next few years, I intend to increase production tenfold. There's been a great volume of Shade activity discovered in Sibilius Mount and if we utilise the fuel, we can end the blackouts occurring every week. Why only yesterday, the household devices went off without warning, and the emergency generator took an hour to kick in."

Miriam added it was more like two hours. Uncle Joe exaggerated further and said it was more like five.

Grandpa Wallie referred back to his son's earlier comment. "You say everyone is reliant on everyone else. But you've never experienced living on a spaceship for years on end, without sight of land or sea or freedom. People nowadays will never understand the intense feeling of liberty when we arrived and the endless possibilities, it's not the same, my boy, it's not the same. Community spirit isn't here any more, no more than this festival's significance. It's a sham. A facade, hiding an ugly core and you more than anyone should know that, Richard, considering the number of threats you've received when you took over as CEO. Black energy isn't popular. It never has been. And you're putting a lot of pressure on your Hunters to deliver. Ever since your announcement about Sibilius Mount, the threats have been directed not just to you but your kids too."

The good mood was replaced with something sinister.

"It's to be expected. They are only threats, nothing more and we're perfectly safe."

"It was a stupid move. The last CEO left abruptly and ran off to become a hermit in Springhaven. Why did he do that—"

"For the last time, we are safe. The police know. They're only words… and I don't think it is the *time* or *place* to talk about this." Richard continued, his mouth a tight line and brows knit together then more quietly, "Today of all days, I don't want to worry. I just want to enjoy spending quality time with my family, which has been all too brief recently."

"I'd rather not talk about it today either and definitely not over dinner." Miriam directed a furious gaze at Grandpa Wallie.

"I'm sorry, son. I'm just worried…"

Like an axe, Michael's truck came down.

"Ouch! Mike!" Marie's wails pierced the adults' tenseness. "Mum told you to stop!"

Everyone laughed at Michael's naughtiness apart from Marie, who rubbed her head where the toy had struck. He wasn't told off this time, but had his hair ruffled by his grandpa. He smiled, satisfied. The happy mood returned, partially.

***

A couple of hours elapsed over dinner, in which several decadent courses were consumed.

Then, while the plates and platters were cleared by the droids, the family migrated to the adjoining living room, separated from the dining room by a single wide arch.

The focus of the living room was the enormous tree standing at ten feet high, looming over everything. Its far-reaching branches brushed the high ceiling. It wasn't real. Fake trees were the norm because Diomedian trees were rarely anything except small, spindly and starved and the antipode of a lavish festival.

Beneath the tree, partially obscured by the lower branches, were Michael and Marie. They shook and then opened everything bearing their names. Their routine consisted of examining the new present for precisely five seconds before reaching for the next. Their mother sat beside them and gasped in delight when each new toy emerged, asking who had sent each one. The children's responses were always vague because the pull to see the item outweighed the names on the packaging.

Grandpa Wallie looked like a child sitting in his wide-backed armchair, with a cushion bigger than Michael propping him up. He slept off the heavy food. A line of drool ran from one corner of his thin lips and he snored in erratic intervals. Grandma Mitts sat in the chair next to him, savouring her mulled wine, which she could have only as a rare treat. Miriam's eldest sister and brother-in-law had arrived after dinner and the pair were now in discussion with Michael's father on the settee. All three talked animatedly, covering everything from politics to poetry to energy suppliers to taxes, nothing the children were interested in, or Miriam and Uncle Joe for that matter.

Uncle Joe examined the digital pictures on the wall that rotated on loop in the frames, away from the others. The majority of these contained the smiling faces of the children. There was soft samisen music playing from the hidden wall speakers though it was barely louder than a whisper.

A scream erupted from below.

It was startling and shrill and quickly followed by another. And another.

Most of the adults jumped to their feet at the first scream. The elderly couple sat up in their seats and the children stared at the door with large, scared eyes, their new toys now entirely forgotten.

The only people that could have been downstairs were two remaining servants. The rest of the house had been shut up for the night.

Their screams severed abruptly.

Richard ventured outside and looked over the balustrade. He returned quickly and ordered the droids downstairs, his expression neutral as he hit the emergency switch by the doorway to alert the police. The living room and dining room were connected to the corridor by two sets of doors. He locked the living room doors and turned off the lights for good measure. With the help of his brother, they moved the settee and placed it in front of the door to block the entrance. It would serve as an obstacle until reinforcements could make it to the house. Their mother pulled the blinds. Outside, the lights from the nearest houses seeped through the slats and cast strips of colour on the floor, the walls, and the family.

Uncle Joe strode under the arch into the dining room and locked the door too, wedging the drinks cabinet against it to barricade them in, his face crimson with effort. Then, the family fell silent in the semi-darkness.

The living room was on the third storey, so the chance of escape was limited. Going down the staircase wasn't an option and jumping out of the window was dangerous from that height. Certainly, the elderly with them couldn't do it.

Miriam's sister switched on her MID and spoke in a hushed tone, talking to the emergency service. She tried to reconnect for a short while and was cut off. The power went off and the nearby houses were cast into darkness too.

The family waited and prayed. For once, Michael and Marie put their natural sibling animosity aside and held hands. A toy duck swung at Michael's side.

Slow steps creaked on the wooden floorboards.

There was a muffled smash from the level below. Torchlight flashed up the stairs and dimly lit the gaps in the door frame before it was switched off again.

"The police should be here by now," their mother whispered.

"I know," their father replied softly, and crept closer to her to offer comfort.

111

Marie sobbed in fear, tore her hand from Michael's grip, and ran to her mother for reassurance. She lovingly stroked her daughter's hair to comfort her, but over the top of her head, she mouthed the words, "What do we do?"

Their father rose and stood motionless in the middle of the room, holding a lampshade uncertainly in his hand. The guns were in a cabinet on the floor below.

With an element of flourish, Joe pulled out a cigar from his breast pocket. The others looked at him accusatorily, as if the smell of smoke would draw those downstairs directly towards the room.

"Does it really matter now?" he said, and lit the match.

Outside the doors, the flooring thudded as if a weight had dropped on it. The occupants of the room flinched.

There was hushed activity on the other side. The occupants of the room waited with bated breath. Joe's cigar smouldered, the edges flaking off.

In a sudden movement, Richard swept his son into his free arm and carried him over to the metal dumbwaiter in the dining room. The servants used this to bring food up from the kitchen. He placed the lampshade down and pulled up the hatch with one hand and unceremoniously shoved Michael inside. It was just big enough to hold him. The boy motioned to protest. His father shook his head sadly. Now was not the time for disagreement. Michael pleaded with him with his eyes as his father closed the hatch. Although his eyes were blurred with tears, he kept silent.

Michael was thrown into a pitch-black world. He kept as still as possible within the cramped hideaway. There was a crick in his neck and little space to move.

He heard the doors smash open and the screams that followed.

Terror stilled his tongue.

He tried not to match the distorted voices to the family member he loved.

In the quieter moments, he discerned his sister's whimpering. Soon the howls of his family stopped and strange hacking and slashing noises replaced them.

At some unknowable point he passed out in fear.

***

Michael awoke in confusion. He panicked, forgot where he was and tried to stand up, bashing his head. Inhaling the stagnant air in rapid gulps, he slapped his free hand against the metal walls and squeezed the toy duck against his chest. And squeezed and squeezed. Taking deep breaths, he managed to calm down and remembered he was in a dumbwaiter. He didn't know how long he'd been there, but the aching in his muscles suggested a few hours. His eyes tried and failed to accustom to the dark.

No one retrieved him from the dumbwaiter.

Have they forgotten that I'm in here?

What was in our house?

He listened to the room behind the shutter and heard whimpering, the only noise he could make out. He strained his ear for footsteps or movement or cries.

There was nothing else.

Answers could only be given by leaving the hideaway, so he steadied his resolve and lifted the hatch about three inches. He saw a hand through the gap by his feet. The rest of the person was obscured by the hatch.

Holding his breath, he lifted the shutter to the top. His eyes were shut tightly. He shuffled to the edge and dropped down to the carpet to lie flat on his stomach. But he still couldn't bring himself to move or look at the room around him.

Finally, when he found the courage to finally open his eyes, his first reaction was to vomit. It went all over his top and pooled underneath him.

After the heaving subsided, he sat up and gazed upon the destruction. He felt as if he were going to be sick again.

Uncle Joe was directly in front of him. His chest ripped open and the cavity was empty as if his insides had been scooped out with a giant spoon. Strips of material from his clothes were scatted around him. In his outstretched hand was that stub of his last cigar. Michael stared past him and saw the silhouette of the fallen tree, the smashed baubles that littered the floor along with the discarded presents and sweets. Beside the tree, Marie lay prostrate over their mother's body, trying to shake her awake.

Michael called out but she didn't respond. Marie began to tear at her mother's hair.

Michael found it challenging to get to his feet and used the table to help him stand up. Finally upright, with shaky legs, he wobbled past Uncle Joe towards his sister. The carpet was tacky from the partially dried blood and his shoes made sticky noises as he moved. Marie looked up at him without recognition.

He cried her name again and held his arms outstretched, his hands open beseechingly. Reaching out, he touched her shoulder.

She shrieked at the contact, as loud as her lungs would permit.

The sudden sound startled him. He staggered back, tripping over an arm on the floor. Automatically, he picked it up. Initially his brain couldn't comprehend what he was holding. On closer inspection, he thought he recognised the shirt, and further along he noticed his father's wedding ring on the ring finger.

Where is the rest of him?

Dropping the limb like a hot coal, his screams accompanied his sister's, in a harmonic cry of fear that echoed through the ransacked house.

Part Two

"My team are the greatest people I've ever had the honour of knowing.

They're brave to the point of insanity, incredibly and unsurpassably talented, and loyal beyond imagining... Without their help, I have no doubt that I wouldn't be alive today. They're dearer to me than my own kin and I'd do anything for them."

- James 'Red' Martin, in his first interview after the
Sibilius Mount tragedy.

12

Longrider

ATTENTION SHADECO EMPLOYEES!

YOUR COMPANY IS DESTROYING LIVES,
BOTH INSIDE AND OUTSIDE OF MAYTON HILL!
THEIR GOD IS MONEY!
RISE AGAINST YOUR EMPLOYERS
AND END THE CRUELTY NOW!

This message scrolled across the window of the Jeep beside mine followed by a graphic image of a badly beaten woman. You could only see her top half. Her hair was matted with blood and her lips and eyes were swollen, distorting the rest of her features. Her clothes were torn and skin shredded as if an animal had attacked her. Another image followed of a boy in a similar state. They appeared to be mother and child.

These repulsive images flashed all around me. Almost every vehicle's windshield was plastered with violent images. Everywhere the same faces in all their bloodied anguish, the unseeing pupils, the throats slit like an open maw. I could understand the anger behind it and the desire for vengeance, just not the reason why they felt ShadeCo was responsible. Were these people anti-ShadeCo activists or the newer group? I could not understand the growing hatred towards the company and its employees. Why harass staff only coming in to earn a living? Why not address it directly with the police instead?

As I only arrived moments before, my car had a clear windshield. I worked late the previous night, so I was a couple of hours later than usual this morning. The gun project's intensity increased as it neared completion and so my workload doubled in preparation for the launch of the new series. In a few short days, my involvement with the project would cease and I could return to my normal hunting duties, something I eagerly anticipated. Office work is not, and never will be, my forte. I yearned to return to hunting after months of monotonous data entry and lab experiments. The fact Butcher frequently sends me pictures of himself from my favourite hunting grounds is not helping either.

To cater for the massive workload, I had undertaken several successive twenty-hour shifts to complete the more pressing tasks, only stopping for sustenance or a quick doze. Last night, or more aptly, earlier this morning, I noticed the lack of sleep was taking its toll and tried to lie in. Spreadsheets and reports spun through my head all night and prevented me from falling into the deep sleep my body craved. So I was not feeling particularly refreshed. As I made my way slowly through the rows of parked cars to HQ, I made a mental note to check into the medical centre before I went to the office.

The parking lot was very quiet. The only noticeable presence was the armed guards slowly plodding around the perimeter of the lot. One stood nearby, aiming his pulse gun downwards for safety; their cerulean uniforms marked them out from other workers.

ShadeCo employees felt uneasy.

A few days ago a couple of employees' cars were attacked in the parking lot in plain view of HQ and the guards' station. Guards chased the vandals away before any serious damage was done, but there were no arrests. I heard they distorted the footage to avoid identification.

For the past few months anti-ShadeCo activists had been joined by another anonymous hate campaign against the company, blackening its name with illusive slogans, derogatory messages to senior staff and destruction of private property. In my opinion, all of them are ignorant lowlifes who wanted to unsettle ordinary people with their attacks. Black energy is needed to power Diomedia as other energy sources are less effective. More importantly, there is no connection between the woman and ShadeCo. If there was tangible proof then the police would be involved. The two together did not mean anything and probably just be the idea of some warped individuals. Red hired extra armed guards and ordered more droids. Their effectiveness was dubious.

＊

It was hot down here. We were deep underground in ShadeCo HQ away from the majority of the employees and almost at the executive level on the bottom floor. The air moderator was malfunctioning and we had no windows to open. I rolled up my sleeves to my elbows and removed my mask. These were necessary actions in the suffocating heat, but I disliked showing my face in front of non-Hunter, ShadeCo staff. There was a lot of prejudice against Hunters and I prefer to keep the two sides of my life separate. Other workers had removed their jackets, some undid their shirts halfway down their chests and earlier I noticed a couple of people walking around barefoot. One person was sitting in her underwear.

In front of me, the newly-built simulator eradiated warmth and shone like a huge white egg in the heart of the room, nestled amidst wires and cables. After the fiasco with Butcher, this simulator was the best solution to test the weapons outside of the field. I waited for the technicians above me on the larger mezzanine level to open the door.

Eventually the simulator's door slid sideways and I was hit by a fiery blast of air. I stepped inside and removed the guns from their holsters, and I took my position in the centre. The door closed behind me. Outside noises grew softer until there was just a static hum and the sound of my breathing. The lights switched off. I closed my eyes because they were unable to adjust to the gloom, and prepared for the start of the simulation.

A trickle of sweat rolled down my back. I shuddered involuntarily.

My eyelids turned vermillion and I opened them wide. Bright light illuminated the space around me and a virtual world was thrown upon every surface. The curved walls disappeared and I was no longer in a tiny box room but a parched, hauntingly desolate landscape. The rocky terrain seemed to stretch for miles in all directions. The wind whistled along the ground, whipped at my hair, and exposed skin. A low moan from a distant animal rolled across the plain. My nose filled with an incredibly real dusty aroma. I nearly forgot that I was in a simulator. In fact, it was so intricately detailed I could have sworn I visited this place before in reality.

Marching on the spot moved the landscape forward. While I walked, I took aim at a spindly tree to my left. The gun was not physically loaded but programmed to respond as it would in reality. The recoil was certainly present. The force hit back into my shoulder with a jolt, but the impact was nowhere near as forceful as present Hunter weaponry. My bullet penetrated the middle of the tree on the spot I aimed for. Then, lowering the weapon, I continued for another few minutes. Suddenly, the corius discs attached to the skin on my legs started to vibrate and my muscles tightened as if I was on an incline.

I climbed over the 'crest' and after a few steps, the ground changed into a green carpet that rolled out endlessly before me. I took a moment to appreciate the view. There was a savannah below unlike anything I had seen before. Huge trees topped with masses of foliage were irregularly scattered across the plain and they appeared far healthier than any plant found on Diomedia, perhaps this represented an area only scouting drones reached?

Grazing animals bounded up the hill, covered in fur instead of the usual indigenous scales. Many had spiralling horns on their heads. Something slithered over my foot and I instinctively retracted it, even though I knew it was simulated. The tail disappeared into the long grass. A herd of beautiful horses galloped past and whinnied to one another. A predator loped closely behind, steadily gaining on the horses. When it was upon them, it chose its victim and clawed the hind legs of a straggler, bringing it down heavily. I continued moving and did not watch it feed.

The designers must've had fun with this!

The corius discs came to life again and created a weighty sensation to reflect the difficulty of wading through the long grass that had just appeared. Through the grass, I saw an enormous tree ahead. The developer's voice in my ear ordered me to go towards it.

When I emerged from the grass, there was a Shade floating in wait. The corius discs quietened and I could move freely. I heard a click on my left and the Shade surged forward.

I pulled the trigger.

The bullet smacked into it with a ripple.

Contorting, the Shade splashed to the ground, throwing up a ghostly hand in lamentation of its fate before it condensed completely. This theatricality brought a smile to my face, and I made a mental note to share this amusing if inaccurate detail with my father later. He would appreciate the comic value of a melodramatic Shade.

While I checked the gun to ensure everything was in order, another Shade unexpectedly assailed me from behind. Spinning around to face it, I felt the corius discs rumble powerfully on my chest and legs. I fell.

The gun flew from my hand, across the simulator and rebounded against the side. At the same time, the virtual Shade continued its attack and the discs rumbled reactively, preventing me from getting up.

"Stop!" I shouted. My voice quavered with the vibrations. "Stop the test!"

I waited for the shaking to subside but it did not. "Stop the damn simulation!"

No answer.

What are they doing???

Awkwardly, I groped for the knife strapped to my leg and yanked it free. Trying to keep as steady-handed as possible, I peeled off the corius discs attached to my chest and arms and let them drop to the floor. Once they were off, it was much easier to move.

Around me, the fake Shade flitted around the simulator, bouncing against the sides while the discs buzzed. I rolled up my trousers and removed the three discs from each calf, throwing them at the fake Shade. Without these hindrances, I was able to stand. But the room continued to shake like an earthquake.

I went to the simulator door and shoved my fingers into the narrow slit to prise it open. A gust of air ushered in the shrill sound of an alarm.

"Hello?" I yelled.

No response.

Through the crack, I noticed the lower level of the room was empty. The viewing space was dim. The main lights had shut down and the illumination coming from the emergency lights on the upper level barely filtered down. Forcing the door open a few more inches, I created a gap large enough to squeeze through. I sucked in my stomach and wriggled out, leaving the vibrating gear inside. I managed to keep the guns with me; if Butcher taught me anything it was to be cautious with your possessions. I switched on the safeties and shoved the guns back in the shoulder holsters.

The area was completely empty.

Normally fire drills did not shift people this rapidly and usually they give you pre-warning it was a drill. A woman's voice emitted from the speakers asking the listener to proceed to the designated safety area at the front of the building, floors above my current position.

They'd left me in there! They could at least have had the decency to tell me instead of abandoning me in the simulator!

Furious, I sprinted up the steps, taking them two at a time until I reached the top, where I was greeted with a similar situation. Vacant workstations everywhere. Coats were slung over the backs of chairs and a few bags sat forgotten underneath the desks. Beside the stairs, the simulator control station was deserted. Everyone had fled. *Could this be a terrorist attack? Activists are getting worse. Good thing that father's team aren't working in HQ today — their team building exercise was well-timed; it would be difficult to get to the generator rooms from here.*

As I passed one of the workstations, I picked up a recyclable cup containing tepid coffee. My colleagues must have fled just a short while ago, perhaps fifteen minutes at most. I swallowed the liquid and crushed the cup in my hand before striding over to the closed exit. My sole aim from this point onwards was to reach ground level as quickly and directly as possible. If this was a terrorist attack, I needed to run and ask questions later. I wished I had a normal handgun with me rather than a Shade-effective one.

There was a small porthole set into the exit at head height and I saw thick dark smoke choking the corridor outside. Emergency lights flickered above me, feebly. I returned to my desk to retrieve my discarded mask and attached it before I ventured into the corridor.

The smoke poured in as soon as I opened the door, covering me. At the same time, my mask's eyepieces adjusted to thermal setting to navigate through the building. In this mode, smoke was not an issue, though the colourful thermal images looked confusing at first. It took a while to accustom to the turquoise and green surroundings.

Several minutes elapsed before I encountered anyone else. I trailed one hand against the wall as I made my way steadily towards the emergency exit. Suddenly, a red-yellow figure rounded the corner and hurried towards me. The mask indicated that he was unarmed. He moved to pass by and I grabbed his wrist and gestured back towards the way he had come, towards the exit. I assumed he had become disorientated in the murk.

He shook his head. "I have to return to my office," he explained, his voice muffled by his respirator.

"Don't be stupid. It's not safe!"

"I need to get back to my office," he explained again patiently, as if I was the irrational one.

He shrugged my hand off, took a few steps back and dashed away. I tried. Now I had to focus on my own safety and carry on.

By now, the heat was increasing with every step. My surroundings gradually changed from the relatively cool greens to yellow.

Several more minutes and I finally reached the emergency exit. *What a relief!* I pushed the door open and felt the warmth of the handle through my gloves. I walked cautiously onto the landing. The metallic staircase smouldered red and orange. I peered over the railing and saw white light smothering the bottom level; these images confirmed there was a fire.

Throwing off all caution, I sprinted up the stairs, taking them three at a time to quickly ascend four levels.

Another three floors remained to ground level. Suddenly, the building gave off a great groan like a girder rent in two, and the ground began to shake. The tremors felt as strong as a major earthquake and I was thrown painfully against the wall. I thought it was the end. My heart beat as loudly as a kettledrum. I crouched and covered my head and neck with my arms. The tremors shook through the building. Some panelling fell over the banister, clanging all the way down.

But I began to feel the shaking subside. When it was moderate, I steadied myself with the railing and continued climbing as quickly as I could.

When I reached the ground floor landing, I went down a short corridor and opened a second metal door, which I slammed shut behind me. My eyepiece displayed this new area in indigo and dark blues, which signified the heat of the fire had not reached here. It was much cooler too, and I breathed a sigh of relief. My clothes were drenched with sweat.

I entered the foyer and was immediately hit by its normality in contrast with the alarm and voice asking everyone to go to the designated safety area. The foyer looked immaculate. The cuboid seats in the waiting area were positioned in neat lines, potted plants were spaced artfully around the reception and along the glass panels at the front of the building, security droids stood to attention to scan any workers before they entered the main building, pleasant music emitted from invisible speakers. Both sets of entrance doors had been released to allow people out en masse and avoid overcrowding due to the usual filter system.

I vaulted over the security desk and bypassed the droids, sprinting across the marble floor. Momentarily, I stood by the entrance and looked down the steps at the car park below while I switched my mask's settings to standard mode. Instantly, the garish objects reverted into familiar hues and a crowd of people emerged from the phantasmagoria. The majority of ShadeCo employees were outside in the designated evacuation point for all emergencies, excluding Shade attacks. However, the procedures had not been adhered to, each team was not standing in orderly rows and no one seemed to be responding to the roll calls.

Some workers approached the fire engines with interest. The trucks were parked haphazardly beside the stone steps leading up to the building and were unmanned and accessible to anyone who desired entry. Paramedics waited for their services to be required near the entrance; their fluorescent-green jackets made them easy to identify. Police officers weaved through the crowd, stopping regularly to question people and noting down information on their MIDs.

I turned around and raised my gaze upwards. From the outside, ShadeCo HQ seemed strong and invulnerable. Above the foyer windows, the blanched facade loomed over the lot and cast a sizable portion in shadow. No smoke emitted from the domed roof. I was relieved to be at ground level. Then I descended the steps to be swallowed by the mass of bodies, where I pushed my way through.

Jostling through the crowd, I carried on walking until it thinned out. At the perimeter of the ShadeCo facility, I noticed a line of armed police droids securing the area and barring anyone from leaving or entering. When I was almost beside the perimeter fence and far from the HQ building, I hopped onto the hood of a car and sat down to watch the scene develop.

I watched the crowd swirl and ebb around the front of the building. As one, they surged forward to help when medical droids returned carrying the workers who had been trapped in the lower levels. Most seemed to suffer from smoke inhalation and were brought round quickly. The raw flesh of one unlucky individual indicated nasty burns; the paramedics rushed to him first, forcing the crowd back to treat the wounded.

At the edge of my vision, I saw someone break away from the mass and gradually advance towards me, waving. I recognised the man as one of father's colleagues, which was odd because he should be off site this week.

"Hi!" I called over. "What are you doing here? I thought you were at the team building event."

"Oh, that was cancelled ages ago."

"What do you mean? So you were all in work today?"

"Yeah."

"My father?"

"I think so — I was mostly in the ground floor reception today and didn't go to the generator rooms much but I think I saw him when I first got in. Don't worry. I'm sure he's okay."

At this point, we were interrupted by a policewoman. She tipped her cap, looking at us behind tinted goggles. Her voice was deep. "Excuse me, could you spare a few moments to help with our enquiries?"

We both nodded acquiescently. I folded my arms and remained seated.

"You probably are aware that there's a fire raging below the building. And we have reason to believe that it was started deliberately and we're trying to get some leads. I'd like to know if you saw or heard anything suspicious in the last couple of hours. Anything at all?" She poised to type our responses on her MID.

Fatigue hit me suddenly and it was hard to think properly. I shook my head. "I don't know."

"Nothing at all?" she pressed. "Every other worker I've spoken to today has seen lots of suspicious behaviour, are you sure you haven't seen anything? It doesn't matter how small the detail, at this point anything could be of assistance?"

I recalled the man returning to his desk. "Well..." I paused and the officer made encouraging noises. "When I was leaving, there was a man going back to his office, he was probably five nine or ten. I had switched my mask onto thermal setting and I couldn't make out his features. When I tried to stop him, he shook off my hand and darted away. I was on sub-seven floor." The cop wrote it all down eagerly.

"What was your impression of him?"

"He didn't really seem malevolent, if that's what you mean, just focused on getting something from his office. I thought it's peculiar because there's obviously a fire and it's unsafe."

"Is there anything else?"

My father's colleague informed her about the messages on the car windscreens earlier this morning but she knew about them already. She seemed more interested in speaking with the guards and I pointed out where she could find them. There was a station beside the perimeter fence. "I doubt if they're still on shift," I shrugged. "But it's worth taking a look."

She thanked us for our cooperation and departed to search for them.

My father's colleague turned to go too. "I better get going. If I see Harald, I'll ask him to call you."

"Thanks. I appreciate it."

He departed and headed towards his vehicle. I remained where I was and tried to call father's MID. It failed to connect and stated that it was an unrecognised device. *Odd... he can't have another faulty MID, surely? He had the other one fitted just a few months ago!*

The chaos outside ShadeCo increased. The crowd was frantic, they'd moved further away from the building.

Another set of police vehicles whizzed past me and parked close to the entrance.

The ground shook again and the earth gave a great roar. I was thrown forward and off the car bonnet. People screamed. The crowds shuffled further from HQ and were getting close to me now. Long cracks appeared in the tarmac and a few vehicles shifted position. A thick line of smoke rolled out of the building and rose into the sky. I dropped onto my haunches and leaned my head back, tracking the smoke until it dispersed and disappeared from sight.

13

Longrider

Further information, they said. We will contact you when we have further information. There is nothing more you can do. Go home and try to occupy your mind with something else. Maybe see friends or family for their support.

As if it were unreasonable to be so concerned. To be focused on nothing else for over a week. The inaction was increasingly frustrating. I heard this advice repeated countless times by the police, missing person organisations, and other well-wishers. It is sickening.

They do not care. Not really.

It feels as if the fallout from the attack turned everyone's senses into pulp.

After the fire, I went to my parents' house to check on father. His car was still in the garage and after a search of the house, I found his MID in the pedal bin in the kitchen. The only way to remove a MID is by cutting it out and it is usually extracted by someone other than the wearer. I tested the device and it still worked so this action did not make any sense. On top of that, I've received conflicting information about his whereabouts. Many of his colleagues saw him at the office, but a few said he wasn't, and no one has seen him since the attack. I could not understand why he told me he was attending a training exercise when it was cancelled. Another lie or did he forget to mention it? This last year he seemed to be drifting away from me and I couldn't understand why. It wasn't the first time he had disappeared but this time it felt different, particularly because of the timing. It filled me with foreboding. It confused me. Nothing seemed to add up. So, I reported him as missing to the police.

A week elapsed and there is nothing to report. Not a single word. Not a single useful syllable. And no sign of him.

As I crouched over the edge of the couch I frowned at the MID screen on my forearm. The last unsuccessful message faded into my skin until it vanished.

I required someone to discuss this situation with. Someone to offer reasonable and practical advice. Someone sympathetic to my concerns. Someone available to talk, now.

Normally in a situation like this, I would seek father's counsel. But he was the person I was looking for. He was gone. I felt I had mis-stepped along a narrow mountain path and was watching myself descending in slow motion, the earth slipping under my feet with no one to pull me back. I needed to find him, as I knew he would me if the situation was reversed. I doubt he would have left of his own accord.

Butcher.

He was likely to be unreachable for the next few hours, perhaps more, and I was not sure how far I could trust him. There was something mercenary about him, and not just the fact that he was a freelancer. His focus was money, and for what I could not say. Perhaps adding to his peculiar art collection; his recent purchase was a four-foot-tall hand with gnarled fingers and palm up to create a bizarre chair.

On the flipside, he had a practical skillset adaptable for locating a missing person.

I stood up, and stretched, looking at my reflection in the closest window. I saw my pale face and shadowed eyes from lack of sleep.

Outside, I watched a cat creep across the ground with a respirator covering its face like a muzzle to protect it from Shades in case it ventured outside the city walls. Its body was low to the earth and each paw placed carefully as if it were hunting.

My breath misted on the glass, making an orb. I drew a big question mark with my index finger then wiped the symbol away with my palm.

There are clues everywhere, just which to pursue?

Mother managed to get through to him just before the attack. He had not said much of note, apart from he would come home early from work because he felt unwell. She replayed the call to me and there was no hidden meaning there that I could decipher. He clearly had no idea about what was to happen in short order.

I provided the police with all the details they required including his ID number and profile, an item of clothing for DNA samples, details of his other friends and relatives that he might contact, and a list of places that he frequented. They fed me the bland statement that I would be contacted when they found anything.

Inevitably, my thoughts turned to mother, now languishing dramatically in a hospital bed. Being a natural prima donna, at the news of my father's disappearance, she fainted spectacularly in the middle of a restaurant. She struck the waiters who tried to calm her down whilst finishing off a couple of bottles of wine in record time, then admitted herself to hospital. It was not the first time she had done something like this and the nurses were quite familiar with her.

When I visited her earlier, she rewarded my efforts with tirades, moans and demands. Mother chided me for not hiring a private investigator as soon as possible to find father, though she did not offer to contribute to the fee. I tried not to take her diatribes to heart. As with everything she does, they are overblown and emotional — the polar opposite of father's logical and measured approach.

In actuality, I researched the private investigation path and did not have funds or inclination to hire someone to conduct the search for me. It totalled more than a year's wages, an absurd amount.

Instead, I devoted myself to the task. My strategy was threefold.

The first stage involved collating as much evidence as possible, dipping into police records where necessary. The second stage concerned sorting valuable data from the detritus. Finally, the last stage was practical action. Presently I was stuck in the indeterminable area between stage two and three and uncertain about how to proceed without advice. I needed Butcher's, if I could get in touch with him.

Stage one's findings consisted of his colleagues' accounts of the day. I messaged all his contacts with my queries, the password to his MID files stored was mother's only useful contribution. I personally questioned his colleagues to discover exactly where he was and what he was doing during the attack. Most confirmed he was working in the generator rooms when the bomb went off and he elected to remain in the building. Yet a couple adamantly claimed that he called in sick. Overall, my gut feeling suggested the former.

But what could have happened if he remained behind?

A number of possibilities crossed my mind. The one that stuck was he had been taken captive by the terrorists. Police confirmed that the fire started due to a bomb rather than arson and suggested a new militant faction of the anti-black energy activists were responsible. My father had been alone. And stayed behind whilst all his colleagues fled to ensure everyone got out okay. Perhaps they knew he did not have a MID, so he could not be traced. The identity of the perpetrators was still unknown, and it's possible they had people on the inside. And there was ample opportunity to smuggle him out of the building because ShadeCo was chaotic for hours afterwards. People flitted in and out of the building so quickly it was impossible to track everyone.

I admit there were holes in this explanation. The perpetrators had not issued any demands for ransom in a week since the attack. And research on other missing individuals indicated they were middle-management staff members; executives or Hunters would have made more high-profile hostages. But police said that Red was a target, as CEO, and father and he had a connection from their hunting past, but they had not worked together directly for years. And it was unlikely that the company would give in to any demands, were they to be made, for the safety of a few individuals. As harsh as it was, I knew Red well enough to know how he would respond. He would not succumb to blackmail.

Yet, I was unwilling to dismiss the captive theory altogether. It was more likely than him simply running away, which is what the police seem to think. That was too out of character for consideration.

The living room was cool, the temperature took a slight drop, and gooseflesh emerged along the length of my naked arms. It was the perfect condition to think. Heat always made me feel sluggish and ineffective.

I drummed my fingers on the windowsill. Rereading the articles seemed the best action, to recheck for information I might have glossed over. I returned to the couch, sat down and activated the MID compatibility on the coffee table. I quickly read through the articles again. I continued until I reached the last one on the list. This was the most important document because it contained a collection of police statements delivered to the press about the attack. Many supported my hostage theory. The police suggested the bombing was too well coordinated to be an individual acting alone, and they were working with the theory that small teams infiltrated the facility. Unfortunately, this was speculation. Nor did they reveal anything about the terrorist agenda except ShadeCo's closure. Even on second reading, it did not give any clue about where they might be based or who they were.

If they want money, why haven't they issued their demands yet? If they wanted ShadeCo to close, why not reiterate it when everyone will listen? Why else would you take hostages?

I had come full circle and to the same conclusion. I was going crazy. It was obvious I had reached a point where I needed a fresh take on the information, input from a different perspective.

Again, I wondered how long Butcher's business would take. I glanced at my MID once more. Over an hour had passed. I checked Butcher's coordinates and he still appeared to be in a cafe on the other side of town. According to the MID, he has been there all day, except when I went there earlier, I could not find him and none of the staff saw him either and he's not a wilting wallflower. Judging from the background noise when I called him, it sounded as if he was in the field. The wind's hollow whistle is unmistakable, you do not get it within the walls of any major settlement. He must have somehow distorted his MID's signal. This surprised me, as I did not think he had such technological prowess.

Stretching my arms, I decided to go for a walk and clear my head. Fleeting visit to the cafe aside, I had been holed up in my apartment and needed the exercise.

14

Landmine

$\mathcal{J}$ looked down at the MID at my wrist. The screen lit up with a name in large letters and underneath was a tiny picture of the matching masked face.

Three times now. What does she want?

What was so urgent was beyond me. I decided to answer to warn her not to interrupt again later on.

"This isn't convenient, Longrider. Spit it out," I said, careful to use her alias instead of her first name. She was finicky about that, no doubt because of ShadeCo indoctrination.

"I need to talk to you. In person," she replied, mirroring my low tone. "I'll tell you the details when I see you. All you need to know is that I require your help in searching for my father. He's missing… well it's not quite as simple as that but I'm not at liberty to speak presently. We can discuss it in person. Where are you? Are you in the field?"

I definitely wasn't about to reveal my location. And I wasn't going to shoot back to town because her father went AWOL. Months of planning to get to this moment, and I wasn't about to waste it. They weren't going to get away this time around.

"Look, I'm in the middle of something important. And a 'please would you help me' wouldn't go amiss either. When I'm finished I might contact you, might, mind you, not definitely. Whatever it is, it sounds risky. And I'm busy. I'm hanging up now."

Before I disconnected, I heard her groan angrily. No doubt she'd be pissed off, but if she really wanted help, she'd wait. If she found someone else in the meantime, that'd be better.

Bastards! I've got you this time!

I laughed quietly and waited for my moment to strike. Not yet.

I was hidden by a cluster of boulders halfway up a hillside. I had a clear view of the surrounding area, and anyone looking up couldn't see me from this vantage point. My clothes and gas mask camouflaged me further. I couldn't wait to pay back those little shits for destroying my Jeep and taking my supplies, including that goddamned stupid goat.

Looking down onto the plain, I watched the small group huddled around the black Jeep I'd used for bait. Even from here, I recognised them. Their bizarre masks were unmistakable. No sane person would choose a mask that greatly restricted vision.

Without a doubt, they were my previous attackers, and they were repeating their moves on the second vehicle. However, round two would be on my terms.

The group's armoured vehicle was parked close to my own and it shone like a trophy against the bare ground. One I was determined to win. An eye for an eye and all that. I wanted it to compensate for my destroyed Jeep, and they could have this current shitty claptrap. Their fuckoff tank was mine!

Unknown to them, I'd tracked them through the desert for hours. I'd hacked into their MIDs to get their route, then accelerated and arced around to halt directly in their path and lay the trap. The second vehicle was just a cheap replacement and though the paintwork was recent, it was old and nearly ready for scrapping. This time, I'd emptied the vehicle, and everything I needed was on me. I'd left it unattended and unlocked as an invitation. They'd fallen straight in, exactly as planned.

They failed to scout the area. I assumed they weren't trained in hunting and I had been proven right. They were opportunists. Zooming in further, I noted their determined movements as they stripped my vehicle of its remaining supplies. The slimmer man guided the others with the precision of a conductor, waving his gloved hands at various sections of the Jeep as they followed unquestioningly. He moved away from them after a while and rested his arms akimbo on his narrow waist. He glanced once in my general direction, staring at the rocks for a few moments before turning away. Instinctively, I felt he was the one to watch and any trouble would originate from him.

A gush of air echoed around the hills. A tyre slashed. The Jeep dipped down on one side.

I crouched in wait. Two guns were at my hip, one of them set to stun. I'd modified some of my Shade hunting traps. The translucent webbing surrounded the Jeep on three sides. It could capture larger creatures like these blundering idiots if they got closer. Their vehicle was just out of range of the nets. So far they lay untouched. The leader took a few steps back.

Just a little closer.

I held my breath. He stopped moving and shouted something to his companions. It didn't carry well. The words were lost. He glanced around like a rodent sensing a predator but unaware where the threat lay. Then he bent down and picked up a stick. Though I could not see the net from my position, I'd a general idea where it was and he was near. He took cautious steps forward and prodded the ground with a stick. The dust was shook up. The net fell silent again when he stopped poking it.

He turned to move on and halted abruptly. His foot snagged. With his next step, the net sprung up and ensnared him. In confusion, he cried out and fell to the ground in a mess of limbs and webbing. Weights attached at various points around the net prevented him from sitting up properly. He struggled to break free and yelled for help. And the more he fought, the more entangled he became.

The other two looked up blankly from inside the Jeep and, after a pause, lurched over to him.

Time to move.

Keeping low and relying on my camouflage to keep me hidden, I strode down the hill. My pulse gun was already at hand, and a lasso of rope hung on my shoulder. When I was almost upon them, I lengthened my stride, my excitement increasing. Revenge was a dish best served hot and I planned to savour every steaming morsel. The adrenaline pumped through me like an electric charge, heightening senses, strengthening muscles, and quickening my movements.

The shitheads didn't know I was here, even now. Their backs were turned. They stooped over their leader and frantically tried to release him from the netting, getting tangled in the process. It was impossible to release it like that. The best way to escape was to move slowly and gently, the exact opposite of what they were doing. They pulled it, attempting to tear the net apart. They started to cut the net with their knives but the cords were strong. It would require a few minutes to create a big enough hole to slip through. I used this to my advantage.

The leader finally spotted me and called out a warning, but I was already on them.

I hit the nearest man with a stun pulse.

It blasted him several feet into the air. His gun flew from his hand and he landed painfully on his back. He didn't get up.

The other man snatched the gun from his belt and took aim. The distance between us was small and I closed the gap in a heartbeat. Using my momentum, I twisted his arm up as he let off a shot. The flickering pulse flew into the air and whipped through a wispy cloud, disappearing into the higher atmosphere.

With his free hand, he rained punches on my ribs and arm. With the adrenaline coursing through me, I ignored the pain and managed to yank his wrist into an unnatural angle so that he loosened his hold on the weapon.

It clattered to the floor. I kicked it out of reach.

Squarely, I swung round and palmed him in the throat. As planned, he doubled over, gasping for breath and clutching at his neck, spluttering.

I aim my weapon, lowered the focus and the pulse exploded at his knee. He squealed like a piglet as he hurtled backwards. What a noise! It was as if puberty hadn't happened! He keeled over onto his side and I stamped on him a few times with my heavy boots until his mask cracked and he was clearly unconscious.

With the immediate threats dealt with, I walked over to the ensnared leader and loomed over him. The afternoon was swiftly becoming evening and my long shadow was thrown across the fallen man.

"What do you want, ShadeCo scum?" he spat with as much dignity as he could muster. His voice was muffled by the mask. "Are you going to kill me too like you've killed the rest of our captives? My kinsmen will seek you out and hurt you and all that you hold dear, just as you did to us. We won't tolerate it any more!" He glared up defiantly despite his helpless situation.

"Shut up." I kicked him in the chest and knocked him back. "Quit with the martyr act! I'm taking what's owed, nothing more."

Out of the corner of my eye, I saw his fingers edge towards his knife, which had fallen near a tear in the net. I leapt forward to ram the heel of my boot onto his hand and heard the audible crack of bone. I cut short his cry with a stun shot to his forehead. He shook on the ground and the net held back the violent spasms. Froth started to fuzz over the side of his strange mask and his limbs twitched uncontrollably.

Lowlife piece of shit! Call me scum!

For good measure, I kicked him in the stomach, spinning him onto his front.

Wasting no more time, I touched particular points of the net in the correct order and deactivated the trap. It fell still. I threw it off easily and searched the leader for something to open the armoured vehicle. I didn't doubt he was the driver. The way he controlled the other men suggested it was unlikely he'd let them drive for him. Also, from the looks of it, the other men were too thick to perform the task even if it was set to auto drive. I rummaged through his pockets, but there wasn't anything on him of note.

I sat back on my haunches. If it was coded to respond to his DNA then some blood would do nicely. My hip flask was empty, so I took out a short blade knife and cut a vein below his wrist, catching the blood in the container. When I'd filled it to the brim, I tore a strip from his jacket's lining and tied it round his wrist to staunch the blood flow.

When I'd finished, I picked up the netting and untied the loop from the stunned man's ankle and left him on the desert floor along with the others. I let them keep their weapons — none of them had Shade effective guns or ammo and I wasn't about to lend them any. They'd be able to protect themselves against most predators when they woke up but probably would be helpless against Shades. They should pray for rain.

Wasting no more time, I sprinted to the armoured vehicle. When I got close, I flicked some of the blood at the door. It activated immediately. Recalling the door opened sideways, I stood back and avoided it hitting my head as it opened with a whoosh of air. There were several rungs leading up inside and I bounded up them and dove into the belly of the vehicle.

It was murky inside. The driving cabin lay to the left, separated from the main section with wire mesh. There were two seats there, wide enough to be armchairs and made of soft brown leather, perhaps goat skin, with faded patches on the seats and armrests from wear. The dashboard was covered with unusual controls, whirring and spinning independently. I reckoned I'd be able to drive it. The front window was large and wide giving the driver a good view. But in the back end of the vehicle, the windows were narrow and touched the roof, so only tall passengers could look out from them when seated.

I opened the panel in the mesh and climbed through, clambered over the passenger seat to the driver's side and took my position behind the steering wheel. The comfort of the leather seats was a pleasant surprise. I swung my backpack over my shoulder and dumped it onto the passenger seat, then took off my mask and rested it on the dashboard. There was a heavy smell of body odour in the air and it wasn't all me. It'd definitely need to be aired.

Examining the space around me, it was unclear how to start the damn thing. I was concerned that time was passing and knew the group would be regaining consciousness soon.

I poured some of the blood onto my hands and clutched the steering wheel. *I'll have to do something about that when I get back if I want to keep driving it.* The pressure-sensitive panel responded and the wheel suddenly became workable. The vehicle switched on with a dull hum and the controls lit up for greater visibility. Underneath my seat, the engine grumbled to life and the door wheezed shut, automatically sealing me inside. Gentle plantasma music played from the speakers, which seemed at odds with the vehicle's brutal form.

Now that it was working, I had to test drive the thing before returning to Mayton. The roads are narrow inside the city walls. The tank was more than twice the width of a standard car and it would be difficult to drive in the settlement unless I had it under tight control. *Right...*

Next I checked the fuel level, which was okay. If I needed more, I could just disable a Shade and filter it into the tank. Directly behind the steering wheel, the monitor displayed a navigation programme. It opened on a list of options, including saved locations. I instructed it to go to the last pre-set destination. It might've been a stupid move, but I was curious where these people came from.

The steering wheel turned independently under my hands and the vehicle slowly rolled forward. I didn't know where to place my hands or feet whenever a vehicle was driving itself. Mine usually stayed on manual. In the end, I rested my hands on the steering wheel and let it take me to the previous location. In the mirrors, I saw one of the men crawling towards the leader of this sorry pack. He shook the man's shoulders.

I checked my MID and glanced at the news. It was all about ShadeCo. Vaguely, I had heard of the disturbance at HQ but hadn't visited the site in weeks and was out of the loop. As a freelancer, I wasn't tied to a particular one, so the attack didn't affect me much because other companies readily took my captures too. Valya must be worried, though. Maybe that's why she sounded so urgent.

Three hours elapsed. I was heading far into unchartered territory to the east. *Is this a good idea? I can't see anything for miles...* Most of Diomedia is unexplored and the majority of settlements are on the coast or, at most, a few miles from the ocean. Drones explored the rest of the continent and it was only a brief surface investigation. The area to the east was largely unknown, as was the continent on the other side of the ocean. Whenever I hunt, it's usually within a fifty-mile radius of Mayton.

I went past a thin stream, rivers are rare on Diomedia. Mountains out here rose sharply and fell just as quickly, reminding me of a sound graph showing high-pitched sounds in uneven intervals.

When I was about to turn back, the vehicle started to slow and came to a gentle stop in unfamiliar territory. The wheels crunched over barbed wire and just beyond there were large, jagged metal spikes that would tear tyres to shreds. Behind the wire and spikes were layers of fencing with a number of vicious looking droids patrolling between in teams of three. A single path led through each set of gates to a small, unassuming windowless building, half submerged in the rocky terrain; it was barely bigger than my house. Perhaps it had subterranean levels. The navigation monitor indicated I'd reached the pre-set destination.

They call this home? I scratched my head.

A few of the droids stopped moving and pointed in my direction. I imagined them watching angrily, despite not being capable of such emotion. My vehicle was probably within range if they decided to shoot.

I've seen enough. Time to go.

Hurriedly, I switched the engine on. Stated Mayton's coordinates and gripped the steering wheel tightly. The vehicle shot backwards. It vaulted up the hill and leapt over the crest. Under my bloodied hands the steering wheel turned on its own will to regain control. All four wheels landed back on the ground and spun round until I faced forwards. I was flung from side to side in the chair. Very quickly, the drive smoothed out. I felt more comfortable away from that place.

I looked at the map displayed on the central screen on the dashboard. Four hours from town. It gave me a lot of time to digest what I'd discovered. What the hell was in there? Who were these people? They didn't speak the common tongue. I wanted to see what was inside and saved the coordinates of the base on my MID.

Valya's request was convenient. She'd be persuaded to help me if I did her a favour.

15

Longrider

Second to hunting, mechanics have always been like another sense to me. My passion for vehicles and all things motored is another pastime instilled in me by my father. Some of my earliest recollections were of him fixing up an automobile from an odd pile of scrap into a fully functioning machine. So, when I saw the monstrosity outside Butcher's house, my interest was most definitely aroused. *What a beast!*

I circled around and surveyed it from every angle. It was monstrous, aggressive and most importantly, intimidating. Its body consumed the driveway and mounted the garden path on either side. It easily stood twice my height and far wider than any other vehicle in the neighbourhood. It was far too big to be considered a Jeep and more akin to a tank with massive wheels rather than caterpillar tracks, and there were hover plates to reduce pressure on the terrain: the ultimate off-roader.

I parked my Jeep behind it, which looked like a palm-sized carmeneon lizard standing next to a two-metre-tall gi' mont dragon. Why Butcher required such a vehicle was beyond me.

Reaching up, I rapped my knuckles against the side. The plating emitted a low resonant clang. I sprung up the three rungs to the vehicle's door and pressed my nose against the window while I held onto the handle for balance. Most of the interior was hidden by heavily tinted windows, and the only object I could see, through a sepia filter, was a single chair.

This could be helpful in intimidating any terrorists if I'm able to track them down...

"Valya..."

Leaning casually against the door frame of his house, unmasked and with an amused expression on his face, Butcher watched me. *How long has he been standing there?* I leapt down and stepped away a few paces, mortified he caught me investigating his property without permission.

"Where did you get this beast from?" I deflected.

"That? Just something I've been working on for a while… just a little project to while away the time." His voice sounded unnatural. It was probably a lie, sounding too smooth, too forced and unnatural, almost practised. He continued in the same strange fashion. "It's equipped with all the latest navigation equipment, and latest field traversing technology. It can cross practically any terrain and the body's strong enough to withstand an explosion, which seems to be necessary now. And it has enough space to hold several cages comfortably."

I nodded and noted the unusual salesman quality to his voice.

He's lying but I'll see how well.

"I bet it burns a ridiculous amount of fuel. What are the costs of running a vehicle this size?"

"Too much… I haven't had it long enough to know exactly."

"Did you sell your old one? You know — the one you bought after they couldn't fix your savaged vehicle, the replacement that was practically falling apart anyway."

"Yeah…"

"Where did you sell it? Or was it a trade in? You must've got an amazing deal to get something this size because it's easily a year's wage, even for a freelancer. And you don't really appear the saving type—"

"I've got funds, don't you worry about me." Butcher turned to go back inside the house and called over his shoulder, changing the subject. "I suppose you're here about your father? Didn't he show up yet?"

"No, he hasn't." With one glance back at the tank, I followed Butcher.

Though I had visited his house numerous times, it never felt properly lived in, as if Butcher merely used it as a recuperation centre between hunts or other excursions. Judging from the unkempt appearance, he had not returned home for a while. The dilapidated house droid half-heartedly wiped off the light glaze of dust gracing many surfaces; the patchwork of soldered metal across the droid's central unit reminded me of our fight. The droid finished cleaning the kitchen table, which now shone with moisture.

I followed him to the kitchen area, taking a stool by the counter. I pulled my mask over my head. In the interim, a drink of water appeared in front of me. Butcher was staring at me, dark eyes intense.

"So how did you *really* get that monster?"

"I told you already," he said. He reeled off the name of a few merchants.

I could not resist needling him further. "All of them? Was this a joint project?"

"All of them. It was a joint project. Valya, I'm not in the mood for this right now. What d'ya want? If he's turned up dead, then I'm warning you now, I'm not good with crying, so if you're gonna get emotional, find someone else to offload on. You won't find much comfort here." He leaned back against the fridge and gestured for me to continue with a sarcastic roll of his hand.

"He's not dead! Don't even say that! What I'm after is your help with my mission. I'll explain more after you've read this."

What a certified asshole. I don't really know why I even keep company with him; he's rude, arrogant and insensitive.

I tried to keep my expression neutral as I transferred the archive from my MID to his. Once he received it, I clicked the appropriate list of documents and directed him to the correct location. This particular file contained information about the attack, footage and my own surmises.

His nostrils flared occasionally as he read the screen, his eyes darting left to right. I allowed him to digest the material and left him reading. I picked up my glass and sauntered slowly around the room, sipping the cool water while I did so. There were some peculiar ornaments in his home, items I considered too grotesque to be called art, although I suppose it is subject to taste. I picked up a shrunken head from a side table and turned it over in my hand. It had a sneering expression barely perceptible through the many wrinkles on its leathery skin, which I rubbed with the back of my thumb. Another *objet d'art* was a painting dominating the far wall, which from one angle looked like a weeping woman and from another looked like she had been flayed. I noted the many dashed brush strokes lacing the canvas, particularly around her face and breasts, and wondered if he were the painter.

His deep voice resonated across the room. "You've found a lot of information already, Valya. But I don't understand why you're showing me this. Shouldn't you give this to the police or a missing person organisation?"

142

"I've already done that. Don't you think I would go to the authorities before I ask anyone else to get involved? The police didn't seem interested in what an 'amateur' had to say, though I provided them with copies anyway. They said all of the missing people will invariably turn up one way or the other. All rather unhelpful. You understand I don't enjoy asking for favours... I like to handle things myself. If there was another option, I would pursue it." I glanced down at the tiny head in my palm. I drew my fingers around it and impulsively threw it at him. He caught it easily with his left hand, as I knew he would, and grinned at me.

Clasping my hands at the small of my back, I returned slowly to the kitchen area. "The disappearances aren't on the police's highest list of priorities. They're concentrating all their manpower on investigating the threat to ShadeCo and protecting senior staff and their families. They're treating missing people as separate incidents and no one is spare to work with me on it. This document, by the way, is information I've inferred from different police sources. They certainly would not tell me outright. So you can see my predicament. The missing people disappeared around the attack, but they're overlooking the obvious link and they're not taking it up...

"And my fear is that unless I act soon, Father's going to end up another permanent face on the missing persons list. This not knowing is frustrating beyond belief."

Butcher gave me a searching look, getting my measure and evaluating the situation. Eventually, he spoke. "I understand... but I don't know what you want me to do about it. I'm not a detective—"

I interjected. "I need your skills as a Hunter. Tracking a Shade is like tracking a human, all you have to do is search for the clues." I leapt back onto the stool. "Look, if I could handle it on my own, I would. We know each other well enough now to have a certain level of understanding. I don't usually impose myself on others but I need help now. And if Father's been taken by a terrorist group, I'm definitely going to need backup and I know I can trust you and you won't slow me down. No one else fits that profile, just you."

The last piece of flattery seemed to work because a smile played across his lips and his expression became less guarded. He glanced down and examined the document again, presumably familiarising himself with the data. "You definitely think he was taken hostage then?"

I nodded, slowly. "Yes. I think that if it were any other reason, he would have turned up by now, one way or the other. If you have any other theories then I'd like to hear them."

His eyes scanned the screen. "And you think that the terrorists who attacked ShadeCo took the others too?"

Again, I nodded affirmation.

"Okay… have you got any idea who the terrorists are or where they might be?"

"Not at the moment," I admitted. "It's all surmises and I'm stuck on that aspect. I'm aware that you're new to the material, but have you any ideas?"

"Hmm." He drummed his fingers on the worktop and contemplated. "My vehicle's previous owners might offer a clue. Though for what I'm about to tell you, you must swear to tell no one. Not a single word out of those dry lips of yours. I don't want you gossiping to your friends about this."

I laughed. His earnest expression was priceless. "Who am I going to tell?"

He did not find it amusing. His deep-blue eyes fixed on mine; the angry glint I saw there warned me it was definitely not a joke. I raised my hands in submission, he would not proceed if I did not agree. "Okay. I swear to tell no one."

"Give me proof."

I pulled off the glove on my left hand and retrieved the knife from my leg holster, nicking my palm with it. I clenched my hand and let several drops of blood drip onto the counter. He looked at the scarlet drops and back at me. I gave him my word as a Hunter I would tell no one.

It sufficed.

"Ever since my Jeep was destroyed a few months back, I've been tracking down the people who did it. I also lost a fair bit of equipment and whisky too, but the primary loss was the Jeep. It hasn't been an easy course, I couldn't find a thing about their vehicle online, the one now parked out front. In the end, I just trolled through the desert searching and waiting and searching some more. I was on the verge of giving up when I saw some noticeably large tyre tracks in the muddy straits near Springhaven, so I went from there."

I nodded for him to continue.

"I followed them for two days until I'd the opportunity to attack them. I looped in front of them in my Jeep and used it as bait. While they were sabotaging it, I snuck up and took their vehicle and left them in the desert."

"What happened to them?"

He waved dismissively. "They'll be fine." He rubbed his eyebrow with his thumb, one of his tells. He was lying. It was the same unnatural tone as earlier, but I ignored it.

"Why do you think that they're linked with my father, at the very least?" I did not see the connection.

"I'm getting to that part. When I spoke to these people, they called me ShadeCo scum and attacked both of my vehicles because there was ShadeCo equipment inside. Once I had the vehicle, I used the navigation unit and went to a pre-set destination out of curiosity—"

"Butcher!" I was shocked. "That's very dangerous."

"Well, it wasn't my best decision. Anyway, let me finish, woman! The destination was a well-protected building deep in the desert, nowhere near the other settlements. It looked small from outside but I reckon there must've been more to it underground because it had fences, barbed wire, armed droids protecting it, the whole shebang. Why'd it need to be protected if there's nothing to hide? Why's it so far away from any other settlement? It was in the wastelands after all."

I ran a hand absent-mindedly through my hair as I digested this snippet of information. It was definitely suspicious. If they despised ShadeCo and all it stood for then they could have orchestrated the attack on HQ. And if they took hostages they would keep them away from any towns or villages, so they will not get rescued. But they have not counted on someone like me. I will not give up. If we are prepared, we can take them on — perhaps. It would require considerable planning. Also, Butcher had not actually promised assistance. Although it was not positively the correct location, it was more than I had before and the greatest breakthrough so far.

Trying to curb my excitement and keep my voice neutral, I queried, "Do you think that the missing people could be in there?"

"Yeah… if someone took them as hostages like you believe. It was a lucky find. I doubt there are a lot of places like that just hidden in the desert. In all my years as a Hunter, I certainly haven't stumbled on any."

"That is just my thought. It seems suspicious…"

"We won't be able to get close in the vehicle. There are spikes on the

145

ground that'll shred the tyres in seconds. And there are droids, probably guards, and who knows what else."

If he was thinking about ways to get inside the building then he was thinking about coming too.

"The spikes shouldn't be problematic. I noticed your vehicle has hover plates on the sides and they reduce pressure on the ground, so the spikes won't puncture beyond the superficial layer. But I agree we need to scout the area first and establish the risks, otherwise it would be suicide. Perhaps a reconnaissance mission is in order before we can come up with an infiltration plan. We need to find the best way to get inside without detection." I cast a wry glance at him and smiled, feeling some of my anxiousness lessen now there was a possible location. "Once we're inside that's where our skills come to the fore. If we have the element of surprise, and the right weapons, we could recover all of the hostages."

Butcher pushed his seat away from the table and abruptly got up. I watched him as he strode through the kitchen and up the stairs leading to his bedroom.

"What are you doing?" I called out.

"Wait there. I'll be back in a minute."

There were a few clicks and I heard the creak of a rusty hinge, shortly followed by some rustling. I pushed the stool away from the bar and stood up. I heard the box shut and his footsteps across the bare planks. At the top of the staircase, he reappeared cradling a gun close to his chest, one hand on the barrel and the other wrapped carefully around the stock. Even from a distance, I could see that it was an old weapon, albeit well kept.

When he neared, I gasped. "Is that…"

"An M-800 pulse rifle," he declared nonchalantly, as if he were not holding a weapon with inexpressible destructive capacities; it was illegal just to own one, let alone use it. "I've upgraded the energy pack to make it compatible with today's technology, which made it simpler to get spare ammunition. Canisters from Earth are hard to come by now."

I sat back, surprised. "They stopped producing those before we came to Diomedia. Do you know how much trouble you'd be in if you were caught in possession of that weapon? How the hell do you still have one?"

"I'm careful. This is the first time that I've got it out of the trunk all year. It's pretty old but it's able to do the job."

146

"Those things can do serious damage!" They were also extremely temperamental, though I left that part unsaid. I felt unsettled even being near it.

"If we come across heavily armed people then you'll regret not bringing it along. Do you want to do this properly or not? If there are only the two of us then we'll need every advantage we can get to get the hostages and ourselves out of there in one piece. I don't want to get myself killed for this, so I'm not helping unless you've got a decent, structured plan."

I nodded, but still felt uncomfortable. Any shot from that gun would tear a person apart, muscle and skin rendered from bone in milliseconds. They were lethal and messy. Normally, I was not squeamish about weaponry. I have an impressive collection of my own, but nothing as brutal as that rifle.

Eventually I said, "Please only use it as a last resort. I don't want to kill anyone, especially not that way."

"If these militant activists are capable of taking hostages and killing innocent people then it's likely they don't give a damn. They're going to attack us and we need to be prepared. In the end, does it really matter? We won't be the ones mopping up afterwards."

In an attempt to win me over, he placed the gun on the table and allowed me to examine it. The long-barrelled weapon was dark and menacing against the pale tabletop. Hesitantly, I ran a finger over the stock. The strength of the recoil from the M-800 was legendary; only a person Butcher's size could wield it. With his permission, I lifted it up and assessed the weight. It was heavy, especially if we found ourselves trekking through the field. After an extensive investigation, I delicately placed the gun back on the table. Butcher let out a long breath, and I realized he'd been holding it.

He might be right. We needed to prepare for any eventuality.

16

Landmine

$\mathcal{M}$odifying the vehicle at a mechanic's wasn't an option, so I took my chances and allowed Valya to alter it and replace the central unit so I could drive it without blood on my hands. For this favour, I agreed to join her on her mission to find her father. And then my house automatically became the planning centre. Not out of choice. She just wouldn't leave. I locked her out a few times, but the droid kept letting her back in, clearly still malfunctioning.

In the end, I just let her be. She didn't want to be alone any more and could *tolerate* my company, which in Valya talk means *I'm fond of you even if you're annoying.* At any rate, my house has enough space for two people without feeling suffocated. And my fridge was well stocked with provisions, so we didn't need to go out. This was one task the droid could still do without a problem.

As Valya had completed stage one and two before she even asked me to join her, we immediately started work on the third stage. And the first confirmed action for stage three of the operation was to acquire an itinerary of our weapons, ammo, traps and vehicles to get a clear idea about our resources. The list was long. Between us we'd a large arsenal stocked in our homes — more weapons than we could carry. We definitely weren't lacking there.

Valya wanted to include the new tank in the strategy. At the moment it couldn't be driven without pouring the previous owner's blood on my hands. I'd spread it further by adding the blood to a flask of synthetic plasma, but the supply was still limited and quickly running out. Neither of us had contacts working in a lab to allow us to replicate the blood. So the only way to carry on driving it was to neutralise the vehicle in the same way that you would to a second-hand vehicle. Only then could my DNA be coded to the system and allow me to drive it normally. She was finding the necessary parts to change the central system. These items were custom-made and weren't liable to turn up for a couple of days, which would be another delay. I wasn't one hundred per cent convinced she'd be up to the task.

Valya was unable to unwind. The two-day delay for the vehicle parts made her anxious and she was constantly getting up and walking around my living room, like a wall guard marching from one post to the other.

Speaking of which, I heard her bare feet pad across the floor behind me. She peered over my shoulder at the MID projection desk, I turned around in my seat and raised an eyebrow at her. Getting the hint, she carried on pacing the floor.

The second item was to obtain a satellite map of the area. Not so easy. The scouting droids' images of the continent were blurry leading up the facility and a three-mile radius around the base was a solid block of grey — highly suspicious stuff. It seemed that something was being hidden there. The tank's navigation unit was no help. Its rendering of the graphics of the landscape is limited. It gives us a vague idea of the area and it's not detailed enough to form a plan on. Having a precise map is essential. Knowing where the danger would come from was vital. When I went there, the only entrance was the building's front door. It couldn't be the only entrance or exit... could it?

"Valya," I called over my shoulder from my seat beside the MID projection desk. "We need to get a decent image. Do you have any ideas?"

"Are you sure that these aren't workable?"

"Come and have a look."

She came up behind me and sighed. "That's no good! It's too blurry."

"Any ideas?" I looked back at her. She stood with arms folded and hands cradling her elbows. Her eyes narrowed as she pondered.

"My cousin, Kimi, owes me a favour, she works in the Getman observatory. You know the one on the tallest mountain in the Malinowski range."

"Friends in high places!" I joked.

She winced and pinched the bridge of her nose. "That was terrible,

Butcher. My cousin is up to date with the situation and the only other person I confided in apart from you. Kimi offered to help me before and I'd declined because I didn't think she'd be much use in the field. She's an astrologer and more focused on theories than the practical side of things. She's incredibly clumsy and has the heavy, flat-footed tread of a giant. I'm exaggerating of course, but for a slender thing she's loud and stomps around. If we brought her along, they'd know we were coming before we even set off. But she does have access to the satellites and can hijack them for our purposes. It is better that than going in blind."

I agreed wholeheartedly.

While I instructed the droid to prepare us some grub, she went up to my bedroom and made the call privately. The droid was temperamental, and short-circuited mid-task on a few occasions, so I oversaw the preparation. This droid sometimes couldn't tell when food was off. Yesterday, it cooked an omelette resembling roadkill and smelt like garbage, which is where it ended up. It hadn't been the same since Valya shot it. Housedroids don't come cheap, easily a couple months' wages for a new, decent model or a month's if you want a second-hand one.

When Valya finished the call, she came down and briefed me on the conversation. Her cousin would help us tomorrow and she'd arranged to meet us at the observatory the following evening before her shift started.

The droid brought us over two large bowls of steaming ramen. It smelt good. I picked up my chopsticks and dug in. The meal was perfect.

Valya seemed anxious. I watched her stir the soup distractedly around the bowl with a spoon, not eating much at all, obviously worried about her father. When I finished my meal, I shuffled around to her side of the table and gave her an awkward, brief one-armed hug.

Then she shooed me away with renewed energy. "Okay, let go of me now please. I'm not going to break. I'll finish my meal and then we can carry on…" She paused. "Actually, on second thoughts, I'll carry on. You should probably take a look at the droid. There's something wrong with it."

Her last comments came as we watched the droid repeatedly reverse and then accelerate into the wall. It was definitely fit for scrapping. On the plus side, I'd a very clean metre square section of floor.

"After this mission, you can buy me a new one."

"We'll see." She laughed, clearly thinking I was joking.

***

The following evening, we were finally on the way to the observatory. Our side of the road was clear.

"We should make good time," commented Valya, opening up a beer and taking a swig. I reached over and took a can from the sideboard as well.

It was rare to see Valya out of her normal ShadeCo gear. She'd decided it was too recognisable and was going 'incognito'. Her hair was un-gelled and tied back with a black band and some goggles rested on her forehead, replacing her normal canvas mask and chrome respirator, which were currently perched on the dashboard beside my gas mask. Personally, I thought she was being overly cautious for a trip to the observatory — it was full of astronomers, not terrorists.

"Valya," I said, gesturing to the field on our left, "is that what I think it is?

She squinted and stared towards the area. A couple of light-density Shades hovered close to the livestock in the field just outside of Mayton's walls.

"You've got good vision! They look, no, they're definitely Shades. They're far too close to Mayton."

Valya called the wall guards to handle them. Any on-duty Hunter at one of the energy firms would be able to help capture them — possibly a trainee. Low-risk stuff.

We passed the clear line where the farmed fields end and the desert begins. The olive trees stopped abruptly and dry ground took its place. I keep my livestock in a farm at the outer edges that had the lowest rates and gave special discounts for freelancers. Two for the price of one, and the farmers tend them as part of the fee. When you're a freelancer, you have to organise these things yourself. Company Hunters have it easy.

The miles zoomed by. Mayton and its surrounding hills shrunk in the rear-view mirror. The domed houses turned into tiny white specks and disappeared into the landscape. Outside it was hot, hot, hot. Ahead the motorway wavered in the heat and cut up as it neared the horizon. The sun began to set and the glare cut through the hired Jeep's tinted windows. Very soon, it would be night. The overhead lights along the motorway turned on in a relay.

Forty-five minutes later, we arrived at our destination, in the middle of the Malinowski range. All these mountains are fairly low, no more than six or seven hundred metres, but they have wide plateaus. With the dark rock, they looked like morgue slabs for giants, just waiting for a body.

In the distance, the observatory's mountain erupted from the ground, showing just the plateau at first then growing up and up and up. As we got closer, it dominated the other smaller steppes.

"They chose that mountain for a reason. They needed a bigger mountain to check the dust storms. The softer rock around here is quickly eroded by the harsh winds," Valya told me.

The visible sides were steep, almost vertical. I could see the road to the top cut into the rock face. From our low position, we were only able to see the curve of the satellite dish hit by the last rays of light.

The motorway forked. The right path led to the observatory, while the left eventually led to the small San Cristobel settlement in the north. The vehicle automatically veered to the right and onto the narrower route. The road gradually tapered to just one and a half cars wide. At the base of mountain there was a checkpoint — the sole point of access. A steel fence surrounded the base of the mountain so that a car couldn't bypass the checkpoint. From time to time, the station's barrier lowered into the ground and allowed a single car to leave before shooting back up again. Several cars waited on the exit side. There was one car ahead of us on the entry side, and our vehicle jolted to a halt behind it.

The car in front of us went through and we pulled up. The checkpoint's window slid open and a bored-looking woman poked her head out. She peered inside and asked us to open the boot as a br-3.0 droid gave it the once-over. After the droid completed the check, she questioned us about the visit. I leaned back and let Valya do the talking. The woman seemed satisfied enough.

"Scan your MIDs," the attendant demanded. "Hurry up! Other people want to leave."

Valya and I raised our arms. The assistant disappeared inside the booth.

We waited for further instruction.

Another minute or so elapsed before she re-emerged and informed us in her energy-draining monotone, "Park in space fifty-five. This is your allotted space. Do *not* go anywhere else once you've reached the top because the other spaces are for staff members only. And after you park in space fifty-five, you need to scan your MIDs again in the main building for access to the observatory and scan again to sign out. That is mandatory too, as is your allotted space, number fifty-five. I notified Ms Connolly already. She's waiting for you in the observatory lobby."

Finally, with as little enthusiasm as she could muster, she said, "Enjoy the wonders of the stars."

The barrier dropped into the ground and we were permitted entry.

"She's a bundle of joy," commented Valya sarcastically as our vehicle whirred into motion. I grinned at her, thinking exactly the same thing.

***

The path up to the top was narrow, to say the least. The wheels pressed against the railing, barely holding us away from the edge. Valya clearly wasn't comfortable with heights and gripped the sideboard so hard her knuckles turned from her usual pasty to full-white. With a burst of energy, we finally leapt over the pinnacle of the mountain and onto its flat plateau, coming to a stop. Valya noticeably settled down in her seat.

This was a first visit for me, so I was interested to see what the fuss was about. On first impression, it was bloody big. Four satellite antennae sat in a row on our right, all at least thirty metres high and pointing in the same north-west direction. Further along from these was the memorial, a black marble stab with names of the lost passengers from *The Traveller* and those from *The Hopeful Voyager* who had died on the journey etched in gold. At the base, fresh yellow flowers lay in wreaths to honour the dead. As we passed it, I tipped my head in respect for the unfortunates.

We drove slowly onwards and looped around a statue of the observatory's founder, Dr Byrne Getman, before drifting into the car park. We rolled along until we reached space fifty-five. The car reversed automatically without straightening up. It was within the space boundaries but damn, it was nearly diagonal... *bloody autodrive*. The doors unlocked and we fixed on our masks before heading out.

Up here there was no protection from the wind. It whipped at the hems of my trousers, at the sleeves of my shirt. It howled around us in a long moan and tried to force us against the vehicle when we stepped out — powerful stuff. Every step forward was a fight. I kept close to Valya, in case she was shoved over by it. On the plus side, there wouldn't be any Shades. Harsh winds interfere with their forms.

We made a beeline to the observatory, cutting across the parking lot. The entrance doors slid open as we approached. We scanned our MIDs and the screen read that we had access the facility for the entire night, if we needed it.

"It shouldn't take that long. I think no more than a couple of hours," Valya stated, passing through the entranceway.

Inside, the lobby was simple, nothing like the formidableness of ShadeCo with its huge glass front and marble for every surface possible. They could've used another coat of paint, honestly. The bare-tiled floors were more befitting of a hospital, which reminded me of Marie. I hadn't seen her in ages and the usual guilt tried to creep up. I pushed the thought away and pretended a sudden interest in the framed images of constellations hanging on the wall, some slight movements on them — probably a live feed.

Craning my neck upwards, I saw a web of thick metal scaffolding supporting the telescope itself far above us, and a few people were walking along the platform that surrounded it. Maintenance droids were fixing the metal frame around the telescope and blue sparks flew around them while they worked.

I dropped my chin and turned to Valya. "Where's your cousin? I thought she was here."

"She is... just over there." She waved and a woman ahead of us waved back. Her casual clothes, an oversized sweater and slightly-too-short trousers, didn't fit the image of an astrologer or astrophysicist or whatever Valya said she was. In fact, the woman herself didn't really fit the image either.

The family resemblance was obvious. Their angular faces were almost identical, though the cousin had softened hers with a short haircut that skimmed her chin. She had the same platinum shade though hers darkened at the tips. Despite the loose clothes, she was clearly straight up and down, not a curve in sight. Again, like Valya.

Then she came over and I noticed the first big difference between

154

them, their height. Even with flat shoes, she hardly needed to lift her gaze to meet mine and I'm tall myself. I saw the unmistakable flicker of interest in her eyes.

"Hiya! *Long*-time no see, if you get what I mean," she said, smiling at us both — a bright beaming smile. She seemed friendly enough, though Valya was frowning for some reason and didn't seem impressed in the slightest, especially when Kimi pulled her into a determined hug. It was funny to see her tense up on physical contact. Her arms pinned to her sides as if her life depended on it. Her jaw clenched.

"Who's your friend?"

Hold up. Was that the once-over again?

"Kimi, this is my…" She paused here, stuck in the grey area between friend and acquaintance, then finally settled on, "associate, Michael."

"Michael," Kimi purred and offered her hand. "I'm so pleased to meet you."

Taking her hand, I replied, "Likewise", and winked. She giggled, as I knew she would. *Gets 'em every time.* She moved nearer and brushed her hand against my bicep.

Valya groaned and slapped Kimi's hand away gently, squeezing between us and forcing Kimi to take a step back. "Please, we don't have time for this *now*! Kimi, back on your leash! We're here for business, *and nothing else*, so please lead the way." She gestured for Kimi to go in front of us.

Kimi rolled her eyes. She turned around and led the way, her hips swaying as she walked.

I chuckled and shrugged my shoulders at Valya. "What?"

"You know what." She snapped and stalked after her cousin.

Earlier in the Jeep, Valya told me Kimi was senior level and had access to all areas. Kimi led us into a lift and we descended several floors, arriving in a short corridor. Kimi halted and raised her forearm at the security check. We stopped too, watching the sensor pass a scan over and through her body. The locks inside swung back and the door slid sideways.

Kimi entered first, Valya next, with me in the rear. Over her shoulder, Kimi warned us to keep away from the screens, but that was easier said than done, the room was barely big enough for one person, let alone three of us. It was practically impossible not to lean against one of the monitors or switches piled on top of each other. We dodged Kimi as she ducked under our arms and around our torsos to check every screen. She repeated, "Sorry, sorry, sorry", whenever she bumped into us, which was often.

Without turning away from her work, she explained what she was doing with a lot of enthusiasm. "You know, you're both privileged to be here. Only a select few have access to these controls because they operate the Thian satellite directly, the second largest in our arsenal. I don't have permission to alter the largest one that you saw when coming up. A look-but-not-touch clearance. We have to be pretty quick in here, too. Non-staff are not really allowed inside even with a guide, so that's why it's so important to not touch anything! I know it doesn't really look much but it is. We've taken images of deep space that presently grace the ceiling of Mayton Hill's town hall, showing the recent spiral galaxy discovery."

Valya and I exchanged glances and shrugged.

"You haven't heard of it? That's a shame, you should check it out. It's sublime!"

Valya didn't look impressed, her arms above her head out of harm's way. I can't say that I was too enthusiastic either, and my mind wandered to the cost of the vehicle alterations. Even with Valya's labour contribution, they would make a dent in my already-undersized savings.

Someone's elbow prodded into my rib, probably Valya's.

"This one is the nearest satellite to the coordinates you've sent me yesterday." She typed in a code from memory and altered the displays. After repeating this action several times on several different monitors, she squeezed in between us and we watched the largest display in the centre. It was blank, just grey static. From the fuzz, a picture slowly emerged. It filled the space from the left-hand side until the entire image appeared. The base and its various defences were tiny on the screen, barely visible pinpricks on the landscape. Not really what we were after.

I stifled a yawn.

The elbow struck again and Valya hissed out of the side of her mouth, "Pay attention!" Then to Kimi, "Can we amplify the image further? Can you take it closer?"

"Sure." Kimi tweaked another set of controls.

The image on the centre screen plummeted hundreds of metres then stopped. Valya fixed me with a stare — a silent request for my input. The building's shape was familiar, but it was impossible to be a hundred per cent certain from the aerial view that it was the right building. I could have sworn, too, that there were three layers of barriers around the base. But there seemed to be nothing there now. Odd. Then the building slowly dissolved into the ground too.

"What?" Valya started. "What just happened?"

Kimi frantically checked all the displays and darted around each monitor. The building reappeared on the screen and so did the layers of defence, though they again disappeared after a minute. Something was making it distort. I'd never seen anything like this.

"Can you get the feed on this location linked to my MID?"

"I can. No problem. I've spoken to my managers." She noticed Valya's thunderous expression. "Don't worry, they're trustworthy, and they said I could use it unless it is required for specific research. We only use the Thian satellite, if our main one, Ganymede, is otherwise engaged. And if I have to re-alter the satellite's sights elsewhere, I'll be quick and change it back straight afterwards and give you the heads-up too. How long do you need it for?"

"About a week, possibly two, and even that will be probably longer than necessary… but it's better to be safe."

While she worked, Kimi began barraging us with questions. "You haven't given me the details about your plans yet. What are you intending to do? I know you're trying to track Uncle Harald, but how? You're a mystery wrapped in an enigma." Kimi pressed her index finger on the base in the centre of the screen. "Do you even know what's in there? How do you know it's the right place? It might just belong to a crazy gun-toting hermit or something weird like that. If you need help, I could come with you. I'll just take some annual leave and—"

Kimi was a useful contact but untried in combat situations. She didn't seem that clumsy to me, but then again, we were in her familiar territory. From what Valya told me, she couldn't handle a gun and fainted at the sight of blood, so she'd just get in our way.

"Thank you, Kimi. But it might be dangerous and I don't want to put you in that situation. I think Father is being held hostage there. We have supplies to take his captors on and we're going to get in and out as quickly as possible, and you're not used to those types of situations. Besides, I need you here to man the satellite. These images are vital to the mission."

If this mission comes to nothing, Valya will be shattered, I realized. My instinct was her father was dead, but that wasn't something she wanted to hear.

"I think the fewer people that know about this, the better. Sorry, Kimi. I can't reveal any more."

Instead of this putting her off, Kimi's eyes widened in interest. Her voice barely above a murmur, as if someone was listening in, she whispered, "Valya, do you definitely know he's there? What if the worst has already happened?"

Valya cut her short and told her to quit with the interrogation. She raised her MID. "The copy, if you please?"

**

Kimi chatted away, walking slightly ahead of us as we strode past the memorial on the ground level. She slowed her pace when we reached her great-great-uncle's name, who had apparently been on board *The Traveller*. She kissed two fingers on her right hand and reached out and touched the etched name.

She then continued her small talk, something about which constellations could be observed tonight. A star is a star as far as I'm concerned, no matter what shapes they make in the sky.

Before we got into the car, Kimi raised the taboo subject again.

"I know you're upset, Valya, but, I *really* think you should let the police handle this instead. You've never done a rescue mission like it before, and I think you're in over your head, even with Michael. He's only one person. Sorry," she said, turning to me.

Valya made a noise of disgust, muffled by her respirator. Kimi pressed on.

"I know you're exceptionally trained, and your skill with a firearm is second to none, but is it really enough? Promise me you won't put yourselves in needless danger. If you want to talk about it, I'm here and if you need anything else, just let me know."

Valya turned away. Kimi took a step nearer and gently brushed her hand across my bicep again, mouthing, "*Anything*". The invitation was

158

badly timed, so I simply took her hand and shook it, then stepped aside to let her say goodbye to her cousin.

I unlocked the Jeep and the driver's door slid back, skimming the side of the car next to it. I rolled my eyes at the auto drive function yet again. Kimi approached her cousin with open arms, and surprisingly, Valya not only accepted the offered embrace, but reciprocated it. Before I could refuse, Kimi bounded away and pulled me into a quick squeeze too, strangely strong for a svelte woman. In my ear, she whispered. "Feel free to come here anytime."

"Come on!" Valya yanked at my arm and drew me up into the vehicle. "Kimi, back off!"

Once inside, the doors swung back automatically. The wheels were already moving as Kimi yelled goodbye. We rolled towards the exit.

I watched Kimi wave frenziedly in the rear-view mirror. Her sweatshirt rose up, revealing a section of flat belly. Looking at her toned figure, I thought, if we get back from this mission in one piece, I'll take her up on that offer.

17

Longrider

$\mathcal{E}$xploiting the last of the former owner's blood, we managed to drive the tank back to my apartment block and park it in the secure underground residential area. The lot was out of view to the public and, even if a few of my neighbours expressed interest in the vehicle, they were private people and could be depended upon to keep their mouths shut. Another benefit was the tranquillity once workers had left for the morning and before they returned around 20:00, it was currently just after 13:00 and vacant. We stowed our technical equipment and supplies in my allotted utilities locker along the wall.

I was well aware of Butcher's issues with his newfound tank. He required the vehicle altered to recognise and respond to his commands so he could control it, and I would be added too as another driver because you never know what might happen in the field. With the materials I purchased at minimal cost due to frequent friend rates at the local dealership, I bought Butcher's services for the mission to rescue father. Though I omitted that I would add myself as main driver and could override his commands, if necessary. If he wanted to back out once I fixed the vehicle, the inhibitors would come in handy. Best to keep something in reserve for a tricky fellow like him.

As my first step, I performed a thorough search of the interior. Butcher trailed me, checking where I checked, lifting what I lifted and probing what I probed.

"You didn't change anything inside. Is everything okay?" Butcher enquired. He appeared concerned.

"Yes, everything is fine, though you might want to CO_2 spray the controls. Some dust has settled in the cracks, which is inevitable if you take a vehicle out in the field. You can attend to that later."

He nodded.

Next, we checked under the bonnet. The vehicle had a flat front. Butcher lifted the bonnet up and locked it in place above our heads. The mechanisms inside lay vertically, different from anything I was used to. The same skills applied, though. I inspected the engine, pollutant filter, brakes, battery and fuel tank. All of it seemed relatively new, perhaps no more than a year, and in good condition. The circuitry was fine and responsive when I tested it. Butcher still lurked behind me, watching every action I took. I knew he wanted to learn, but it was distracting. He brushed up against me and I felt his warm breath on the nape of my neck.

"Would you mind moving back a bit please?"

He shifted two paces to my right.

Within a few minutes he was peering over my shoulder again.

"For fuck's sake, I'm not going to break the damn thing, so would you back off a bit?" I turned and shoved him with one hand. "Give me some room!" He took another couple of steps backwards and folded his arms.

"Are you sure you know what you're doing? You said you've never seen anything like it before."

"Outwardly, that's right. But when you drill down to the mechanics, it's similar to other Jeeps or larger vehicles and I'm entirely familiar with them. Don't worry. Just give me a little space and a little time and I'll have this working for you without a hitch. I'm going to check the lower section now." I ducked down and crawled beneath the vehicle.

The tank itself was high enough to work underneath without a mechanical lift. I crept along on my knees until I saw the outline of the under-chassis panel. My droid passed me the drill. I removed the plate and shone a torch over the mechanisms and methodically checked the parts. All appeared in good order aside from a coat of dust over everything. Field dust infiltrates even the most seemingly inaccessible places. To give Butcher something to do instead of standing around like a lemon, I sent him on an errand to fetch a long weight. That should occupy him for a while. *I wonder how long it'll take before he realises it's a joke.*

"Take your time." I called out.

When he was gone, I crawled over to the back right of the vehicle and removed the old bio-recognition unit and secured the new one. Then I placed my hand on its front panel, entered my details and pricked my finger with a needle to put a small droplet of blood on it. When Butcher returned, I would add him too.

After this, I crept out from beneath the tank and attempted to open the door without blood. Even with gloved hands, the door swung up obediently and scraped the ceiling on the lot. Then I leapt up the rungs into the vehicle and started the engine with two clicks of my fingers. Everything lit up inside and the system welcomed me by my first name. I took my position in the driver's seat. I sat down and the chair began to give me a back massage, ripples rolling up and down my spine at the perfect amount of pressure. It was delicious.

"Very funny! Very funny," Butcher laughed self-deprecatingly. I was glad he was not annoyed. "A long wait! They kept me there twenty minutes before it clicked… You've got it working?" His head and shoulders appeared in the doorway. He took off his mask, climbed inside, and sat down beside me. His chair began to rumble too, vibrating even more than mine. He groaned with pleasure and closed his eyes. "This is the life."

"Vehicle, off."

Butcher turned towards me and raised a questioning eyebrow.

"I need to turn it off to install you as a user too."

"Before I turn off," the vehicle stated in a high, electronic female voice, "in future please refer to me by my name: Contemporary Automotive Navigation Traveller, or C.A.N.T."

"It's called Cant? Is that usual?"

"The previous owners used a rare bio-recognition unit that didn't interact with the driver. Usually vehicles with intelligence are given names and communicate with you. I'm not talking about your common Jeep but vehicles like this one."

"But Cant?" He chuckled. "The instructions are always going to sound strange: Cant find home!"

"Cant navigate," I added.

"Cant switch off… Imagine shouting it out? A vowel slur and I'll be making a few enemies."

"Butcher, you've called me that a few times…"

"Yeah, well… you don't seem to mind," he said, winking. "I know you can take it!"

Cheeky bugger! I ignored him and said, "You can add yourself as a registered driver and we'll be ready for tomorrow."

✳✳✳

The following day, I woke up already alert, knowing it was the day we would go.

I lay comfortably in the guest bed for a few minutes longer, staring at the single crack in the whitewashed ceiling. Unsurprisingly, I was in excellent spirits and glad we were finally acting on our mission.

Butcher's tank ran excellently when we tested it out yesterday evening. We had all the equipment needed at our fingertips. We considered many situations and arrived at solutions to each. I felt positive that the mission would prove fruitful.

I sat up and stretched my arms above my head as far as they would go, reaching up so high my shoulder blades and elbows cracked. I was in such a good mood that even sleeping on Butcher's guest bed had been agreeable, despite a lumpy mattress and pillows flatter than an ill-timed joke. The temperature in the house was crisp and cold and, as I slithered out of the warmth of the covers, gooseflesh rose across my exposed skin. During the night, I spread one of Butcher's jumpers across the bed for extra warmth. I pulled this garment over my head. It was several sizes too big and the sleeves entirely swamped my hands. I put on my boots and sauntered over to the kitchen for sustenance, waking up the semi-repaired house droid.

From the level above, Butcher growled, half-asleep. The top of his head was visible through the railing for a moment before he threw the covers over himself, presumably to muffle the noise I was making. The morning was almost over and he did not appear to be rising anytime soon. However, we needed to get a move on; he would be getting up regardless. To somewhat soften the blow, I told the droid to make hot drinks. The gurgle of boiling water reverberated around the house. Butcher groaned again.

"I'm making hot beverages, d'you want one?"

Through a massive yawn, he called back, "An Irish coffee."

"Right…"

He explained. "It's an old Irish tradition, passed down on my father's side, to stimulate you first thing. A standard nutritious morning beverage."

"Right… I'm sure it's very stimulating." It was hard to tell if he was serious or not. I made two black coffees, minus the whisky. I needed him to have his full wits for the day ahead and I did not want him sluggish with alcohol.

***

We finally departed in the early afternoon. Cant careered down the motorway, obliterating the speed limit just a few miles out of town. It was more of a suggested speed limit. On the navigation monitor beside me, our progress was plotted by a small yellow dot blipping across a map of the local terrain.

Experience taught me to prepare for any eventuality, and so there was enough equipment and food in the vehicle to allow us to camp out for several days without the need to search for further supplies, though we should only be out for one. The aim was infiltration and rescue, so Shade-hunting equipment was minimal and only for defensive purposes. The back was stacked full of our luggage. To secure it further, I crossed some climbing cables over the boxes to keep the equipment in place. The trunk containing Butcher's gun took a special precedence on one of the passenger seats, restrained by two seatbelts and away from the potentially damaging influence of the other luggage. He was very fastidious about the weapon and did not want to risk harming it. Clearly, it had significance that he had not shared.

A heavy drumbeat pounded from the speakers — Butcher's choice. I mentally tuned it out and checked off all the items on our list in the unlikely event we had forgotten something. I always did this, perhaps slightly compulsive, yet this meticulousness had kept me alive in the past. It was not too late to go back. We had both methodically double-checked everything was packed before we left, so hopefully my uneasy feeling would be simply that: a feeling. For the first time, I started to think that another person or two wouldn't have gone amiss.

The hours passed. Butcher and I discussed the usual common topics of weaponry, training and hunting, rather than the mission ahead. It was infinitely interesting to listen to the viewpoint of a freelance Hunter and his unconventional methods of carrying out the trade. In all honesty, it sounded much more complicated and my previously harsh view of freelancers had softened, slightly. They had to rear their own livestock to use as bait, along with maintaining and paying for their vehicles, equipment and ammo. At ShadeCo and Hayward Bros, they provide Hunters with anything needed. Most Hunters affiliate themselves with a company.

Eventually our vehicle veered left onto an underdeveloped dirt road off the carriageway and we continued on this route several miles into a withered-tree forest. Half a mile of steering through the sun-baked trees brought our vehicle to the edge of a small, yet fast-flowing river.

This was the site of our only planned break, which we had chosen because of Shades' hatred of water.

We parked a short way from the riverbank. Butcher exited and I snatched one of the food bags resting on the luggage and followed suit. With his rifle aloft, Butcher explored the area, checking for Shades lurking nearby. My eyepiece identified one hovering nearby, detached from the usual tree or boulder. I was mindful of the creature as I carried our supplies close to the water. It was unwise to relax before this duty was complete.

Drawing my guns, I moved carefully closer to the Shade. My eyepiece verified it was the only one here. Judging from the solidity of the creature's form it was high-density. It would be valuable ore, particularly if we used bait. I wondered if it was evaluating us too. Who could say? It is difficult to study such creatures outside of their host, because they will even attack recording equipment.

We were cautious.

Its form started to darken to pitch-black, the clearest precursor of an attack, yet it shied away from the riverbank and did not move forward to approach us. I watched Butcher take a few determined steps forward, and

I analysed his technique. The double-barrelled rifle was poised to shoot, he was looking down the crosshairs, and his finger lingered near the trigger. He walked a few more paces towards the creature. At ten metres away, he dropped down onto one knee to steady his aim. At this range, the chemicals in the bullet were concentrated enough to kill. All he needed to do was shoot.

I waited.

Why is he holding back? What for?

I knew he was perfectly capable but I was ready to take the shot, my gun already in my hand.

Butcher pulled the trigger.

The creature splattered in mid-air. The viscous mass hit the parched dirt and speckled some of the rocks, frothing and sizzling. Several inky bubbles grew and burst with a soft plop. Butcher straightened up and swung the gun's strap over his shoulder and approached the Shade, now that it was condensed.

Disappointedly, he nudged the sludge of the former Shade with the toe of his boot; I knew what he was thinking. Dead Shades have monetary worth and it seemed wasteful to leave it. We had no choice though. We had not packed a container. Hunting Shades was not on our mission agenda.

Placing my gun back in the shoulder holster, I returned to our supplies and unpacked our afternoon meal. I unfolded a wide scarf and laid it on the ground as a makeshift blanket, placing a few food items on top inside their sealed containers. I set an alarm on my MID to alert us to leave thirty minutes later. I picked up a stickyfruit and reclined, gazing around the landscape.

My previous good mood was steadily dissolving as the day progressed, replaced by anxiety. Doubt nagged away in the back of my mind. If Father were not at the facility, I would have to start the search from scratch. I would have no idea where to begin. I tried to push the worry aside and shoved a fruit segment into my mouth, savouring the sharp taste.

Heavy footfalls preceded Butcher before he slumped down beside me, his rifle bouncing against his back and shoulder. He leaned over, grabbed a container from the pile, and rested it on his lap, claiming it. He then gave me a sidelong glance, daring me to say anything as he took out his hip flask and drunk a quick mouthful of its amber contents. I crinkled my nose at the distinctive bitter smell.

"You could've at least brought something decent," I commented.

"Thought you'd turned teetotal?" He grinned back. His eyes crinkled with mirth, clearly recalling my hungover promise months ago. "Do you want some?"

"No thank you... and you shouldn't have too much." I took another bite of the fruit in hand and glanced away. "You won't be much use if you're drunk."

His grin deepened and I could feel him watching me. He took another generous gulp before re-screwing the cap and returning it to his pocket. "A swig of this won't affect anything and the effects will wear off soon enough..."

Conversation dropped and there was a comfortable silence. We were quiet apart from the sounds of chewing and the fizz of the cascading river, its waters bursting and jumping against the steep bank wall. I lay down and watched the meagre clouds glide across the sky.

We will probably reach our destination just before dusk. We will not have to conceal ourselves for too long.

A shout broke me from my reverie. It echoed from the forest nearby, but the trees muffled the sound, sparse as they were. I bolted upright, alert. Butcher shovelled the rest of his pasta in his mouth and stood up. We shot alarmed looks at each other and instinctively reached for our guns and masks. It could be the anti-ShadeCo group

There was a second, fainter scream. With guns in hand, we went to investigate.

The second scream was not followed by a third.

The forest was silent.

And that silence was ominous in itself. Someone in minor pain makes more noise than an individual who is seriously wounded. The person could be passed out, or dying.

Butcher and I darted behind a couple of trees and crouched, not daring to approach until we assessed the situation properly. We could stumble blindly into a trap. My eyepiece indicated that there was one person in the clearing. I rested my palm on the withered trunk and peered around.

Up ahead, between two undernourished plants, I saw a girl slumped in the dirt. She lay face down in a nest of roots with her arms curled underneath. Most of her hair had loosened from its restraints and spilled like liquid gold around her head. It was not possible to gauge from this distance whether she was alive or not and the thermal setting on my goggles indicated her body was warm. Her fatigues suggested that she was a Hunter or possibly a trainee, though most are accompanied by a mentor. She was alone.

The screams must have come from her. The wind's shrill whistle was the only discernible sound as it blew through the forest and disturbed the red dust. The girl's bare legs and arms were powdered with it and she'd be buried soon.

"I wonder what happened here," I murmured.

My finger loitered near my handgun's trigger.

"Well?" Butcher whispered, his eyes remaining fixed on the clearing and the girl.

"She doesn't look like she's in good shape… and we can't just leave her. She'll die. We need to bring her into the tank. Are you picking up anything else? My equipment is indifferent and I haven't spotted anyone else." I kept my voice low regardless.

"Same."

"What do you think happened?"

"Impossible to say. Maybe she was attacked. Maybe she wasn't. Don't reckon a Shade got her though because she's not shaking… she might already be dead."

"I'm not getting any readings at all, Shade or human, so whoever or whatever it was made a sharp exit. I say let's get closer." As I stood up, I felt the clasp on my shield belt around my waist. It was active and would protect me from bullets or pulses, though would be ineffective if I was caught in an explosion.

Cautiously, we approached. Dry branches and roots snapped underfoot and sounded painfully loud to my ears. The roots were raised and I was careful with every step lest I sprain my ankle or worse, which would bring the mission to an abrupt end and waste all our efforts. I continued to scan the area for signs of movement.

Butcher was about a metre to my left. He turned out to be surprisingly nimble for a man of his proportions, and did not allow even a single branch to break despite the cross-web on the ground.

Suddenly, my shield belt activated and its pulse repelled a small item a half-metre from my torso. It shot off a considerable distance.

"Did you see that?"

"It looked metallic. Watch yourself!" he replied.

A few metres away from the girl, I noticed she had several needles sticking out of her, one in her shoulder, two in her neck and two in her arm. A pale-blue liquid trickled down from the wounds intermingling with blood and staining her skin. I stooped down and inspected some of the tacky substance between my thumb and forefinger. Through the respiration's filter, it smelt like aniseed. Judging from her prone form, the perspiration dampening her skin, and her laboured breathing, I reckoned the substance was a poison of some kind. I reached out and felt her wrist for a pulse. Erratic.

Her left foot was caught in a snare. I pulled the wire taut and cut it easily with a knife.

Butcher stood beside me with folded arms, keeping guard. I informed him of my supposition and told him we needed to bring her back to Cant *tout de suite* for urgent medical attention. He ran a hand through his tangled mess of hair then swung his rifle onto his shoulder, bent down, and picked her up like a tired child. Her head rolled back and her delicate limbs dangled limply over his arms.

Our pace was much faster on the return journey.

I trekked a few paces ahead. When the forest cleared, I ran over to the vehicle, threw off the camouflage netting, folded it and put it aside. I retrieved the Medex Cube and medical kit from beside the passenger seat while Butcher placed the girl on her side in the recovery position.

I positioned the Medex Cube next to her waist and set it to its task. A red beam about the width of a thumb shot out of the side of the unit and scanned up and down her body twice. In a generic androgynous voice, it announced she was suffering from omaxzin poisoning and identified the antidote. Fortunately, we had packed for a number of eventualities, including medical emergencies. I fetched the syringe that held a universal antidote for many alkaloid poisons.

I felt for a vein in her forearm, stabbed the needle in, and pushed the plunger down. While I was doing this, I had a good look at her face and recognised her as a ShadeCo trainee. *Red's niece!* I could not believe it. Where's Tobias, though? As her mentor, he should not have let her go out alone unless she had a number of successful hunts under her belt. It didn't seem to fit with his character, so perhaps he was not aware that she's out here? I doubted Red knew about this either. Considering the anti-ShadeCo feelings, it was unwise for trainees to hunt solo. Anyone could have come across her.

The liquid disappeared and I hoped it would work rapidly. Medical care in the field was never going to be as quick or efficient as hospital treatment, but this should suffice.

After this, I sat back on my haunches and connected my MID to hers, it identified her as Sophie Connolly. Out of curiosity, I checked her main contacts. High up the list was Harald Ericksen, my father. She must know him through Red!

"Is that it?" Butcher asked disinterestedly. His arms were folded across his chest and he seemed bored.

"Yes."

"Then we'll have to move her and get going. We're already later than your schedule."

I was taken aback. "We can't leave her like this. What if a Shade comes along or a predator? She'd be easy pickings!"

He shrugged his shoulders nonchalantly. "That's life in the field."

"Butcher!" I cried indignantly, shaking my head. "We're not leaving her. She's Red's *niece,* for crying out loud, and he's practically part of my family too. I can't leave her out here alone and look him in the eye again. That must be some sort of sign. Besides, she's a trainee Hunter and she'd have to be pretty handy with a gun to pass the initial stages; those tests aren't easy, not that you'd know. It could be prudent to have another Hunter with us, even one who isn't fully qualified." Butcher drummed his right fingers against his upper arm while he listened. "I can see that you're not impressed by the idea, but she might be useful."

We argued for several minutes, neither refusing to budge. He was adamant she would slow us down. Eventually, I offered to meet him halfway to break the deadlock.

"Let's say if she recovers full use of her senses before we reach our destination, she can help us. If not, she stays tied to her seat. As far as I can see, she owes us a favour."

Butcher was dubious. "She's young, Valya. And drugged up to her eyeballs. I doubt she'll be much use for a long time. She was also stupid enough to get caught in a trap! And as far as I'm concerned she'll hold us back even when she regains full use of her senses—"

"We've still got quite a fair distance to go, and you never know. She might be fit enough to help by then. The antidote will counteract the poison soon, and when it does, she'll be fine. They don't usually let Hunters go into the field alone before they've had several successful hunts, which suggests a considerable level of skill. But I guess that's another thing you wouldn't know, being self-trained and all."

He slapped the side of the vehicle, his voice edged. "My background doesn't come into it — she's a liability! I really don't understand you. First you only wanted my help. Mine alone. And now you're willing to let a random girl join us and waste time in the process? Didn't you tell me earlier that *time was of the essence?*" His voice raised a few pitches to imitate mine. We held eye contact for a moment. He continued. "If you want to take her, that's your call. It's your mission. But if she becomes a burden, she's your responsibility. And I'm not carrying her anywhere else except into my vehicle. Got it?"

"Understood."

He stared at me, disapproval emanating from him like hot air on a sweltering day. He looked her over appraisingly. "At least she's carrying real weapons," he said, nudging me with his elbow somewhat playfully. Then he bent down, picked her up, slung her over his shoulder, and mounted the rungs into the vehicle. I followed quickly because he was certainly correct on the time element.

We resumed our positions in the front once the girl was safely nestled amongst the boxes of supplies. When the doors sealed, I took off my respirator and goggles and placed them on the dashboard. "If she doesn't improve, then we'll leave her inside the tank. But if she wakes up and is alert enough, then I'll ask her to assist. Does that seem reasonable enough?"

He grunted in response and started the vehicle. Sophie might come in useful later. At present, the number of people we were about to face was an unknown. If there were dozens, then Butcher would be grateful for her presence. During the lectures I gave to her class, she seemed astute and knowledgeable about hunting and the only one to challenge my answers. I knew she was top of her class for firearms module and I remember watching her in action at the firing range, pulling off some shots that even I might struggle with — on a bad day, of course. I felt she could be a useful asset to the mission.

18

Landmine

*W*e were back on course just before dusk. I checked the rear-view mirror. The girl was propped up in the back, mostly hidden by boxes and crates piled in front of and beside her. Hell, there was even a sleeping bag and a rolled-up camo-netting on her lap. Her head flopped forward and her chin rested against the top of the sleeping bag, her hair across her face and her arms slack.

She was zonko. Her chest rose and fell gently. Sleep was probably a side-effect of the medicine. I hadn't paid attention to the earlier diagnosis. It didn't matter. To get in that state on the field was careless.

What's Valya thinking? How could she think that this girl would be useful? Even if she wakes up soon...

Valya noticed me staring at the girl and twisted in her seat to face the other way. "She's not an unknown. She's James Martin's niece, you know, ShadeCo's CEO. I've met her a few times and taught her class before all this trouble with ShadeCo and father. My first lecture with them didn't go to plan." She began discussing how the trainees led her off topic, and I was again glad to be a freelancer. I wasn't forced to give these lessons.

It must have been obvious I wasn't listening because Valya abruptly stopped speaking. After a pause, she changed subject. "The antidote is working its magic. She'll wake up soon. I can already see colour returning to her cheeks, earlier her face looked like soured milk, didn't you think? Not easy with that tan..." She reverted suddenly to the earlier subject. "You know, teaching is useful. I got an insight into the quality of the students. Her entire class — all of the remaining trainees — are set to graduate, which will be a record if it happens. A couple of years ago, only one person passed. And Red let most of their trainers go. This year should be promising. Can you believe it? The girl's bright—"

"She could be a genius for all I care, Valya. The problem is she's inexperienced and careless and almost lost her life in the field because she fell into a trap. That's not someone I want watching my back."

She gave a bark of a laugh. "You don't even know her. It was bad luck—"

"Doesn't matter, you make your own luck. I'm just looking at the facts," I shot back.

"She's either been poisoned or drugged up for your lengthy acquaintance of half an hour and I don't think that's a sound basis for personality analysis."

"Okay, would you have let your guard down like that? Even while you were a trainee?"

She considered it, chewing her lower lip. "Well, no. But I wasn't a typical example of a trainee; hunting has been my life ever since I could walk or even crawl. Father took me out on my first hunt when I was twelve, so I'm not a typical example. Some people have to work on the hunting instinct. You're being very severe when it's almost impossible to prepare for every hunting situation that you might face in the field. She might have fallen into a trap set by the anti-ShadeCo group because the forest is sometimes used as a training spot. Or it might well have been set by a non-human and there's no way that a trainee or even an experienced Hunter could predict that."

"With a snare?"

"You never know."

"A snare? A centuries-old form of hunting and you think that some alien life form adopted it to attack unsuspecting humans? Really?"

"Actually, regarding the snares, it's more like millennia."

"Is that important?"

"My point is you can't possibly consider everything."

Yet she believes we've considered all the scenarios for assaulting this base. Her mind is very selective.

"Besides," she continued, with the wry, knowing smile of someone holding a winning trick. *Here comes the barb.* "Weren't you attacked out here a short while ago?"

I didn't take the bait. Instead, from the back, a gentle voice asked,

174

"Where am I…" Then trailed off. Valya jerked her head around so violently I thought she'd break her neck.

If I hadn't heard her speak, I'd have thought she was still out of it. Though she was upright, her eyelids drooped and only a small part was visible, like thin slices of egg white. Her lips had a slight droop to them. She looked like Marie when she was heavily sedated after one of her episodes.

"Sophie, don't worry, you're safe now. You've met me before but I don't think you've met my friend, this is Landmine." Something was really distorting Valya's judgement. Maybe worry morphed her self-professed logical brain. Our task wasn't going to be *safe* by anyone's standards. "We are in the middle of a rescue mission, so we can't take you back to Mayton until we have completed it."

"I don't, I live… in Winsford."

"Okay, Winsford. As you've unexpectedly, but not inopportunely, joined us, we might require your help. Of course, that depends on how long it takes for the poison to neutralise. It should be fairly soon." The string of drool hanging from the girl's lip finally detached and plopped on the sleeping bag. *Is Valya seeing what I'm seeing?* "Not too long, really. At most, the Medibox estimated just over an hour. Let me know if I'm speaking too quickly?"

Due to the girl's slowed processing speed, she took a while to digest the information and respond. "It's fine… I'll just rest a bit… please."

It was enough. Valya nodded and left her alone.

***

Several hours passed before Cant stopped. Our position on the navigation screen began to pulse to indicate we'd arrived. We parked about a couple of miles from the base. Cant emits stealth scramblers masking our presence, even in the case of motion or heat detectors. Our shield belts would emit the same pulses when we got out, though we only had two, so if the girl stays near us then she'll be hidden too.

The area was very uneven. Hills shot up from the ground as frequently as valleys dropped down into it. Both of Diomedia's moons were thin crescents tonight and emitted little light to expose us. All part of the plan. Troublingly, the area was much more open than our map suggested, or I remembered. There was limited cover from boulders and trees, very different than the rugged terrain in my memory. *Weird. Have they been moved?*

I'd an unnerving feeling we weren't going in unannounced.

"We're reliant on stealth, so we need to wait until the dead of night. When we're out there, pay close attention to your eyepieces because if there are Shades around we need to avoid them. If we engage, the shots will give away our presence. As we need to wait, let's go over our strategy with Sophie before we scout the area."

I'd to give it to Valya. During the last part of the journey, the antidote did its job and neutralised the poison. The girl was now alert, the side effects having worn off as well.

I let Valya do most of the talking because she knew her strategy better than a domestic droid knew how to clean a kitchen... apart from mine. The first step was to place a pulse scrambler by the first fence and detonate it. The detonation would disengage the gates and deactivate our weapons too. But to the guard inside, their defences would appear intact. This'd allow us time to enter the vicinity and remain incognito on their scanners for a while. If we ran into any trouble, we had the knives, stun guns, and my old rifle, which wouldn't be affected by the scrambler. Our other guns would reactivate within a few hours.

The girl listened raptly to Valya's explanation. But she still seemed like a novice. We'd be quicker with just the two of us.

When Valya paused during her monologue, I asked her, "I take it you've decided what you want to do?" I gestured to the girl with my thumb behind the backrest.

Valya turned around properly in her chair to face the girl in the rear. "I'm just going to ask you a few random questions, nothing too challenging. Name a captain of *The Hopeful Voyager*?" Even a pupil at primary school would know an answer to this.

The girl answered hesitantly. "Captain... George Stanton..."

"Where is the academy situated?"

"Fifteenth Street, just past the Exchange shopping mall," she replied, surer this time.

"What year will you graduate?"

176

"'Seventy-two."

"What is the most efficient bait for a Hunter?"

She smiled widely, dimples in her cheeks, and answered, "Goats."

This is wasting time.

"Hey, is the interrogation over? We need to get going," I finally said.

Valya reached for the Medibox sitting on the dashboard and clambered into the back so it could scan the girl. The device confirmed that she was now clean. So I assumed she would now be tagging along.

"It's your mission, but I think you need to actually ask her if she's up to the task, instead of assuming she's happy to sign up." I finally spoke directly to the girl. "Have no illusions about this, it's dangerous. If you don't feel up for it, you can wait here, as long as you don't touch anything."

"She knows it's dangerous," Valya interrupted, with an irritable edge to her voice.

Valya carried on and related what happened to her father. The girl was shocked.

"Harald's always at the academy. He helps the trainees and sometimes Tobias and I go to visit him at HQ. I like him a lot. I always thought he is one of those people who energises a room with his presence, a very charming man. And Uncle Red always speaks highly of him."

"Red would. They were former teammates and always saying how great they are. Honestly, they haven't worked on the same team in decades but whenever they're together, you'd have thought it was only yesterday. But I'm glad you think so too." Valya smiled at her then she brought the talk back to the mission. "These last couple of weeks have been tough. And we don't know exactly what is waiting for us in there. Initially, I thought we could handle it ourselves. However, now we're so close, I'm not sure. If we only have one shot, I want to increase the chance of success. You're almost a Hunter. A talented one. And we know you're physically fit and able. I understand it's a considerable undertaking and a colossal favour to ask of anyone but if you join us on this mission, it would repay any obligations you might feel towards us for saving your life. We need to get started right now, so please decide."

She has a keen blackmailing technique.

It took a heartbeat before the girl agreed, without reluctance. Her clear-blue eyes sparkled with fervour. "I'll help any way I can!"

177

Shit…

I rolled my eyes. "Valya, remember, if she gets hurt, it's on you. Cant, turn on blackout windows and inner spotlights." The lights embedded in the roof shot on so we could begin getting the equipment ready. "Have you got much ammo for your weapons?"

"I've got a few rounds… I didn't think I needed to use them…"

"Fine. You can borrow a couple of ours. You'll definitely need a stun gun. Not that one!" I interjected. Her hand darted away from the trunk beside her, which contained my rifle. "I'll get the equipment. Make room, both of you." I scrambled over the seats and boxes to the back to unpack the gear.

As I unloaded the equipment, I remembered there were only two shield belts. That was going to be a problem. They aren't affected by the pulse scrambler and offer protection from a range of weapons. After much deliberation, I found myself undoing my belt and passing it to her. She accepted tentatively, securing it above her normal one.

"I'll need to stay near both of you when we go outside to avoid being detected," I stated.

Valya raised her eyebrows. I ignored her. She smiled and turned the shield belt's buckle forty-five degrees to activate it, and the girl, who'd been carefully watching her, copied the action on her own belt.

The rest of the weapons were evenly passed out, five each, two pulse, two stun, and one Shade-effective, along with the ammo and an assortment of knives. It was enough to hold off an attack of ten, twenty times our number if we had a good enough position and food and water. We didn't know what we faced inside. Valya underplayed the danger during her speech and the girl looked terrified. She was so young, barely out of her teens and not yet a Hunter.

"Ready?" I asked them both.

"Ready," Valya responded.

"I'm good," the girl said.

178

19

Landmine

$\mathcal{O}$utside, the darkness was deep and my vision was restricted to three metres in every direction. My eyepieces switched automatically to night vision and the landscape materialised in various shades of jade. Valya and I ascended in the planned north-westerly direction. My weapons rattled at every step in their holsters and the dry ground crunched noisily underfoot, sounding like I was stepping on cereal. Glancing back, I noticed the girl only just leave the vehicle. She started to sprint to catch up until Valya spoke into her MID and told her to slow down and be quiet. Without boulders or trees to offer the illusion of protection, I felt exposed. Every part of me prickled with anticipation, expecting to be hit at any point. Vulnerable.

Valya ran just ahead. I kept close enough behind to receive protection from her shield belt. These belts would have to be switched off if we engage in close combat. For long range, they're fine. The girl trailed in the rear. We darted through a slalom of knee-high shrubs and didn't break our stride even when the slope became severe. We wove along the hill until we reached one of the only large boulders in the area, wide enough to provide cover for all.

The girl caught up, her breath ragged from fear and exertion. We allowed her a few moments of respite while we peered around the boulder.

Valya whispered to me, "The satellite image shows that we should carry on north-west to the next significant shelter, a silverblade tree, about thirty metres away except there appears to be a wide and shallow cavern in the way, which was not on the map. We can either go around or try to scale it. What do you reckon?"

"It doesn't look like a naturally formed cavern. It looks dug out."

"Around or over?"

"With all this equipment? Probably go around."

Valya went first. She went in a crouching run, ten metres, fifty, a hundred, two hundred, until she reached another cluster of rocks, the largest of which was waist-height, then ducked down.

"Go ahead and follow her," I told the girl.

She sprinted along the same trail, mirroring Valya. I watched her reach the cluster of rocks and Valya forced her down onto her knees. I followed quickly and ducked too. We gave it a moment then peered over the rocks. I couldn't see anything ahead except a few lizards scuttling along the ground. It was open, and silent. Even the sound of the carmeneon late evening call was absent.

Valya spoke, keeping her voice low. "I'm not entirely certain the readings are correct. My eyepiece reckons it's clear. But then, the satellite images are proving unreliable and there're a lot of devices able to give our equipment inaccurate feedback." She paused. "We need to confirm we're not being followed. I thought I heard footsteps. Did you hear anything?"

All three of us listened carefully. I strained my ears. I definitely thought I heard extra footfalls when we were running. We turned around to view the area we'd just travelled.

It was empty.

The girl straightened up, presumably because she thought no one was there. I grabbed her arm and yanked her down again. We held our breath and waited in tense silence, watching the barren area.

After a while, I let go of her wrist and gestured downwards with my palm indicating she should remain here and keep low.

"Should we just make a run for the top?" I suggested.

"It's too risky to just go straight up. There's another tree higher up the slope. Let's aim for that."

With one last glance around, Valya pushed herself off the ground and advanced diagonally, going down the slope slightly before zigzagging upwards to a couple of withered trees. The girl went next and I followed behind. Her pace slackened to barely faster than walking speed. I shoved her forward and ordered her to hurry.

The large tree called us. I was convinced we were being followed. Valya seemed to think so too. We reached the tree, slamming into the trunk and sinking to the ground. There was a slight niche at the base and we squeezed into it as much as possible. We didn't move for a jumpy quarter of an hour, waiting and watching the landscape.

Turning to me, Valya said, "Butcher, we can't sit here forever. If there's someone following us, then they've probably stopped too."

"Continue?"

She stared hard up ahead to the apex.

"We should carry on."

I was watching the distance when it happened. Between the tiny trees above about four metres away, people suddenly started appearing out of the ground.

"Oh, shit!"

One. Two. Three. Four. More to our left. More to our right. Their stares were identical. They wore masks without features in the darkness, and they steadily advanced, their weapons pointed directly at us.

We were outnumbered five to one.

Had they been hidden there the entire time?

To our immediate left, we heard the click of a gun. We spun. A man was about two metres from us. He wore camouflage mesh as a cape, scrub woven into it so that he looked like a tumbleweed. His white mask shone out of the brush like a ghost's face with the intricate tribal design found on the same people who destroyed my Jeep.

"Put your weapons down and place your hands on the back of your heads. No sudden movements," he growled in a muffled voice. "I *said*, weapons down!" This was slightly louder, but still barely above a whisper.

He took a step closer to Valya.

Then it all seemed to happen at once.

With a desperate growl, she leapt at him and swiped her arm across his gun so that the pulse he fired spun harmlessly into the air and lit up the valley like a flare, illuminating us. As the flash faded, the pair tumbled, rolling down the slope together. They wrestled for the gun, getting extremely near the edge of the cavern. They detached and both scrambled on all fours for the man's weapon.

The others were stationary, perhaps struck by her bold action. It didn't stay that way for long. Another couple of men charged. The first kneed her face and she fell backwards. All three piled on top of her and many swift hands disarmed her. They were efficient and noticeably noiseless. Their bulk hid her from my sight, except for her feet and lower legs wriggling this way and that.

I went towards her and quickly found myself surrounded by another ten people. They didn't do anything at first, just sizing me up. My antique rifle was in my hands and I shot quickly. One of their blue-grey pulses connected with mine and neutralised both. Another shot spun me sideways. The rifle fell from my hands and rolled over itself, clattering a few metres down the slope. My right arm dangled lifelessly. I reached for the other gun at my hip with my left hand.

Where's the girl?

Out of the corner of her eye, I noticed her sneak behind one of the attackers and stun him. The attacker fell forward, rigid as a log, landing with a *thump* and she took his place in the circle around me. Suddenly, I was hit by a stun pulse and dropped too.

Just before I passed out, I saw her turn and run up the slope towards the facility. The group ignored me and went after her. The dark spots in my vision joined up and then darkness.

Interlude Two

Longrider
Twenty-Six Years Before

A universal fact for any party, soiree or gathering, is that guests will eventually, irresistibly, be drawn to the kitchen and this one was no different. Domestic droids handed out bottles of beer and full glasses of sparkling wine to guests as soon as they finished a previous drink. Nibbles in arty bowls lay on the table to whet their appetites — dried cuttlecod fins, amber balm stalks and small spherical nuts from desert trees.

Conversation flowed effortlessly between the close friends, punctuated by frequent bouts of laughter. The house had a relaxed mood that it normally lacked. Everyone was finally unwinding from a long period of intense work. The intoxicatingly tangy aroma of frying onions mingled with their voices, drifting out of the kitchen and eventually winding its way to Valya's bedroom. The girl's nostrils twitched at the delicious smell. For a moment, she stopped work on her digital painting and lowered her stylus to breathe deeply.

It smelt good. Frying onions and mince, which meant only one thing — her father was making meatballs. She became concerned that he was not getting the recipe correct without her help. He always needed her help when cooking. With this aim in mind, she stopped painting, saved her work, and sprinted down the corridor.

When she reached the dining room, she squinted in the dim light and her eyes were drawn to the bright kitchen doorway. The aroma was more potent here, as was the squawk of adult laughter. They were having fun, and she wanted to join in too. She walked intently towards the door, holding her tablet ahead of her like a venerated tome.

Tentatively, she approached the half-open door and peered in. Six people were standing around, including her father. To the side and towering over all of them, was Uncle Red. Her father had told her he was their group leader. At that moment, he leant against the counter, close to a young woman. They were entirely ignoring the others, and speaking in urgent hushed voices.

Valya knew the woman too, she was called 'Frosty'. Every time she saw her, she was struck by how lovely she was. Her skin shone from some inner illumination and she had a personality to match. Everyone adored her.

There was a chubby man talking to her father. Valya could never remember his name, it was long and hard to pronounce, so she called him 'Squish' on account of his size. There were others, too, who she could only catch a few glimpses of through her obstructed view. Valya knew that none of the others were her mother; she was out with her friends and wouldn't return for hours.

As she opened the door and moved into the kitchen, she found that the adults were too engrossed in each other's company to notice her straight away. She hesitated temporarily in the doorway before gathering her courage and stepping forward a few paces. A counter obscured her from view. As she walked closer, her father went to the fridge and retrieved a bottle. He noticed her standing there and his face beamed with delight, cheeks slightly pink from the alcohol.

"Valya! I wondered when you'd come join us!" He placed the bottle on the counter and strode over to her to pick her up. "Have you come to help me cook?"

She nodded eagerly and thrust the tablet under his chin, initially unaware that the others were looking at her. As soon as she glanced around, they chirped, "Hello Muffin!" in unison.

She blushed in embarrassment at her nickname and tried to wriggle out of her father's grip. He held her tight, anticipating her reaction.

"No. You're not going anywhere!" he laughed, sitting her down on a clean space on the counter.

"So, little one," started the grizzly leader. "Would you like a beer?" The others chuckled as if he were joking. However, he stepped forward to quickly allow her a sip from his glass. She winced and pushed it away.

"Red!" Frosty shrieked. "You can't let her have that! She's only four!"

"It's all right, it's only a mouthful, it wasn't that bad, was it?"

Valya pulled a face again and shook her head, indicating she didn't want to try any more.

Uncle Red's whiskers shook as he laughed. It was a deep rich bellow and very infectious. The others started chuckling too, as if he'd told a great joke. She thought that although he was as big as a bear, he wasn't scary. Since they were laughing, she started to giggle too, though she wasn't really sure why.

"Valya, can you pass me that bowl, please? I think some of these are done."

Her father indicated towards the large dish directly behind her. She turned around, lifted it with all her strength, and handed it over to him. He scooped out individual meatballs from the pan with a spoon and placed them in the bowl.

Her father brought up the topic of threeshot, his favourite sport. The adults began arguing over the outcome of the last game. Frosty gave a wide, theatrical yawn and Valya chuckled because her feelings toward the sport were mutual.

"Do you not like threeshot, Valya?" she asked.

"No."

In mock surprise, her father exclaimed, "You're meant to say that you support the Mayton Rangers like me!"

She paused, considered his statement then replied confidently, "No. Threeshot is boring."

The group burst into laughter again. Her father pretended to turn into an angry monster and threatened to eat her brain unless she changed her mind. Red and Squish joined in. Valya fought them off as best she could, squealing in protest. The game came to an end once she told them to stop or she'd pee. Unsurprisingly, they backed off and let her calm down. Her father turned his attention back to their dinner and instructed the droid to lay the table.

✳✳✳

At the dinner table, Valya was propped up on a stack of cushions to boost her height and with a napkin around her neck. After settling down properly, Valya had her first opportunity to examine the one man she didn't know in the group. Her first impression was he looked funny. This was mainly due to his unusual hair which, in her opinion, hung like long black sausages around his face. He hadn't said a word in the kitchen, and was silent at the table as well. He seemed pleasant enough, so she decided she liked him anyway. Squish was next to him and chatting animatedly, while the young man said almost nothing and smiled often. Frosty and Yossi were obscured by her father and Red.

Somewhere between stabbing the first meatball with her fork and guiding it towards her mouth, they started talking about her favourite topic: hunting.

Red lifted his glass. "Well, here's to our first successful hunt with our new comrade, Tobias. Even if he is originally from Springhaven, he's not a halfwit and did us proud. Congratulations, everyone!" He waited until the others had raised their glasses too before he finished his drink in one glug. Valya didn't have any of her juice left, so she lifted her meatball instead.

"It went really smoothly, didn't it?" her father said, still holding his glass up. He took another sip. "Normally at least one element of the hunt never turns out as planned, but there weren't any hitches whatsoever and hopefully, we won't get too comfortable if we have more days like today. It just goes to show you how much of a difference an extra body makes to a hunt."

"I just followed procedure." Tobias waved away the compliment. It was the first sentence she'd heard him say. His voice was low.

"Nonsense," interjected Red. He pointed at the newcomer with his fork. "You're an asset to the team. And you've more than verified your capability. I wouldn't have offered you a permanent role otherwise. It's hard to find someone decent who hasn't already been snapped up. Why I remember a couple of years back we asked a candidate to come with us on a hunt. He was only just out of the academy and they should've sent him back because he couldn't shoot. He accidentally shot Harald in the ass." He grinned. "Needless to say, we didn't ask him to come again."

"I'm glad you brought that up again, Red." Harald rolled his eyes.

"Any time, mate, any time. It was bloody funny."

"Not for me, I couldn't sit properly for a week!"

The others laughed at the memory, apart from Tobias who smiled politely.

"In all seriousness, you are *all* exceptional individuals and I'm lucky to say you're on my team. You're highly skilled and have natural hunting ability, which is not something that can be taught. We've a reputation as the finest, most reputable and dynamic team in ShadeCo and I hope that it's the case for a long time. That being said, recently I've really been feeling my age, it's a tough job and I doubt I'll be in the profession for much longer, I might hang up my weapons and get a desk job at HQ, work my way up and concentrate on the project to cure Umbras."

The others protested.

"No, no, I've been thinking about it for a while. A few years at most and then I'm moving on. ShadeCo has much more potential than energy collection alone. It has so many resources available and a considerable archive on Shade behaviour that we should be tapping into. It should have a medical wing researching cures for Umbras. Imagine it. Hunting without the risk of infection? The number of lives that could be saved? The potential..." He sighed heavily. "It is a pity not everyone sees it as a priority. *Butcher*," he said the name as a curse, something disgusting, "was a narrow-sighted, tremulous conservative, afraid of innovative thinking. I'll charge you all to shoot me if I get as rigid-minded as that. I've no regrets about him, or his family for that matter. We did the right thing for the greater good. Nothing can change unless you gamble once in a while."

Valya's father shifted uncomfortably in his seat. "Can we change the subject, please? Little ears," he explained, glancing at his daughter.

"What do Shades look like?" Valya piped up, resting her fork on her plate.

Red stroked his whiskers. "They're..." he paused again for a moment, "like a living shadow. Yes that's right, imagine if a shadow had unattached itself and could move of its own accord. That's what a Shade looks like."

Frosty cut in. "Sorry, Red, but I don't think so. Shades are more similar to a dark mist, because they can hover too. I've never seen a shadow hover, have you?"

"I'm not saying they're *literally* a shadow, I'm just saying they take on the appearance of one. Didn't you watch the one earlier creeping along the ground? With the density of trees and the hour of the hunt, the creature looked just like a shadow. We wouldn't have been able to see it without our masks."

"They don't do that very often though," her father said, taking Frosty's side. "That's only when they're trying to sneak up on would-be victims, but we've usually spotted them by that point. Normally, they're levitating."

Red kept pushing the point. "The second one we captured today crept along the ground, and by doing so, it was caught in the net." Both Harald and Frosty still looked sceptical. The man with the strange hair was eating happily and ignoring the exchange. Red wouldn't allow him to remain impartial. "Tobias, what do you think? Do you agree with me or with Frosty and Harald?"

"A Shade is a Shade, whether it hovers or moves along the ground," he said, shrugging. "As long as we capture it, I don't care what it looks like."

"Very diplomatic," Red said, shaking his head.

"What do they smell like?" Valya asked, curious.

"Oh dear, you're very inquisitive today," Red replied.

"Mother doesn't let me talk about hunting because she says it's bad for her nerves."

Harald told her, "You don't want to be close enough to smell one, Valya. When you go to school, you'll find out more, but one of the places Shades can get into you is through your nose."

Her nose twitched reflexively, although she knew that she was safe inside the house. There were anti-Shade defences in every home now.

"Daddy, why did you become a Hunter?"

Exhaling deeply, he looked at his daughter with pride in his eyes and squeezed her cheek. "It wasn't a quick decision. It wasn't just because Grandpa was one of the first Hunters. It's not necessarily a family profession. I fell into it. I enjoy the comradery and—"

"The money!" Red butted in.

"I'll drink to that!" Yossi piped up and finished his beverage in one gulp amid the laughter of the others.

"You're terrible, Red!" Frosty shook her head, though she was smiling at him fondly. Then she told the girl, "Most people become Hunters because it's exhilarating."

The conversation changed. Harald asked Tobias a few questions about himself. He had grown up in the small settlement of Springhaven up in the mountains. As he was a quiet young man, soon there was silence and Valya saw her opportunity to ask her most important query yet.

"When can I become a Hunter?"

Temporarily stunned, the others stopped eating and talking and turned their attention back to the little girl.

"When you're old enough, maybe," her father answered evasively. He ruffled her hair playfully and hugged her head to his side, straight into a spot of gravy that had landed on his apron. When she pulled away, she wiped the sauce off the side of her face with the back of her hand.

"But when will that be?"

"After you've finished school."

The girl counted on her fingers how many years she had left before she could become a Hunter. She had used both her hands and still had two more to go when she sighed, realizing she had a long time to wait.

Her father observed her dejection. "You don't have to wait long to *train* to be a Hunter. I can start training you at ten."

Counting on her fingers again, she reached six, deciding that was acceptable, if not ideal. Ideally, she'd start today. She happily stabbed the last meatball with her fork before shoving it whole into her mouth, her cheeks puffing out. Being with her father's friends felt right, and for once, she felt perfectly content.

One day she'd be a Hunter like them.

Landmine
Twenty-Six Years Before

"Oh, Michael! You can't go running off just because you feel like it!" his aunt groaned, running her fingers through her frizzy hair and taking several breaths to calm down.

She knelt down to his level and rubbed his shoulder tenderly. When she continued, her voice was even, but the edge was still present. "What's upset you? You know, you can talk to me about anything. I promise I won't shout."

He did not answer. She sighed and scrunched her hair again.

Michael underwent tests and doctors confirmed nothing was physically wrong with him. He simply chose not to speak.

His hair hung in uneven bangs around his face. He refused to look at his aunt and fiddled with his hands. From head to toe, he was covered in mud and silage and smelt like manure. Michael appeared embarrassed, although it was due to being caught by the farmer rather than true repentance.

"An hour ago, I thought you were safe in school and you were in fact traipsing around the farm. You know, your teachers will stop making concessions because of... you know... and properly punish your misbehaviour soon. Did you set off the fire alarm?

He didn't respond.

"Do you not care for the last manic hour I've run around searching for you? I took the rest of the day off work to find you, despite the fact we need the money. Marie's treatment isn't cheap." She sighed again. "Your father's wealth would've helped. Unnatural to allow the inheritance to go anywhere but to your own children..."

Michael braved a glance at her, still not saying a word.

Leaning closer, she asked in a confidential tone, "Is someone bullying you? We can sort that out if they are. But we certainly can't have you running away all the time, it's got to stop, Michael. It really has! This worry is wearing me down."

The boy's frown deepened. He stared hard at his aunt, anger in his deep blue eyes.

She finally said, "Well, go and take a shower. Then you can play until your sister comes home." She checked the time. "She should be back from the hospital in a couple of hours and I'm sure she'll need you to cheer her up."

Without saying a word, he broke away and dragged his feet as he walked towards the corridor. With every step, he trod mud into the ivory carpet, leaving a footprint trail behind him. He didn't want to be in this house. He wanted to be back at the farm with the animals, with the sheep, and goats, and chickens. They didn't constantly question him. On the other hand, he was starting to feel hot and nauseated, and regretted eating animal food.

"Take your shoes off!" his Aunt Maple hollered from the other end of the corridor.

Obediently, he rested his hand against the wall for balance and tugged one shoe off then the other. As soon as he reached the bathroom, he slung the mucky shoes onto the tiles and stripped without shutting the door. He pressed his hand against the switch on the wall. Automatically, the shower sprung to life and water gushed out of the shower head in a torrent. He stepped in and the water's temperature adjusted correctly to his body's needs.

He turned his face upwards so his cheeks, nose, and lips were lashed by the powerful spray, closing his eyes as he relaxed.

For a long time, he remained there. Even after the water ran clean, and the skin on his fingers crinkled.

***

Several hours later, the small family sat at the dinner table: Michael, Marie and their aunt. She made one of his favourite meals, pasta with a creamy truffle sauce, but he wasn't hungry. He strategically fiddled with his food and noticed his sister Marie wasn't eating much either. She gave him a small, conspiratorial smile, which rapidly faded.

"Mikey, you're really pale. Are you feeling all right?" his aunt asked.

191

He pushed the plate aside and rested his forehead against the table. The back of his neck and head felt unbearably hot.

His aunt's chair scraped against the floor. "Do you want me to help you to bed?" she offered, stroking his shoulders.

Slowly, he sat back up and was sick across his plate and the tablecloth. Startled, Marie jumped away from the table, while his aunt stepped away with a cry of alarm, narrowly avoiding spoiling her sandals.

"Marie, can you get the droid and take him to bed while I clean this up? Get the droid to bring the sick bucket, he might need it again."

"Okay!" Marie called over her shoulder.

One of her arms circled around Michael's waist as she gently steered him to his bedroom. Even though she was two years older, he was quite heavy and almost as tall as her. When they reached his bedroom door, she clumsily kicked it open and they stepped into his messy room.

Letting go of his waist, she took his hand and guided him to bed. She ordered him to lie down. But he would not listen, folding his arms and sitting down in defiance. Exasperated, she grabbed his wrists and tried to force him. He pulled back stubbornly and as he was sturdy and she slight, it was Marie who lost the match and ended up in a mound of covers and limbs on floor.

"Mikey!" she cried, rubbing her elbows, which had taken the brunt of the fall. "You're sick. You need to go to bed."

Folding his arms again, he turned to face the wall. Being ill and going to bed meant you went to hospital. He didn't want to go there. A second wave of nausea seized him.

He scanned the room for the sick bowl. He tried to convey his need to his sister by groaning and rubbing his belly.

"What? Are you going to be sick again?"

Too late, Michael heaved onto his bed covers. The droid arrived belatedly with the bowl.

***

While his aunt and droid were distracted with cleaning his room, Michael crept into the lounge and turned on the HV. He went to the listings and selected his favourite programme; it automatically started from where he left off earlier. The images were comforting as he fell into a half-sleep.

He felt his aunt nestle under the blanket beside him, putting a reassuring arm over his shoulders. He liked his aunt, but she should smell differently — like mints mixed with flowers, like his mother. He did not return her hug and kept his hands rigidly on his lap away from hers.

Soon his sister bounced onto the settee on the other side of him. He shuffled closer and leaned his head on her shoulder.

They sat and watched HV together. Though he didn't care for their programmes, he felt, for the first time in over a year, as if everything was okay. Yesterday, they found out the police believed that they were attacked by a team of robbers and not Umbras infected individuals, as first assumed. Marie found it impossible to speak about or even recall what happened, despite therapy, to the frustration of the police. For a while Michael could forget why he was here and escape the scene in the family mansion on the second hill.

Part Three

"The truth is often harsher than the realities we create for ourselves. Yet, it is only a pretence that we are in control. It is only pretence that the relationships we forge are true. Break one piece and the rest will shatter and fall."

\- Minister Irenka Gorski

20

Longrider

Am I blind?

Darkness everywhere, although my eyes were open.

I blinked.

Gradually, the mental mist started to ebb.

Vague memories of the assault began to come back.

The back of my head ached; the dull throbbing served as a focal point for my senses.

My surroundings started to get clearer. The effects of the drug they gave me were subsiding and it became easier to hold onto my thoughts.

I was blindfolded and gagged. The taste in my mouth was rubbery. I concentrated on regulating my breathing.

Outside?

No, I was resting against a cold concrete wall. I managed to move my feet on the bare floor, which felt chalky and solid.

Time?

No way to tell how long I've been here.

My limbs throbbed.

I was kneeling on a freezing floor. The cold penetrated my clothing, despite the warmth of the rest of the room. It was as musty and humid here as any lower floor office in ShadeCo, wherever *here* might be.

A bead of sweat trickled from my hairline, trailing down around the tip of my nostril to my chin, where it fell. My top was soaked.

My arms were suspended above my head and my wrists were tied together with cords across what felt like a thick metal pipe. My ankles were tied to another. Rattling the restraints only served to tighten them.

Feeling useless, I flexed my fingers, then folded my hand tightly into a fist, which I would have gladly punched someone with. To be captured so easily, with so little resistance, was maddening.

What a fool I am! So utterly naïve to believe we could infiltrate the facility without detection. It was my mission and the responsibility fell entirely on me. *Caught before we had even begun. How could I have been so rash?* I put the others in danger before we penetrated the first layer of defences. Before we were even in sight of the base.

Where are Butcher and Sophie?

I strained my ears for the sound of movement, or talking, or any sign of life. There were no sounds at all, so if Butcher and Sophie were confined then they were not with me.

Yet I still had hope. Aside from my tender limbs, I felt otherwise okay. No major wounds. I felt a bit weak from lack of food, my stomach groaned noisily in response, but that could be easily fixed.

I would not end it like this, trapped, soiled and alone.

Leaning as far forward as my restraints allowed, I pivoted back and forth to loosen them. It might have been my imagination but they seemed slightly slacker than before. I kept going until my wrists became too tender to continue. My blindfold loosened with the motion and it dropped down enough to see with my left eye. I violently shook my head and the blindfold dropped past the other eye. I nodded my head a few times and it slipped over my nose and rested around my neck.

Weak though it was, I flinched against the sudden light and I blinked until my eyes accustomed to it.

As I suspected, I was alone. The room looked insignificant and windowless, probably no more than four by four metres in size. In the far-right corner there was a stack of interlocking chairs with my goggles and respirator lying on top. No weapons left. They had taken my shield belt. Running across the wall beside me were two metal pipes about the thickness of my forearm. My wrists were connected at a cross-section where the pipe disappeared into the wall, my ankle fastened to the lower pipe running along the floor. Ahead was a solitary door. Above me a solitary fan circulated hot air, no vents or loose panels. I looked at the bare stone floor for a means of escape and found none.

How to escape?

Perhaps there was a loose tile in the floor, or a weakness in the walls.

Need to break free first.

I swung back and forth to loosen the constraints.

Come on...

Just a little more...

Suddenly, I heard a shuffling scrape of footsteps outside. I stopped testing for weak points and sat upright. Two figures were framed in the door's oval, frosted window. They lingered outside for a moment and then the door slid back. For a heartbeat, they stood in the doorway and momentarily regarded me.

The attackers had changed their unusual battle camouflage and were now garbed in lycean attire, wearing jackets with sharp upturned collars that were narrowed severely at the waist and scarlet trousers. Instead of the wedged boots normally paired with these suits, the man wore durable leather shoes and the woman had stiletto heels that arched her feet painfully.

Both were tall and willowy, and the woman looked fragile. The pair was obviously related, possibly brother and sister, judging from their similar manes of dark hair, dark skin, and even their identical expressions of distaste. An opaque half-mask covered the left side of the man's face. I had seen ones like it before in the minor injuries' unit at Mayton hospital and knew this kind of mask was either utilised for multiple wounds too close together to be repaired by traditional surgery or burns.

The man strode across the room to the stack of chairs, passing me without a second glance. He swiped a gloved hand across the seat and the equipment clattered onto the floor. He kicked them into the corner with the side of his boot. He lifted two chairs and positioned them in front of me. They both took a seat. The woman delicately folded her legs and straightened her trousers. The man crossed his arms across his chest.

At this proximity, their pale brown eyes were golden and lent them a feral appearance. The man's mask pulled his face into an unswerving sneer.

He spoke to the woman in a fast, lilting language. My translation processor must have been damaged during the fight. Only one or two snippets came through. It was impossible to follow the conversation.

I waited for them to switch to the common tongue.

Finally, the man addressed me directly. "Ms Erickson. I understand that for the last six years, you've been a Master Hunter at ShadeCo and an acclaimed Hunter for the previous six. And considering your background we'd assume you were hunting on the field outside the base." I tried to keep my face neutral. "Now, I'm no expert in this regard, but our Hunters tell me the area we found you in is normally a dead zone for Shade activity, so you're not going to fill your quota here, my dear, definitely not. But perhaps it's something far more substantial you're after… Your munitions in our vehicle certainly look suspicious, and, though as I say, I'm no expert, your arsenal contains little if any Shade-effective equipment."

The woman interjected. "What were you doing with one of our missing vehicles?" Her voice had a nasal quality that would have been irritating under any circumstance. "The owners shall be pleased to have their property returned."

I stared at them mutely, unable to reply. The man reached forward and tore the tape over the gag away. Exhaling, I spat it out. It flew out of my mouth and landed on his lap in a globule of spit; his wormy mouth twisted in disdain and he pushed it away.

My lips were sore and dry. The last drink I had was before we left Butcher's vehicle. Hours ago.

"Where's my father?" I kept my voice level. "Where're the other hostages?"

The man raised his eyebrows. The woman turned and said something to him in their foreign tongue.

"Where are the other hostages?" I asked again, increasingly frustrated.

They did not answer. The woman leaned forward slightly and knitted her fingers together over her knee, while the man did not move a muscle, still sneering.

"I don't know what your aim is. Black energy isn't going to go away, it's far too vital to our society for that to happen," I croaked. My mouth felt like a desert. "The authorities are bound to catch you. And they won't negotiate. They'll catch you and punish you, as you deserve. Just release your hostages and be done with this sorry business. You never know, they might go easy on you for helping them out."

When I finished, the man simply stated, "I don't think so. No. The three of you might prove useful yet."

"Three?" Did they mean Butcher, Sophie and I? "What three? What do you mean *three*? Who are the others? Who else do you have—"

With irritation, he reached into his pocket, took out a roll of tape, tore off a piece, and forced it over my mouth again.

"I expected as much. I suppose that'll suffice for now. Let's attend to the others," the man said to his companion.

They stood up and left, turning the lights and fans off.

I returned to the shadows and resumed testing my bonds.

I have to get out of here...

21

Landmine

*W*ell, fuck.

I guess that's what you get when you value your account balance over your instincts.

What a fucking mess.

The first person I'd seen for days and he hit me. It wasn't particularly powerful, but it was fucking annoying I couldn't retaliate. If I could, we'd see a different outcome. I smirked. He punched me again and his ring caught near my eye. That one stung. He stepped back and cracked his knuckles in satisfaction.

"ShadeCo scum! How dare you say that to her! You don't want to anger me further. I've learned and lived with cruelty over the last few months, and more than willing to put this new knowledge to the test."

"Fuck you, you prodigal piss stain!"

It doesn't matter what I say now. They intend to kill me and that's that. Perhaps they knew I stole the tank. Revenge is clearly something they do heartily. At least I'd get some amusement while I could. I grinned to his sister, watching from the corner. "You keep staring at me, darling, do you want a ride?"

The woman's face drained. "Disgusting... I think we should start with the next phase."

I stared at the woman, giving her an obvious once-over. I couldn't have given a fuck about her but this seemed to be the best way to anger her brother. The colour went to the man's cheeks, turning them crimson. I'd the satisfaction of making him lose all the composure and superiority he'd affected when he entered the room just a short while ago.

He spat, "What an insolent... repulsive... yes, let's skip straight to stage two with this one. He doesn't deserve any courtesy. We offered you the chance to cooperate and answer our questions, but you destroyed any consideration or mercy we might've had for you. At least the others behaved with an iota of respect.

"You forget your position. You are *our* captive. And *we* will do what we like with you. And ShadeCo will listen once we are done. And they'll finally leave us alone."

He made a swiping gesture with a device on his hand and my chair's headrest started to shudder. At the edge of my vision, I noticed metal tendons creeping over my scalp. They knitted in my hair and dug into my skin until my head was locked in place. My body was already tightly secured to the chair. The bonds across my arms constricted and the veins popped up distinctly, particularly on my forearms.

The woman took out a syringe from her satchel, which contained a pale green liquid. *Poison?*

Was this the end, strapped to a metal chair in this basement in the middle of nowhere?

It could be worse.

At least it's not Umbras.

Even so, I tensed and prepared myself. The woman selected a vein in my right forearm and inserted the needle, pushing down the plunger. I watched the substance disappear. She took out the needle and a trickle of blood dripped down my arm. The woman stepped back next to her brother, where they observed me with anticipation.

Minutes passed and nothing happened.

My throat was dry. I could do with some water. My lungs felt as if someone had tied wires around them, tight, yet not tight enough to restrict breathing too badly. More like a chest infection than strangulation. I coughed to clear it and waited.

The invisible wires began to tighten. Suddenly, a sharp intense pain shot through my lungs and spread to fill my torso. It was followed by two more cramps, but both lightened into a tickling sensation.

My lips stretched into a thin line as I tried to fight it. I clenched my jaw. The tension extended to the other muscles on my face to contain it. However, it burst out and I let out a cry.

A cry of laughter. *They've given me some sort of laughing potion?*

It boomed from my stomach, filling my ears and resonating deafeningly around the small space. It wouldn't stop. Tears formed and poured out of the corners of my eyes. I collapsed against my restraints, if they weren't there, I wouldn't have been able to stay upright.

The pair started at the noise and they looked at each other in confusion. Apparently, they hadn't expected this either. They turned on each other and started arguing and my translator started to work in my ear but I could barely hear over my own forced laughter.

"What's going on? Why is he like this?"

"I don't know. He should be having pain spasms. The concentration must have been too weak."

"Why did you dilute it in the first place?"

"It would have killed him if I didn't!"

"That would have been better than this. This doesn't send any message to anyone except about our stupidity! I put you in charge of this for a reason, Seraphina. I can't micromanage everything that happens around here!"

"I'm sorry. I'll make another batch."

The man shook his head at her. He looked at me and threw back his head in an exasperated sigh.

"Did anyone else touch it?" he demanded.

"It was with me for most of the time…"

"When was it *not* with you?"

"I left it distilling for ten minutes, that was the only time I was away from it or it was not on my person."

The man latched onto that. "A sabotage! We'll find the person and—"

"You don't know that, Alvise," she cut in. "You can't accuse people without proof. We don't know anyone tampered with it. I might have got the formula wrong. Just leave it be. The other two officials' patience is getting thin with our expeditions and they already say you're abusing your position and neglecting your duties to the community as a whole. If Yadav and Jose heard about this they would veto our campaign. They can still do that. It was my mistake, Alvise. Let's leave it at that."

"Is there any way to counteract it and start again?"

"I am not sure. I'll have to check my references. Probably by the time

I have an antidote, it will have subsided anyway."

He sighed. "Just sedate him and place him with the other Hunter temporarily. Let them stew in the cells together."

The syringe came out again. She refilled it with a clear liquid from a flask in her satchel. She plunged the needle in my vein again, less carefully than before. My cheeks and stomach ached in merriment.

I watched. And laughed. And laughed.

22

Longrider

The door swung open. A couple of droids filed in, carrying Butcher between them. They deposited him beside the pipe network, secured him there, and exited just as rapidly. His chest heaved erratically and his top was specked with dried blood around the collar. His head was covered by a canvas sack.

For some inexplicable reason, he was laughing hysterically and the noise was only slightly muffled by the bag. He was literally horizontal with laughter, though his arms were fully stretched above his head by the cuffs. His arms weren't quite long enough to reach and his shoulder lifted off the ground. It must be hurting him.

I shuffled over to help, straining against my bonds to grip the top of the bag with my fingertips. The string cords were loose and I managed to free him of the sack. Underneath his tanned face was crimson and wet with sweat, his hair slick against his skin. A prominent vein protruded from the middle of his forehead and another was visible along his neck. He had a cloth gag, soaked with saliva.

Using my knees as a lever, I assisted him into an upright position and together we manoeuvred his body until he was propped up against the wall. His chest rose and fell jaggedly. Manic laughter aside, I was pleased to see he was otherwise physically unhurt.

Probably the same could not be said for Sophie.

If this group discovered she was Red's niece, I doubted that she would fare well with their anti-ShadeCo sentiments. Their intentions appeared malevolent.

***

Who could say how long it had been? The hours and days merged together in a timeless procession. My legs continually cramped and my ankles and wrists ached with outrage, only temporarily alleviated by shifting position within the restricted confines. My clothes were stained with piss and excrement and astringent sweat. It smelt like a farm in here.

The brother-and-sister duo had not returned, and no one else visited us. It was easy to despair with nothing except time to think. I wondered how long did they intend to keep us like this? What did they want to do with us? Had they made ransom demands using us as leverage? And would anyone care if they had? If they wanted information, why didn't they speak to us directly instead of letting us stew in our own filth? Do they intend to eventually kill us?

If the lack of knowledge was painful, the fact I was responsible for putting us here was excruciating.

At intervals, droids came in and injected both of us with high energy substances, keeping us alive and hydrated. Beneath the gag, however, my lips were still dry and cracked at the edges. I longed for some chilled, refreshing water.

With little to do, we slept intermittently. It was not rejuvenating because I was frequently snapped awake by the sporadic whir of the fan, or Butcher shuffling his feet, or a drip from the pipe, or the ache in my limbs. The laughing spasms made him retch from time to time. Through the gag, which was fortunately porous, he vomited bile over himself. *Poor Butcher. What a mess I have got us into.*

After that, his laughter began to subside, his chuckles sounding wearier. He shut his eyes and rested his head against the wall.

***

Finally, the woman returned alone.

I was half-delirious. The pain in my wrists and hands was excruciating. Initially, I did not even realise she was there. She took one of the chairs and sat in front of us, this time wearing the unusual black mask with pinhole eyepieces. She spoke in the common tongue. "I trust you're more open to talk now? If so please nod and I'll remove your gag."

I nodded and she lowered my gag as promised. Immediately, I croaked a request for water. I sounded like an ancient woman sighing dust. She held a flask to my mouth and I guzzled the cool liquid greedily until the container was empty. I thirsted for more, though none was offered.

"We want to know what you were doing outside the facility. Were you looking for more people to abduct or was it something else?"

"I have no idea what you're talking about."

She sighed and raised her palms disappointedly. "Maybe we need to leave you here longer." She stood to leave, turning towards the door.

"Wait!"

Stopping, she cocked her head slightly to one side.

"Please don't leave us here! What've you done with my father? Where is he?"

Not unkindly, she said, "We haven't done anything to him. You're the first people we have kept here. I don't know where he is."

I leaned back against the wall and groaned. She watched me, and at length, sat back down and leaned forward confidentially.

Her voice sounded far away. "Can I assume that was why you were at the facility?"

"Yes." *I'd been so sure.* "He went missing a while ago. After the explosion in the main ShadeCo office, the missing person records will back that up. I registered him. I assumed you were holding him hostage…"

Where else could he be? Why would he have kept away so long?

We were silent. I tried to hold back the tears threatening to spill. One fell, which led the way for others. They coursed quietly down my cheeks and I closed my eyes, disgusted my enemy was witnessing this.

Her warm hand pressed on my shoulder and squeezed. I looked up at her. "Perhaps you were mistaken."

I stared away from her, fixating on a crack on the wall, and did not reply.

"We will need to check the facts, Valya. I cannot just accept your word. We need supported and unquestionable evidence for your story before anything else." She began to put the gag back in my mouth, then thought better of it. "Alvise will want to hear this too… I fear we might have made an error in our haste. I'll return once I can confirm your story."

Out of the corner of my eye, I noticed Butcher watching the door. He turned to face me and began to make sounds. At first, I thought the laughing had started again then I realized he was trying to indicate something about escape. I could not understand what might have changed about our situation. I shrugged my shoulders.

"If you are suggesting we escape through that door, I think you might have forgotten a number of things. First, we're still imprisoned and tied to this damn pipe…"

He repeated turning to the door and back to me.

"Butcher, I don't know what you're trying to say."

Suddenly, the door swung open again. The woman and man I knew filed in, followed by two burly men wearing the distinctive black masks. They took some chairs from the stack and sat in front of me.

Meanwhile, the brother knelt and attached a cog-shaped device to my forehead. It tingled as soon as it made contact with my skin. The man then forced the sack back over Butcher's head and pulled the cords tight. He said something derisively in the foreign language.

"Valya, would you please repeat what you said earlier?" the woman asked me in a low hushed tone.

"I was searching for my father." The cog sent shockwaves over my forehead. They weren't painful, just mildly uncomfortable. "He vanished two weeks ago, though it is probably longer now… I'm not sure how long we've been here. I believed he was held here…"

"Why did you think so? Why in the middle of the desert?"

"It seemed suspicious to me. If there was nothing to hide, why wasn't the facility nearer the main settlements? Why are there so many measures to obscure it?"

"That's exactly my thoughts. And it is why we were monitoring the building for weeks," the woman agreed, turning to her brother. His face remained impassive, arms folded tightly. His foot tapped uneasily.

The man spoke. "We researched your father, too. He is a ShadeCo employee and a former Hunter, like yourself. He is a worthy individual without a mark on his record or a crime against his name. Why would you assume he's being held captive in a ShadeCo facility, when he's an employee? Taking your own staff hostage is unheard of in Diomedia… at least in Springhaven," he added as an afterthought.

What? Were they even listening to me?

"This facility isn't part of ShadeCo. I've worked there for years and never once heard of it. It's not ShadeCo. Otherwise they'd be your employer, too. And I've never seen you at the main HQ, not at any of the mandatory events or meetings."

The man looked at his companions and switched into the foreign tongue. They had a brief conversation. He seemed to be the one they all listened to. While he spoke, he ran a hand briefly over his slick hair, his feet twitching nervously. The woman took his hand and squeezed it in both of hers.

The woman reverted to the common tongue and took out a photo and did not show it to me straight away. "As I said before, we monitored the facility for some time and this one was taken just over three weeks ago."

She flipped over the picture and I gasped.

There he was. Walking in the middle of a group of people about to enter the building and he seemed to be going willingly inside. With him were a few individuals I recognised from Red's huge biannual parties held at his mansion. They were flanked by several armed guards, so perhaps that explained their complacency.

"And no one has come or gone since. We believe that you have mistaken where we are now for that facility. You are actually in Springhaven and currently underground in the council assembly building."

"What! That's not true! You're trying to confuse us." What did the inhabitants on Springhaven have to do with this? They might be a little genetically restricted because they do not welcome outsiders from the main settlements, but I would not have guessed they would be involved in acts of terrorism. They mostly just want to be left to themselves.

Questions multiplied in my head. "I don't understand why you think that other facility is ShadeCo-owned. Those employees you showed me were under armed guard. And I don't understand why you hate the company so much…"

The man was slumped forward, his elbows resting on his thighs, suddenly despondent. "She is telling the truth," he said to his feet and ran his hand through his hair again. I noticed a band of white skin on his ring finger.

The woman asked him a brief question. He nodded and told her to proceed.

"We owe you an explanation. My brother allowed me to tell you about his family's role in this—"

He cut in. "Sorry but I can't. Please excuse me. Seraphina, do what's necessary."

He stood up, bowed slightly, and left. The others shifted uncomfortably in their seats.

The woman sighed and continued. "The wounds are still raw... it's been months and he can hardly tolerate the retelling. It's as if he has relived it every day since. He won't allow himself to forget and soften the grief.

"Presumably, you're aware Springhaven is built in the heart of the mountains. Our ancestors relocated from Mayton Hill because they felt it was securer and we've been here for nearly four generations. Up here, we are above the vast majority of the Shade menace and, on the whole, safe. We limited our interactions with Mayton Hill and Winsford Lake, and in return, we wanted our privacy respected too. And the isolation served us well for many years.

"However, over the last decade, a number of strange occurrences happened and many Springhaven inhabitants vanished without a trace, never to be seen again. We attributed the first few disappearances to Shade attacks, despite our normally low infection rates. But then frequency increased sharply. These disappearances were unusual and as the numbers increased, so did our concern. We knew something horrible was happening and had no idea what or why until a few months ago, when my brother's wife and child were taken from us and then more pieces fell into place."

The woman leaned further forward and her companions moved closer too, though they must already know the story. "On that occasion, there were witnesses. They saw the pair manhandled and thrown into a ShadeCo Jeep, but they were too far away to do anything about it."

I remembered the story from the news, just never made the link with Springhaven. They never really said where the pair came from.

She continued. "We applied to Mayton Hill's police for their assistance in the search for our missing people. But, as outsiders, our claims were not priority and their help was minimal." She shook her head.

"We also applied directly to the ShadeCo executives. We met them a number of times and their position didn't budge. In fact, instead of sympathy, the CEO's response was point-blank refusal to have the matter investigated further and adamant no one in his employ would help us. Understand: we had proof. Pictures and film. But he claimed we doctored them. It was infuriating.

"We knew the guilty party was concealed within the company. So we decided the best method was to campaign against ShadeCo as a whole in a two-pronged attack, for the return of our missing people and for the company's closure. On the most part, this is peaceful although there were some violent confrontations with members of staff trying to shoo us from the premises. And we have nothing to do with the explosion three weeks ago, we do not know what or who started that."

What she was saying was incomprehensible. It was unbelievable that Red would reject their petition. He was a rational, logical man. He would not dismiss clear evidence of a kidnapping and cover for those involved. It was not in alignment with his character. Why would ShadeCo kidnap people in the first place? For all I knew, she was lying to gain our trust. But why would she want sympathy from two bound captives?

"We studied the missing people and noticed a trend. All survived Shade attacks."

That was surprising. I looked over to Butcher and wondered what he made of this. Survivors from Shade attacks are few and far between. Normally, anyone attacked is killed or infected.

"Josie, my sister-in-law, was attacked by a Shade whilst pregnant. Despite contaminating her, the Shade didn't possess her mind, and instead entered her unborn baby. It was unconventional and against Alvise's wishes but she decided to carry it to full term and her son was born perfectly fine: a healthy eight-pound, three-ounce baby. As the years progressed, my nephew demonstrated an abnormally high intellectual ability, artistic talent, and superior athletic skill. He was miles ahead of his peers. If he had lived, who knows what he could have accomplished."

Impossible. Shades, after infection, head directly for the brain. Countless studies have proved it. I did not interrupt her.

"By chance, a few months ago, a small scouting group discovered a guarded base hidden in the desert. Its location seemed suspicious, as you mentioned, even though outwardly the building itself is unremarkable. There was a ShadeCo Jeep outside, identical to the one my sister-in-law and son were thrown into. They thought Josie and Victor might be in there, so they tried to enter, few as they were, and attempt to find out what was going on. Unsurprisingly, they failed, and barely escaped with their lives.

"A few days later, Josie and Victor were discovered near our settlement. It could have been an animal attack…" Her voice quavered and her throat trembled. "But we knew better. They were trying to silence us."

She stared at the ground and wiped away her tears. Her companions lowered their heads respectfully.

"Though we haven't managed to investigate beyond the first room, the main theory about the facility's purpose is that it is used for experimentation, just what exactly is unknown. We think something to do with Shades. And the trend for kidnapping Shade survivors appears to support this. Why, I cannot say, perhaps deliberate cruelty or perhaps research or something else. It doesn't matter. All we want is for the disappearances to stop and, until ShadeCo closes for good, then it will keep happening. We tried to protest peacefully and it just didn't work."

How abhorrent! Could this really be possible? Could they be exposing them to Shades deliberately and giving them Umbras… There is nothing worse than such a fate. If father has it then he's already effectively dead… But I couldn't leave him as a raving creature…

I felt sickened. Even if this was not a rescue mission, I knew I needed to find him regardless.

Seraphina continued. "We were forced to attack, and if a few innocent people died then so be it. We want to be left alone. We intended to use the three of you as leverage because you're all linked to the company. However, if your father has also been taken, then you are mixed up in this too and there is nothing to gain from it. When we stumbled on you, we were in the midst of launching an assault on the base and assumed the three of you were going to attack us."

"But we were going towards the base, too."

"You also had one of our stolen vehicles," she observed.

Butcher muffled something underneath the gag and one of her companions, still seated, kicked him in the ribs.

"Where is Sophie?" I demanded.

"She's safe. Do not worry."

"What do you intend to do with us now?"

"I don't know."

I *had* to get inside that building. "If you're going to launch another attack, Butcher and I can help. We're Master Hunters and all we want is a chance to get inside that base. Please consider it."

"We do appear to have similar aims."

The other two people shifted forward in their seats and took off my restraints. I slipped out of them and rubbed my tender wrists. I stretched my legs out as far as they would go and clicked my toes satisfactorily.

They took off Butcher's bonds, but the woman with a sneer ordered her companions to keep Butcher's gag on. She explained that she would call a meeting to discuss their next offensive and told us we would be provided with sustenance and as much water as we could desire.

After they departed, I slapped my stiff legs and scrambled to my feet by pulling myself up by the pipes. Wobbly, I walked from one side of the room to the other to get my muscles working properly, stretching as I went. It felt superb to be out of the restraints and walking after days of inaction.

"Don't get me wrong, Butcher," I said. He looked up morosely, unable to respond. "They are a means to an end. Cooperation will get us out of here quicker."

The hunt was back on.

23

Landmine

No idea why they'd had a sudden change of heart. A full hundred-and-eighty-degree turn. They were ready to torture us then… boom. Freedom. These people were fucking insane! Must be the thin mountain air, they were starved of oxygen.

And it stunk as badly as a maggot-filled corpse in here.

Valya was apparently ready to trust them. I wasn't. All I wanted was our weapons back, mainly my antique rifle. That gun has been in my family for generations and survived the journey from Earth, and I'd be damned if I'd be the one to lose it.

Standing up on my numb legs and feet, I held to the pipes for support and rested against the wall until feeling returned to the lower half of my body. My arms burned furiously too. But it felt good to be untied. I tried to remove the gag, which seemed to be just a strip of material tied at the base of my skull, except it wasn't budging. Valya tried to help and received a mild electric shock. She gasped and drew back her hand.

"You'll have to wait for the others to return to get it off, Butcher."

She resumed pacing from one end of the room to the other. When they'd first untied us, she was hobbling and was gradually becoming more sure-footed with each step. Sweat pouring out of her in torrents.

I took a step forward and wobbled. Then another that was equally risky. My legs weren't responding properly, but I kept going, following Valya's lap.

After several more laps, Valya halted, barring my way. She grabbed my arm and lowered me to her level so she could whisper in my ear.

"Have you seen Sophie?"

I shook my head. She groaned and knitted her hands behind her head. Even in this dim light, the shine on her skin was noticeable. She smelt sour. Not that I was any different.

"I hope they haven't found out about her family links. We found out quickly enough. They despise Red and it wouldn't bode well for her if they knew she was his niece."

I mumbled my agreement through the gag.

"Butcher, it is clear to me that these people are inexperienced. They kidnapped us because we presented an opportunity, nothing more coordinated than that. They even said we're the first they've ever captured. They're not sure what to do with us... I've been thinking about it. The Springhavians must intend on going back because their first assault was a failure and they wanted to get their own people back, not take ShadeCo employees. If they're going on another hunt and we can join them and rescue Father and this will all have served a purpose."

I scoffed.

She stared at me as if I was about to start the hysterical laughter again. "We need to get inside the facility. I need to know what happened to him. I told them our true intentions to gain their trust. They can identify with what we're doing because our aims echo their own. All we want is to infiltrate that damn facility. And they only want to bring their missing people back, too." For emphasis, she squeezed my arm tightly.

I rolled my eyes at her.

Because trusting your captors is a logical step. For someone so intelligent, she is easily blind sighted.

"They know we're both Master Hunters and they can use us. But we can use them in return." She squeezed my arm tighter. "At least they trust us enough to remove the restraints. They're being cautious as they don't know us, yet I think they want us to accompany them. We can still complete the mission!"

I shrugged her hand off and continued the lap of the room.

Honestly, she believed these people far too quickly. She's too blinkered by her own agenda to analyse the situation properly. The main facts were, they'd attacked us, dragged and bound us inside this complex and let us fester for days on end without explaining why they were keeping us here, or how long, or why. Also, it wasn't as though we were entirely free. Two armed droids hovered either side of the doorway facing each other, tasked with keeping us inside. As far as I can see, this is still a mess.

By now, my muscles had woken up. I stretched down into a lunge on the right leg and then the left leg and repeated several times.

Time passed. Too twitchy to sit properly on one of the chairs, I rested on the floor with my back propped against the wall. Valya was positioned on one of the plastic chairs opposite the only door, eyes closed yet twitching underneath her eyelids. She was on the verge of drifting off to sleep, but kept snapping herself awake.

Suddenly the droids came to life.

"Triple zero-five-two-six active," chanted one of the droids in a monotone, strangely like the woman at the observatory checkpoint. Its eyepiece shone and a web of neon-blue lines lit up along its body, the air underneath it wavering.

"Triple zero-five-seven-three active," the other replied in an identical tone.

Both swivelled ninety degrees to face us. "You are to follow us to floor three, room four," stated the first.

Five-two-six opened the door and a wave of cool air swept in. There was no one waiting outside. Five-seven-three knocked against the back of Valya's chair to force her to hop off, reclaiming it for the stack in the corner.

"Please follow." Five-two-six raised its armpiece, which had a smooth stump where there would normally be a hand. It appeared to be an upgraded version of the battle droid R-two-three-zero-six from Earth.

We walked single file, five-two-six in front, then me, then Valya, with five-seven-three in the rear. The corridor itself was narrow and high, about one-and-a-half shoulder lengths wide by twice a man tall. We followed the droid until it led us to a lift. There was no indication of floor numbers inside. The lift lurched downwards and my stomach catapulted. We came to a stop and the doors slid back into the wall.

We followed the droids out into a highly unusual office with a horseshoe-adorned archway in the middle. On the far wall, there was a portrait of a Latino stunner, smiling sadly at us. To the left of it, another portrait showed a boy, about eight or nine, with similar features to the woman. They seemed familiar. Then I remembered — they'd been the ones on the news a few months ago, when Valya and I first met socially, and at that point just missing persons. It'd be a safe assumption that it was our interrogator's family after what his sister told us. So the room was kind of a memorial.

Our former interrogator emerged, the arrogant bastard, from behind the plants on the side of the room. He approached and bowed slightly to Valya, ignoring me entirely. That suited me just fine.

"I hope you aren't too worse for wear after your incarceration. I trust you have been given food and water?"

Valya replied that we hadn't.

"I see. Well, that can be remedied after this meeting. Please remind me. This is a difficult time for Springhaven. We've been under attack now for such a prolonged period that we adopted a habit of acting first and asking questions later and I'm sorry you've been caught up in it. It was a misunderstanding on our part and we wholeheartedly apologise for the error." He addressed this part to Valya alone. "I understand the situation with your father only too well. It hit a raw nerve because a significant number of our population disappeared and as we are so few in number, each disappearance is felt by the whole community. I feel for your plight, truly."

He touched his hand to his heart. It seemed insincere. I didn't trust this man at all. Valya should be careful.

"Please allow me to introduce myself properly. My name is Alvise Ferrara and I'm one of the three elected protectors of Springhaven. Our setup here is slightly different to Mayton and Winsford which have just one president, in Springhaven we have three elected presidents, and any one of our proposed actions must receive a majority agreement from our permanent council of twelve otherwise they are disregarded. My duty is to oversee the running of the settlement, from sewage disposal to Shade defences. But before this, I was a developer at our droid assembly plant. I was born and raised here, the eldest of five and never lived in any other settlement."

Examining him in the light, he couldn't have been more than forty. His face was wedge-shaped and there was a coin-sized mole on the side of his forehead. He had a small mask covering part of his forehead, as well. On our first meeting, the mask had covered half his face, so he must be healing quickly. The trim frame, smart clothes, and well-manicured hands suggested a life spent primarily indoors. If the tragedy with his family was discounted, he's led an easy life. His smile seemed false and didn't reach his eyes, but I watched it melt into a genuine one as he looked past us. Shoes clacked behind us to signal his sister's arrival.

"And please let me officially introduce you to my lovely sister, Seraphina."

She walked between us and stopped close beside her brother, putting an arm around his waist.

He continued. "She's coordinating our strategies and informed me of your offered service to our cause. We're certainly interested."

Why the sudden change of heart, you tricky fucker? Do you want to use us for cannon fodder instead of your companions?

"The assistance of two Master Hunters is not something to discard lightly." He turned to the droids. "Five-two-six and five-seven-three please bring us some chairs, the new plush crimson ones, if they are not otherwise occupied."

The droids darted off to do his bidding, returning after a few moments with four leather seats. Alvise ordered them to bring refreshments and they zoomed off again.

"Five-seven-three, please remove the gag," he said, turning to me for the first time. "But, if we hear any more crass talk from you, it'll be going back on in an instant. Understood? Am I making myself clear?"

Valya elbowed me slightly. I frowned at her, and then nodded at him. The droid released the gag and sucked the material inside the lower section of its arm, out of sight.

"I spoke to the council about your offer and they have some reservations. Is there anything I could present them with to accept your assistance? I have to convince them of your trustworthiness before their vote within the hour because there's an attack scheduled tonight and, personally, I would like your involvement. We need to be quick."

The group leaned back as the droids brought vibrantly coloured drinks over. I picked mine up. It was fruity, though unfortunately without a hint of liquor.

Valya glanced sidelong at me. I wasn't going to say anything. I didn't trust them. It was better if we didn't go along. She spoke up.

"I've been thinking about a solution to this, and I have a proposal. As you know, Butcher and I are qualified Master Hunters, veterans in the hunting fields. Our weapon training is second to none, it's not arrogance, it's just not possible to reach this level without this ability. But Sophie, on the other hand, is just a trainee. And my proposal is that she can be kept here as a guarantee of our help, while Butcher and I join you and your associates and when we return from the mission, you can let all three of us go. Would this assuage the council's concerns?"

Seraphina was nodding as she listened to Valya. Alvise pursed his lips, his face unreadable. When she'd finished, they excused themselves and walked to the far side of the room beside the lift.

The responsibility for Sophie's welfare fell entirely with Valya, and she'd essentially bargained her as collateral. I wasn't sure how willing the girl would be to remain a hostage. Valya was more cunning than I'd given her credit for, not as soft-hearted as I'd thought. On the bright side, this was the fastest way of getting our weapons back.

After a few minutes, the pair returned and sat down. Alvise leaned forward and took Valya's hand. He held it there for a moment, squeezed, and let go. He tried to repeat the same action with me, but I turned my wrist so he had to shake it properly. I gave him a hard grip, and it was satisfying to hear him whimper audibly and shake his fingers once I let go: a small victory.

"Thank you for the offer. I'll raise your suggestion during the meeting and I'm confident the council will accept it. We have some of our own Hunters here as well and they are aware of your skill. However, this is still *our* expedition and you are in *our* settlement, so I'll be giving the commands. This is non-negotiable." Out of the corner of my eye, I noticed Valya glare at this, her brow crinkled and her mouth twisted in annoyance momentarily. She hated it when someone else was in control.

"The droid will come to collect you for the mission briefing tonight," he said, looking from me to Valya, his golden eyes shining. "Until then, we will have our chefs cook you a meal and also you are free to use the shower rooms. I'm sure you both desire a wash. Seraphina, please show them the way."

24

Landmine

*A*fter the meal finished, Valya went off with Seraphina to collect our masks, while I waited a short time in the dining hall for a droid to escort me to the briefing.

When we entered the auditorium, I saw it had the same layout as a lecture hall, though this one was much grander. A plush royal blue carpet with diamond patterns covered most of the floor, apart from the stage, which had gleaming, varnished wooden panelling. Row upon row of the cushioned pews was already populated by all sorts of individuals: young families, the elderly, rowdy teenagers, businessmen, armed soldiers, mechanics wearing greasy overalls, and more. Springhaven is small; this might well be every citizen. There were only a handful of spaces left. And already, some people stood near the back.

I paused at the top of the steps and scanned the room for a glimpse of Valya and spotted her platinum Mohawk sticking up about four rows from the front. *How did she get here before me?* She faced forward, and I noticed she'd a painful looking purple bruise at the base of her skull. There was a gap beside her, enough for a person and a half. *Ahh, she's saving me a space...* The droid prodded me in the back to make me move.

I descended the steps and squeezed my way through and took the free seat. The droid came to a stop on my other side.

"I forgot the popcorn," I murmured in Valya's ear as I sat down.

She smiled.

"It doesn't matter. I've got something better." In her lap, instead of our masks, she'd a couple of Springhavian ones. "Seraphina gave them to me. Apparently, they offer more protection than anything on sale in

Mayton. Here." She passed me the larger one. "Feel how light they are and they're much easier to breathe through. You'd think they'd be less effective. But they're much more resilient and Shade proof, with a lifetime guarantee. The pinhole eyepiece effect is just for aesthetics and you can see perfectly fine when you wear it. Inside each mask," she flipped hers over, "across the forehead, is a strip of minervium cognitively programmed to our DNA and we can manage the masks with our minds, rather than verbal or manual commands."

The lights overhead dimmed. The crowd quietened as a tall figure emerged in the disc of light on the stage. Alvise. An image spread across the wall behind him showing an aerial view of the facility we'd tried to infiltrate a few days before.

"Firstly, I'd like to thank you all for coming to this meeting at such short notice, and appreciate you've taken time out of your busy schedules to address a most important matter, the kidnappings. After several probing missions to determine the location of this facility and finding out what it contains, tonight we will act. Tonight, it will end. Months of effort culminated in this mission, which we have named Vermillion Spring Viper.

"The aim is to rescue of all our missing people. We will take no further hostages. Any non-Springhavian we encounter shall be treated without mercy, as they've certainly shown us none."

The audience clapped.

"Our strategy is clear. There will be task forces assigned to attack the facility, each with a specific skill set required for the task. We will take three vehicles, labelled one, two and three for ease of reference." The images above him switched to three lists headed with one, two and three and underneath these columns were names of those involved. "Behind me you can see the thirty individuals assigned to the vehicles and they are split into six teams of five. The six teams are listed as Alpha through Zeta and they are to be adhered to at all times. There is one qualified medic per group. We'll also bring twenty battle droids to be implemented in the first assault."

The image behind him reverted to the first image, then panned out and focused on the three perimeter fences and it then switched to showing one of the vehicles and panned in on cylindrical devices attached to the sides. "We fitted anti-defence cylinders onto the sides of the vehicles to neutralise these fences. This will also deactivate our droids, but once through, the ADCs will automatically shut down. The droids will engage the enemy, while Team Gamma attaches explosives to the side of the base at, where we believe, is the weakest point. Everyone else will remain a safe distance from the blast zone and wait for the signal. When you hear the word 'gravity', you need to drop immediately. The explosion itself is set to go downwards, the force arrested at four metres to neutralise any enemy soldiers or droids on the first level.

"Our previous reconnaissance missions have never reached further than the first sublevel, so anything below that is an unknown element and we do not want to risk injuring the captives. Intelligence informs us the first sublevel consists of a circular corridor without apparent doors, lifts or escalators to other levels. However, our experts believe the force of the explosion will create an entrance to the lower levels. From there, we will locate our missing people and carry out the rescue. Now, does anyone have any questions?"

Someone shouted somewhere to my left. "Do we have sufficient weapons?"

"Yes, there's plenty. That was one of our first considerations. Our supply has been bolstered by our new companions," the speaker replied. He looked down at Valya and me.

Another person stood up to speak. "Can we confirm enemy numbers?"

"It's estimated there are between twenty to fifty guards on the first sublevel. The force of the explosion should remove any enemy — human or droid — on that first sublevel."

"Should we take more armed droids?" a woman piped up from near the front.

"This is a search-and-rescue mission. We aim to get in, get our people, and get out. More droids require additional vehicles and additional people to man them, along with increasing our chances of getting noticed before we reach the area."

Another person raised his hand and the speaker pointed at him. "Is this worth the danger? Won't ShadeCo lose interest in us eventually and leave us alone?"

Alvise fired back venomously. "It's been happening for years and years! They won't leave us alone. They won't lose interest. Why do you think we're organising this mission? Why do you think we resorted to violence if the peaceful courses of action hadn't already failed? We are not violent people! They drove us to this! Do you want more innocent citizens to be killed? Have goodness knows what done to them?"

He leapt off the stage to the walkway and approached the heckler in the second row. "Don't be so naïve. These kidnappings have been happening for years and will continue unless we show that we won't stand idly by. No one should experience what I went through. No one, you hear me, no one!"

The questioner raised his hands defensively, apologising. Alvise backed away, returning to the stage and smoothing his jacket and hair.

"Be quiet!" a small girl shouted.

Her mum pulled her back onto her lap, but the damage was done. It started a tidal wave of noise. The crowd sounded as if they could easily turn into a mob. People began to chant, "Down with ShadeCo!" The pews shook.

All the while, Alvise stood silent in the centre of the stage, hands clasped behind his back, legs shoulder-width apart. He tilted his head towards the ceiling, ignoring the crowd, waiting. The sound finally ebbed into a low, angry buzz.

He began again as if nothing had happened. "Would all of the named individuals please head for room fourteen on the fifth floor for further briefing? You've been assigned clearance." Then he added, "This meeting is adjourned. Please leave in an orderly fashion."

We waited for the crowds to thin and then ascended the steps. In one of the last pews, I spotted Sophie sitting next to a large woman with her arm around her and there was a droid on either side of them. Valya stopped suddenly and edged her way along the pew in front of them. I waited on the stairs for Valya to say her piece. She connected her MID to mine so the conversation appeared as a transcript on my forearm.

Valya stared down the other woman until she shuffled away. Then she said to Sophie, "Who's she?"

"My gaoler. She's watched me today. Before that it was a set of droids."

"Did the Springhavians question you?"

"Not much. I saw the speaker and his sister once and that was it. They didn't visit me again. Don't worry, I didn't say anything."

"Good. Thank you, Sophie. Well, if you haven't figured it out already, these people despise ShadeCo and your uncle in particular. In fact, the speaker hates him most of all. There's not enough time for specifics. They probably already found out the link between you both. But all the same, I'd keep shtum as much as possible."

The girl visibly gulped and started to fiddle with her hands.

"Tonight you'll be on your own. Butcher and I are participating in their mission. They didn't feel that you'd be up to it. That's just how it is." Valya glared again at the other woman, who'd begun to turn around and swivelled back again to face the other way. "Here. For protection purposes, though hopefully it shouldn't come to that." She grasped the girl's hand and shook it. I noticed there was something in her palm, perhaps a flick-knife. The girl enclosed it in her hand and quickly stored up her sleeve.

Valya stood up and turned to go. "One last thing. Don't try to escape. It won't pan out well for any of us if you do."

Then she turned on her heel and marched towards me. We left the auditorium together.

25

Longrider

Seraphina's and Alvise's organisational skills impressed me. We departed Springhaven precisely as scheduled, not a second before or after. Everyone on mission was well-versed in the details and could probably recite the briefing backwards if required.

They had assigned Butcher and me to Team Beta in vehicle three along with Team Epsilon. Outwardly, the vehicles were replicas of Butcher's tank, easily accommodating the ten of us. Inside, the layout was different. A metal grill divided the space. Two team members were up front driving while the rest waited in the back on seated rows, facing each other. Two droids were fastened on the back doors, set to activate once the vehicle arrived at the base.

Not long now.

I felt nervous, my right leg jittered and my foot tapped the metal floor of its own accord. It took an effort of will and pressure on my knee to calm it down. Out of the corner of my eye, I observed Butcher turning over his antique gun in his hands, shaking his head and swearing softly to himself. When our weapons were returned, he discovered the plasma shell was loose, its clip probably bent during the original assault. He would only know the full extent of the damage when he fired it. I knew the gun was temperamental and thought the fact he opted to bring Springhavian weapons along too, including an axe and set of knives, was telling.

The driver called back to us through the gap in the partition. "We're getting close, ten minutes, tops. Put your masks on everyone."

As the vehicle started to slow and the engine eased into a low purr, there was frantic chatter from the front. The person nearest the partition asked what was wrong.

"We initiated ADCs but the fences aren't down," the driver replied. Our teammates immediately became apprehensive. Someone suggested we turn back. Another suggested that we get out and fire at the fence.

"Wait, vehicle one just rammed the fence and broke down a section. It's out of action, so we'll have to charge the next fence. Everyone buckle up."

Henny, Team Beta's medic, sat next to me. She was ashen with worry and bit the side of her nail nervously. Clearly, she only came along because of her medical expertise and I felt sorry for her.

Suddenly, we were moving again. The driver took us in several sharp loops to build up speed, accelerated forward, and rammed against the barrier. The vehicle bounced and I was lifted out of my seat although the belt kept me from going too far. As we landed, everyone thudded into their seats and then scrambled back into a more upright position.

The navigator confirmed we had taken down the fence and our vehicle was in good condition. We would try the third and final barrier.

We circled around again. The engine revved loudly. We rushed forwards.

I braced for impact and clutched tightly to the sides of the seat.

This time, the shock was greater, and our vehicle was rebuffed and bumped back. It was still. After unclipping my seatbelt, I went over to the divider and looked through the slit. A section of the fence was damaged with a considerable dent about a metre from the base. One side of the panel had separated from its supporting pole entirely.

Our tank was in bad shape. Vapour poured out of either side of the vehicle's bonnet and the engine made struggling, groaning noises. The driver and navigator frantically clicked switches and issued commands, but to no avail. We would walk from here.

Through the window, I watched the remaining vehicles drive past us, edging ours aside to get closer to the facility.

Our two droids failed to activate. A couple of members of Team Epsilon unlatched them and opened their chest cavities to perform some alterations.

I turned away and checked my equipment. The shield belt was active. My knives were in the lining of my boot with the handles protruding slightly, guns were in my hip and shoulder holsters. Butcher confirmed that he was ready, too.

Once everyone had their masks on, the back doors swung open and a cool waft of air rushed in, rustling my hair. The members of Team Epsilon abandoned the droids and filed out to join the others outside. An orb of light whizzed past us and the pulse smashed into the ground in a pale turquoise burst several metres away. It went up the length of the fence and dispersed at the top of the pole with a crackle.

"We need to get the droids outside. I think the ADCs are affecting their circuitry even though they didn't disable the fences," Butcher said. He pushed the rifle strap further up his shoulder.

He knelt down and examined the droids' internals, rewired them and made adjustments.

Johnny, another member of Team Beta, helped Butcher carry the droids out of the five-metre range of the ADCs.

When were far enough away, they lay the droids down. There was a charging hum then the droids reanimated. They darted upwards and hovered about a metre from the ground, their eyepieces shining with emotionless lethality. Butcher told Emily, another teammate, to instruct the droids to avoid the five-metre perimeter around all the vehicles. She entered a command onto her MID and they shot off toward the base to engage the enemy droids, who in a defensive manoeuvre, moved to the interior tier just outside the main building and were shooting through the fences at us. Without the green half-moons on their torsos, they were difficult to distinguish between ours and the enemy's.

We were very exposed. We sprinted toward vehicle two for cover. My heart thrummed loudly in my ears and I was conscious of every step, every movement, and everyone around me. I shot off rounds from my handgun for cover from the enemy droids as I ran.

An enemy droid stopped in our path and was torn apart by a pulse from Butcher's rifle. The weapon still worked, though he immediately complained it wasn't as powerful as it had been.

Another pulse whizzed over our heads and we all involuntarily cringed.

"Onwards!" Butcher shouted.

We continued our sprint to the last vehicle. It was surprisingly far.

Are the explosives laid yet? Scanning side to side, looking for the bomb squad, I thought about the numbers on the Team Gamma's masks: seventy-six, seventy-eight, ninety, one hundred and four and one hundred and five. Reactively, my eyepiece pinpointed their position with several yellow circles. The first four people were closing on the facility, whilst number one hundred and five was down and unmoving.

It was droid-heavy here. Pulses fired thick and fast. We finally arrived at vehicle two, our team members engaged with the enemy to our right, and sheltered behind it. Butcher swung his rifle strap over his head and shoulder and told me to help him undo the ADC. He rammed the stock of his borrowed handgun against the catch at the top of the ADC, whereas I worked on freeing the other end of the cylindrical tube. The other three team members covered us as we did so. *I wondered what he intended to do with it.*

After much persuasion, we freed it from its bonds. The ADC was heavier than it looked and we realized we needed three people to carry it. Butcher, Johnny and Emily held it between them while Henny and I fired at the enemy droids. As we neared the main assault near the entrance to the base, our shots became more frantic. A number of the enemy droids hovered towards us and the volume of shots intensified.

"Butcher, care to explain what we're doing?"

"We're bringing it closer to the base — near that concentration of droids. They'll all fall down and we can easily disable the enemy ones. Then we pick it up and move on. Then ours will come back to life."

"Okay."

A pulse entered the range of my belt and my shield deflected it. I fired at another shot hurtling towards our group. The two blasts connected and exploded in mid-air.

When the ADC came into range of the closest couple of enemy droids, they simply dropped. I indicated to the others to lower the cylinder and they placed it carefully on the ground. I knelt, aimed at the nearest enemy droid, and fired. It blew apart and debris whizzed past me. Johnny stood to my left, shooting sporadically as a deterrent.

Butcher disposed of the two droids like a hired assassin. One shot to the head, two to the body. Henny cried out in alarm as another pulse came perilously close. It was dangerous to keep still for long.

"Done!" Butcher shouted over the noise.

The others picked up the ADC again and we carried on as before until we reached another set of battling droids, both ours and the enemy's. Both sets fell down mid-fight, and Butcher disabled them while we protected him.

Three more enemy units down.

We took a few paces forward.

"Gravity!" Alvise's voice screamed in our ears.

My eyepiece went scarlet. We were within the blast zone. The others let go of the ADC and we darted back until the lenses cleared, indicating it was safe to drop.

I heard Butcher shouting, "Down, down, down!" I closed my eyes and waited for the impact.

The bomb went off and shook the ground violently, juddering like an earthquake. While on the ground, I wondered how they could be sure they controlled the explosion. *Who knows how much damage this could inflict? It might go even deeper than the first subterranean level.*

The fence collapsed in several places. A beam of light shot into the air as the explosion descended deeper underground and, for a moment, it was daytime. Machine parts hurled overhead, along with parts of vehicle two. A wheel rolled and bumped against a fallen pole.

I opened my eyes and turned my head to check that Butcher was okay. His hands were knitted over the back of his head, facing the ground. He was breathing deeply as if napping. I nudged him in the ribs. He faced me and said, "What are you thinking about?" in a high, imitative female voice.

"Stop messing around," I said, nudging him again. *Unbelievable! I think he's actually enjoying this!* "We need to get moving. You're a strange one, Butcher. Did you get hit on the head?"

"Not yet, there's still time, though," he commented wryly as he rolled back on his haunches.

"Don't tempt fate. Come on, we can't stay here!"

Around us, other teams were already up and moving. A woman near the remnants of the building was unpacking four palm-sized silver scouting balls from a trunk. She inputted a command into her MID and the balls rose into the air, wobbling uncertainly for a moment before darting into the newly-created entrance.

Four screen images projected from the woman's MID, representing the scouts' views. One showed close-ups of several charred human remains on the first level. People caught in the impact, their torn, tan overalls still smouldering. *At least it was quick, poor fools.* Another screen displayed fallen walls, pipes exposed and warped, floors ruptured with tiles twisted and melted out of shape. Everything was in bad shape.

The rest of Team Beta crouched further back. I walked towards them. "What are you waiting for?"

"Alvise needs to give us the go-ahead before we continue," Emily informed me, clearly frustrated. "They're analysing the scouts' data to plot our course before we go in. But this is taking too long. Every second is precious. The enemy might be regrouping…"

It was eerily quiet now the gunfire had ceased. Around us, the other teams were sitting nervously. To my right, I noticed Team Gamma attempting to save a teammate, who had a sizeable hole in his stomach. His entrails were visible and the medic was attempting to hold them in, using a Mediunit to repair the skin. I felt uneasy.

Butcher caught my eye, tilting his head toward the base. "Fuck Alvise. Let's get this over with."

He swung his rifle over his shoulders and back into his hands in a calculated gesture, walking towards the entrance. I stood up and followed directly, my gun aloft and ready. A quick glance over my shoulder confirmed the rest of our team was disobeying direct orders and coming along, with several others joining them. Emily commanded our droids to precede us and absorb initial enemy attacks.

We stepped over the remaining wall of the upper level, now barely at knee height, and looked down into the blast's aftermath. The explosion distorted the staircase to the lower level and the steps had either melded together or disappeared entirely. There was a spot of light at the bottom, but it was too dark beyond to discern anything from our vantage point.

Johnny untied a cord of rope from around his waist and retrieved a foot-long metal spike, stabbing it into the ground. There was a crunch as it secured itself to the concrete and he tied the rope to it with an elaborate knot. He threw the free end into the hole, the rope rapidly unravelling until it hit the ground below.

I offered to go first. I slid down the rope and into the heart of the base.

26

Landmine

$\mathcal{B}$etween the explosion, the shouting, the gunfire and all the crumbling debris, it had certainly been a dramatic entrance. As far as I was aware, search-and-rescue missions were meant to be quiet and lightning-fast, in and out before the enemy even knows you're there. Not sure what this would be counted as apart from noisy.

Once Valya disappeared into the darkness, I quickly followed, sliding one-handed down the rope. I kept my forefinger on the trigger of my rifle in case there were enemies below. My feet hit the concrete and I stepped over some rubble and out of the landing area.

Down here, the lights blinked intermittently and struggled to remain on. Along the dim corridor, the walls were crumbling, and blackened in both directions. The floor revealed twisted and broken piping, which let out a steady stream of vapour. Droids were melted to the floor and inoperative.

Scorched bodies lay nearby. Their lips pulled back in grimaces, noses melted away, and their waxy skin a bloodied mess. I stooped to examine a few. None had a passing resemblance to Valya's father. Fortunately, the masks filtered out the smell. I'd smelt the awful, acrid odour of burnt flesh before and was in no rush to experience it again. There were no enemies indicated on the mask's radar, so I lowered my rifle, pointing it toward the floor.

To my right, the ground had given way and formed a steep ramp into the corridor of the level below us. Valya stooped over the edge and looked down.

"Whoa!" Valya cried, backing away as the tile she'd been standing on fell away and cartwheeled down. "This isn't looking good... I don't know how structurally sound this building is now. We have to be careful. What are the others doing?"

I looked back at the rope, gently swaying from side to side. Several silhouetted heads appeared at the top of the hole. Emily called down almost as an apology. "We can't go against our direct orders." In my earpiece, Alvise's voice had increased in volume to hysteria, screaming at us to wait for the data analysis. I muted the device.

There was a torch function in the tops of our masks, which lit up the area two metres directly ahead. The second level was entirely in darkness and the deep shadows flickered away from the torchlight, making me nervous. I reached for my Shade-effective gun and stared at a potential monster. These masks were Shade-proof, but not able to identify them. Shades are opportunists and the spilt blood above might've attracted one to the area.

Valya placed a hand on my forearm and shifted my aim. "It's not a Shade. That weird movement is coming from the light above." Even so, I reached up and checked that my mask was secure.

"I'll go first. Watch my back," she said.

Valya tentatively placed one boot on the rubble. It held. A scout whizzed past her and disappeared into the lower level. She moved her other foot. A dislodged pipe clanged down the ramp and rattled as it came to a stop. We waited for a few moments. Nothing else fell, so she continued, starting off slow and speeding up as she made her way down the slope. Shortly, she was safely on the second level. She called up for me to descend too.

After a few large leaping steps, sliding a metre and hopping over a section of ceiling, I joined her. I asked if she were okay.

"Fine so far. You?"

"Not bad. I'm not getting any enemy readings down here."

Above us, the others were finally slipping down the rope and entering the facility.

"About bloody time! If Alvise insists on controlling everything this is going to take ages. Who knows how long it'll take him to approve them coming down here? We should carry on without them," I said.

But we quickly heard an 'ouch' behind us as Henny slid down the rubble on her butt, followed closely by the other members of Team Beta.

Another team followed, either Epsilon or Delta. The remaining teams hovered uncertainly above, unsure whether to carry on without Alvise's approval or not.

"Has he given *you* the go-ahead?" Valya asked the rest of Team Beta.

"No," Johnny replied matter-of-factly. "We're tired of waiting. He's not here and anything that he wants to order is delayed by the damned analysts."

I nodded my approval.

The scout returned, feeding footage to our masks to show us three possible directions to take. We could go left down the unobstructed corridor, turn right and shuffle past the rubble to the other side of the corridor, or descend into the jagged hole in the floor to the third level. The other team chose the first option along with the rest of Team Beta, preferring to trust their fellow Springhavians than us outsiders, and the scout attached itself to them. *Who knew where the rest of the scouts were?* Me and Valya decided on the right-hand path.

Overhead, the remaining teams began to clamber down the ramp to our level. Perhaps they'd try the third route. We didn't hang around to find out.

* * *

An hour later and two further floors down, we found ourselves in a doughnut-shaped corridor that looped around without an obvious entrance to the lower storey. The hallway was untouched by the explosion and the ground was surer than the higher levels. The tiles here looked damp and thoroughly cleaned, as if washed in the last half hour or so. Full-length mirrors lined the walls in frequent intervals giving the impression the corridor was wider than it actually was. I shot at one of the panels before I realised it was a mirror and it had shattered loudly, fragments of glass scattered over the tiles.

On our fourth lap, Valya burst out, "There has to be another way! There just has to! Why would there be a corridor without a single door? Or rooms? Or anything? Why is it so difficult to find him!" She punched the wall a few times in frustration. A blood smear remained on the pale surface. "Is there anything that we might have missed? Anything at all?"

I didn't know what to say. If there were an entrance on this floor, then it was hidden. Valya approached one of the inner walls and rapped her knuckles against it at chest level. She crouched and tapped all the way down to the skirting.

"It doesn't sound hollow to me," she said.

There would be one way to know for sure. I told her to stand back and fired off three shots.

"Butcher, are you crazy! This place is already unstable without doing something like that—" she began, but her voice rapidly drained of anger when she noticed the fist-sized hole that appeared at the epicentre of the blast area. She approached and looked through the gap. She gasped and darted back. "As much as it's dangerous, we need to get in there. Fire again, please."

I shot again. The hole widened and was big enough to get a head through. Valya asked me to hold fire. She approached the wall and tested it, deciding it was stable enough for another blast.

I fired a third time. The hole was now easily large enough to climb through. We cautiously approached the gap. My mask's radar showed no enemy combatants but fourteen unarmed individuals.

I poked my head through.

Immediately, I noticed a considerable drop to the floor below, it was too high to drop down. I looked up and noticed that the room was huge, the size of a ShadeCo generator room. The hole must be in the middle of the wall. A short way above my head was a platform attached to the wall. It was near enough to grab onto if I reached up. At the far end of the platform was a staircase leading down to the main section of the room. Being taller and able to reach further, I offered to go first. I climbed into the hole in the wall and reached up easily to the metal platform and lifted myself up and over the side in a fluid movement. Once secure, I grabbed onto one of the supporting poles and reached down to offer Valya a hand. She stretched up to take hold and deftly leapt up, grabbed the same pole I was holding with her free hand, and heaved herself over the platform edge as well.

Straightening up, I checked my weaponry as Valya turned and stared over the railing. She gasped in horror.

27

Landmine

I followed Valya's gaze and met a gruesome sight.

Several metres below lay a motionless naked woman on one of four steel slabs, gagged and pinned down by leather straps across her neck, arms, thighs, and under her huge, pregnant belly. Even from this height, I saw her nipples oozed a brown substance that trickled over her chest. There was a tray of medical equipment resting on a nearby table, and an operating unit extended over her stomach, its monitors blank.

It appeared someone had been operating and suddenly stopped. We'd made enough noise to alert them of our presence.

As I scanned my sights across a room the size of a ShadeCo industrial generator room, I noticed there were actually two staircases either end of the gangway, one leading down to the main area and one ascending to a set of double doors as the only observable entrance and exit.

Beside me, Valya warily directed her aim downward, jumping at every little noise.

She shook her head in bewilderment. "What are they doing to that woman? Alvise was right… this is inhumane… disgusting…"

I glanced again at the woman, now writhing against her bonds. "Let's hope your dad isn't here then."

Valya didn't say anything, but I noticed her hand squeeze the gun's grip tightly.

We cautiously descended the gangway, our footsteps echoing around the high ceiling.

When we reached the lower floor, Valya immediately veered towards the woman on the table and attended to her. I noticed the air quivering around the bottom of the stairs. There was a canister jutting out underneath the bottom step, quietly emitting gas. It didn't have a label. I twisted the dial to stop the flow anyway.

Valya called out, urgency in her voice.

I raced over.

We stood either side of the pregnant woman like surgeons. Valya had undone the woman's restraints and the gag, but she wasn't moving now. I knew basic first aid, flesh wounds, burns, that sort of thing, but I'd no idea what to do with her. My eyes were drawn to the huge, bulging belly with its cross-web of purple pulsing veins running along it. There couldn't just be one baby in there, or even twins, or triplets. It looked unnaturally massive.

There was a dark crescent just over her prominent bellybutton, moving around. I felt strangely drawn to it and wondered what would happen if I touched the skin. I reached out and the dark spot revolved around her bellybutton, away from my finger.

"Butcher!" Valya slapped my hand away. "That's inappropriate."

"Of course it fucking is, but have you ever seen anything like it?"

"No! But my first compulsion isn't to touch the unknown. It might be dangerous. Leave it alone. She's been through enough…"

The shadow suddenly formed a small handprint on the skin. Then it was gone. "Did you see that!"

Valya didn't respond and lay two fingers on the woman's neck to check her pulse. "She's alive. But her breathing is laboured. Help me get her off the slab and into the recovery position."

I lifted her under her shoulders and Valya took her legs. We placed her down gently on her side, bending her left leg into a support position and tilting her head back. Valya took out some camouflage webbing from her backpack and covered her so only the woman's head was visible.

"That'll have to do for now."

We began to explore the rest of the room. Valya checked inside and around the four metal slabs and I strode over to the tall cupboards on the wall.

They were mostly unlocked. I kept my handgun ready and nudged one open with my free hand. At first, I couldn't believe what I was seeing. I was sickened. Rows and rows of cylinders. They contained pale bodies of mutilated foetuses, babies and young toddlers, the oldest two or three, at most. Distorted skulls. Strangely lengthened limbs. A disembodied stomach with obvious stitches here. Conjoined creatures there.

They were humanoid but not human. The containers were ordered by alphabet and number, A-one through to L-three.

I stepped back, horrified.

Two foetuses were hooked to life support, the cables pumping something into their containers. There were tiny masks over their faces, connected to a single tube. Their backs were arched and limbs too long for their torso.

What the fuck is this?

Bile found its way up to the back of my throat. I gulped it back and steadied myself. It was one of the most hideous things I'd ever seen. Was the pregnant woman's baby destined for a space in the collection? Whoever was responsible for this was one sick fuck.

I heard retching sounds close by. Valya had seen. She placed one palm against the wall nearby, bending forward to vomit.

I filmed the bodies for a couple of minutes with my MID, focusing on each for a few moments before moving to the next. I fed the live footage back to the analysts in Springhaven. Let them examine that! This was valid evidence to justify the attack as far as I was concerned.

Valya couldn't bear to look. I finished recording and gently closed the cupboard doors.

"Butcher, there's a hatch over there adjacent to the slab on the far left. I think that's where the other people are. We need to check. Father might be in there. Please be ready with the gun while I lift up the hatch." I put the handgun back in the holster and reached for my rifle. She caught my wrist. "Not the rifle. It's too powerful."

"I'm not getting killed for this," I told her, shrugging off her grip and swinging the rifle into my hands.

"Fine," she said, though her voice stated otherwise. "But don't hurt Father."

She crept over, flipped the latch, and darted back. We both trained our guns on the entrance and waited for the hatch to flip up.

Nothing happened. Valya stepped towards the door and flung it open. The door landed heavily on the concrete.

My view was partially obstructed, but I could see a narrow metal staircase that went beneath an arch leading to a mesh walkway. Pillars on either side of the hatch door hid the rest. Valya started to descend, taking slow, deliberate steps. I looked down the sights of my rifle and moved closer.

Halfway down, she placed her gun back in the shoulder holster and waved me down. She took the remaining steps two at a time and disappeared from view. I followed.

Rows of cages lined the corridors, three metres wide and the same depth. Instead of bars, these cells were glass tanks and lacked visible doors or methods of entry. Two floor strips of green lights grimly lit the room and gave an eerie radiance to the distorted bodies inside the tanks, casting the shadows upwards. All the captives were pressed up against their cage fronts. Their mouths opened and closed like fish out of water gasping for breath and they pummelled their fists on the thick glass. Their captors probably did not have time to bring them along so were disposing of the evidence instead. I couldn't hear a sound, but it was easy to lip read what they were saying: "Help."

"They're suffocating!" I cried and took aim with my rifle. Valya leapt at me and grabbed the barrel, forcing it away. I glared at her.

"The blast might hurt the people inside! Do you still have your axe?"

I took the backpack from my shoulder and unfastened the axe hanging from a loop on the side. With the axe in her hands and using as much force as she could muster, Valya spun round and slammed it into the nearest tank. The impact made a resounding *bong*, startling the young woman inside into leaping back in fright. The girl eyed her warily, holding her stomach protectively.

Valya repeated the action. On the second impact, the axe's blade stuck fast into the glass. She shook the handle, rocking it back and forth until the weapon freed.

Her third and fourth swings were more successful. On the third hit, a splinter sliced diagonally across the surface. She adjusted her grip. The axe arced above her head again, landing in the centre of the weakened spot. A web of fractures spread over the glass. It was close to breaking.

I left her to it and walked down the gangway. *The axe is too slow. Most of them will die before she frees them.*

I turned to the cage on my left. The prisoner was a boy wearing a loincloth, about five or six years old. He stared up at me fearfully with his face and hands against the glass. I placed the rifle back over my shoulder, took out the handgun and let off three rounds into the top of the cage. The front shattered and little pieces of glass surged across my legs, feet, and the surrounding floor. The boy fell forwards onto the walkway and landed on the shards. I stooped down and picked him up. Some of the larger bits stuck out of his skin but he didn't cry out. He was too weak.

There was a steady fizz in the air that was unmistakable. Gas. These people didn't have gas masks like we did.

Carefully, I carried him to the level above and lay him on the ground. Already I noticed that his breathing was easier and colour was returning to his cheeks.

As I descended again, I noticed the axe discarded on the walkway. Valya had taken my lead and started firing rounds into the cages. As each one broke open, she moved quickly to the next, leaving the prisoners slumped across the walkway behind her. The steady whoosh of gas came from every opened cage. I began moving the freed people upstairs.

I carried them to the upper level and placed them beside the boy to keep him company. One person was already dead. I hid him on the other side of the slab, away from the others. They were frightened enough and we didn't need any of them panicking.

With each second that passed, gas pumped out of the vents in the opened cages and into the room above. Those still trapped inside were slumped against the glass and their taps were gentle, if they were moving at all.

"We need to free them quicker," called Valya, jogging to the end of the corridor. We had released one row of people so far. She aimed at the last cage on the right. "I'll start at the far end, you start near the stairs and we'll meet in the middle. When they're all free, we can shift them upstairs."

I let off a few rounds into the nearest cage and the person inside spilled out. I moved to the next. Then the next. And the next.

Several broken tanks later and my elbow bumped against Valya's shoulder. We stood side by side. The victims were free now, but whether they were alive or not wasn't clear. I picked up a woman almost as tall as me, and so large she might've been heavily pregnant, obese, or both. She was covered in red stretch marks as if she'd gained a lot of weight quickly, and recently. I cradled her in my arms instead of throwing her over my shoulder. My muscles tensed under her bulk. Why was she so well-fed when most of the others were underweight? *Was this all some experiment?*

The glass crunched underfoot, impossible to avoid. I stepped over a couple of women immobile on the floor. Valya carried a tiny girl whose skin was rapidly changing from pink to blue, gooseflesh across her bare skin. She was choking and her eyes were bulging from their sockets. I let her go ahead of me up the steps.

A familiar voice called out a hello, echoing around the room above. It was Johnny.

"Hello!" Valya yelled back, bounding up the stairs.

I reached the top, and lowered the woman as soon as I could without blocking the staircase. My muscles ached in protest.

Johnny's masked head looked down from our hole above.

"We need to get these people out of here! Hurry! We think some of them are critically hurt," Valya explained, lowering the limp child to the ground. "There's a poisonous gas being pumped out downstairs."

The head disappeared.

I didn't wait for him, returning to the cage level. There was a woman on her feet using the walls for support. She was having trouble and didn't complain when I lifted her up. The front of her long tunic was torn from the shards of glass.

Valya appeared at the foot of the stairs and picked up a man who must've weighed more than she did. She draped him over her shoulder and painstakingly plodded up the stairs.

"Do you want help?"

"No, I'm fine," she said through gritted teeth, determinedly climbing the stairs one steady step at a time.

Above us footfalls clattered on the gangway. It was the rest of Team Beta along with a few others who must've split from the main group and doubled back. They descended and made a beeline for us. Henny rushed to the pregnant woman and felt for her pulse, pulling a back-up gas mask over her mouth and whispering encouragement to her.

"Wait!"

They looked at me.

"There're more people downstairs. We need to get them up here before we get them all out."

Spinning around, I led the way down. When we reached the cage level, a few Team Beta members rushed past to the two remaining people lying on the ground. I waited by the banister. They carried the pair between them.

I saw Valya at the top of the stairs through a haze. It highlighted the gas problem. It wouldn't be long before dangerous amounts drifted up to where we were.

Once everyone was out, I shut and locked the hatch to stem the flow.

A few of them looked over at the cabinets. Valya explained what was in them. Horror showed on their faces and three of them strode over to the containers to see for themselves. We left them to it.

The medic approached me, leading the first naked pregnant woman by the hand, and requested that I, specifically, carry her up. I placed an arm around the woman's neck, bent down and put another underneath her knees, and lifted her. She was incredibly light and her stomach contributed most of the weight. Her cheekbones were prominent and arms and legs stick-thin. Henny squeezed her hand a final time and let go. The woman reached for her and asked her to stay in a weak voice.

"I need to help the others, but I'll be close. You're safe now," Henny reassured her, smoothing the woman's hair from her eyes. "Don't worry."

Overhead, one of the Springhavians was working on the doors. Suddenly, the double doors blew apart and toppled over the side of the suspended gangway, narrowly missing Johnny and Valya. A cloud of dust seeped in and sprayed us with flecks of debris.

I wove towards the staircase and to the newly opened exit.

28

Longrider

The little girl gazed up at me with grey, haunted eyes. I could only imagine what happened to her to make her stare so.

None of the Springhavians recognised her. Was she born here? She was unable to speak, communicating in a series of grunts and pointed gestures, fearful whenever any male approached her. I carried her to save her the distress.

We carefully ascended the metal stairs and traversed the gangway leading to the exit. We walked through the double doors into a contaminated equipment room containing trays of soiled utensils. I shielded the girl's eyes as we passed through into the decontamination chamber. Above and below us were large vents to sterilize the area.

In the corridor on the other side, we were out of range of the noxious gas. The hostages rested against the wall. I lay the girl near the pregnant woman and she snuggled up to her. Protectively, the woman draped an arm over her shoulders.

Most captives needed proper medical attention but it was too late for one of them. Father was not among them, luckily. In spite of Henny's best efforts, the equipment available was limited and not really suitable for treating gas inhalation. It was probably more for dissection or whatever else they performed here. I shuddered.

I counted the hostages. Twelve were rescued already. Two more remained downstairs and Butcher and Johnny had not returned yet.

Emily glanced around uneasily, upset by the captives' condition. She took off her mask and wiped the sheen from her face with the back of her hand, unsticking her high-necked top from her heavy breasts and flapping the garment to cool down. She announced, "I sent a message to Springhaven to bring more medical supplies. They confirmed the vehicles have been deployed." She addressed me. "The footage Michael transmitted made quite a stir, as it should have, and Alvise is coming with reinforcements."

Somewhere deeper in the facility we heard rapid bursts of muffled gunfire and small explosives. The corridor rolled under our feet and the mirrors swung on their hooks on the walls. I braced myself, one hand on the wall, knees slightly bent. Some of the Springhavians dropped and protected the captives with their bodies. A thin stream of smoke slowly crawled along the ceiling towards the experiment chamber.

We waited in silence for the reverberations to subside.

One of the Springhavians said, "These people need to be taken to the surface. It's not safe here."

The ground heaved again. The building groaned. Those standing stumbled sideways.

Butcher scratched the back of his neck and looked at me. He was letting me decide the next course of action.

"Butcher and I will help get the hostages up to the surface, but after that, we're returning to the facility to search further. There're probably more hostages here and I want to be certain we've found everyone." *Like my father.*

"The captives here are hardly a fifth of the people we've lost and only three of them are from Springhaven," said Emily, resting her hands on her hips. "I haven't found my daughter yet. There have to be more people here. They can't be the only ones."

The others made noises of agreement. Henny, who had been bracing a woman's broken ankle, stood up and directed us to those who should be taken first. There were fourteen hostages and eight of us. Considering the damaged state of the paths to the upper level, it would require two trips to move them all. Even Butcher would be unable to carry more than one person at a time over unstable ground.

242

***

About an hour later, all the captives were by the entrance. Three of the others, including Henny, remained behind to attend to the injured. The recovery vehicles were on their way with further supplies.

We accessed the instructions delivered to our MIDs by Alvise. The scouts' feedback had been compiled into a guide that indicated how to infiltrate the deeper levels.

We could see on the map that a number of teams were engaged in combat in a parking lot located on the seventh subterranean level. This had most likely been the source of the earlier gunfire.

We picked out a route down via the third-floor breach and made our way back there. There was a wire rope secured to a hook in the concrete ceiling by the earlier team. Butcher leaned forward and tugged on it, and the rope held. I went first. Abseiling downward, we emerged through the roof of the fourth. A short way off there was another hook and rope attached to the ceiling, which led further down, bypassing the fifth and went directly into the penultimate sixth level.

The sixth level was similar to the layers above, with one exception. Along the left wall, several metres from the landing point, there was an alcove sheltering a spiral staircase. On the wall opposite, there was an out-of-service lift with a folded, slated door. The mouth gaped widely and a few cords were unrestrained, swinging gently in the breeze of the shaft. Moving closer to the edge, I glanced down and saw the car crashed at the bottom several metres down.

Butcher rapped his knuckles against the balustrade three times to get my attention and waved me over. All of our companions had gone already. With his rifle secured against his shoulder, he stepped onto the top of the spiral staircase and went after them. I took out both handguns and followed.

Each step increased the volume of the gunfire below. My view was restricted to Butcher's back and the walls that enclosed us. After roughly thirty seconds, the walls ended and we emerged into the seventh level. My mask's eyepieces indicated enemy targets below us. Up here, we were extremely exposed. The staircase quivered slightly; the nearest wall or ledge was about four metres away.

Lying diagonally along the ground underneath us, mangled and scorched, was the rest of the staircase, severed from the top half and there was now a drop of several feet to the floor. Others had already dropped and dark footprints stained the paving.

From the high vantage point, I observed the cavernous parking lot easily capable of holding a hundred vehicles, but was currently nearly empty. The few cars there, leaked fuel, which we needed to avoid igniting at all costs. Bodies lay twisted on the tarmac, some in guards' uniforms, others in lab jackets or civilian clothing, and a few Springhavian troops. Each gunshot reverberated around the enormous space.

Below and slightly to our right, Teams Delta and Gamma huddled behind a rapidly crumbling pillar, the enemy's pulses steadily destroying more concrete with every hit. A handful of humans and about four or five enemy droids remained. I suspected that we were now fighting the rear guard covering their companions' escape. At seven levels down, I was concerned about the number of destroyed pillars. We needed to move quickly.

I saw a flash of white as someone popped their head over a bonnet and shot a pulse at us. It whizzed past to hit the wall behind us. Butcher took a few steps down the staircase ahead of me and returned fire. The man ducked down again.

I covered Butcher while he jumped from the staircase. Once he landed safely and was out of the way, I scuttled to the last rung. Glancing once more at the drop, I decided that there was nothing for it and jumped too.

29

Landmine

Hitting the ground, I forward rolled to ease the impact and immediately leapt to my feet. Keeping low, I zigzagged towards an armoured car a few metres away to my left. Behind me, pulses and bullets darted past, hitting the space I'd filled moments before. I ducked behind the vehicle, which was quickly hit with a short barrage of blasts, pushing the vehicle back.

Valya fired from above.

The enemy hid.

In the silence, I peeked over the car's roof and observed my surroundings for a minute. Between me and the enemy was a no man's land. Fifty metres of empty parking spaces, broken vehicles, and droids. The remaining Springhavians weren't daring to get any closer, and neither were the enemy guards.

The ground rumbled and, overhead, the building groaned deeply. I glanced up. The trembling intensity increased sharply, throwing me to my knees. A moan emitted from a nearby cracked pillar, which grew deafening as the two sections separated. People hiding behind it stumbled over each other to get away and the smoke swallowed them.

My whole body shook with the vibrations. I scrambled further from it, watching as the top section crashed to the ground, along with a sizable chunk of the ceiling and furniture from the level above. It smashed down in a cloud of dust and debris, which shot out in every direction.

I tried to shield myself, but suddenly a blinding pain seared through the right side of my face like nothing I'd ever experienced. I gasped and fell.

I reached up with shaking fingers. A metal shard jutted out of my mask, embedded in my right eye and cheek. When I touched it, another stiletto of pain raged through me. With all my control, I held back the cry.

The shard was wedged tight.

Who ever heard of a half-blind Hunter? Damn, it fucking hurts!

I tried to tug at it. The shaft of pain tore across my face, neck and chest and my vision blurred. I found myself laughing from the intense agony.

The dust cloud started to thin. From the rubble, I noticed a hand protruding like a twisted pipe, the owner buried somewhere beneath. A woman lay on her back, unmoving. A few people slowly emerged from the remains, their clothes, masks, and hair coated in grime. I'd counted ten earlier. Now it was four.

Valya darted towards me, a gun in each hand. Then she was sheltering beside me. She put her weapons down and clasped my head in both hands.

"Butcher... oh, that's bad!" she muttered under her breath. "There's a lot of blood..." She retrieved a Medex Cube from the pouch at her waist and instructed it to provide pain relief. A beam shot out the side and scanned me once. Immediately the ache lifted. She put the cube back and tied the pouch shut.

"Try not to touch it! We'll get you back to Mayton and have you treated in the hospital because the Medex Cube can't handle something as sophisticated as eye surgery. On the plus side, I don't think you've hit an artery. Head wounds tend to bleed a lot."

It feels if my skin is pulsing, but it's numb and painless. I reached to touch the shrapnel and Valya grabbed my hand and firmly lowered it.

Her voice sounded far away. "Have you checked the scout feed?" I shook my head. "The scouts' feedback showed multiple exits and the nearest is down here, a long tunnel into the desert. We've got to go down to go up, basically. Alvise already issued vehicles and droids to barricade every exit so the remaining enemy can't escape."

Another section of ceiling about the size of my torso fell down, exposing part of a metal girder above. The plaster shattered into small fragments.

"The building's falling apart around us. Let's go," I said.

I got up, head spinning. I felt her arm grip me tightly around the waist.

It was clear up ahead, but our progress was slow. We watched the ceiling more than anything else because the other sections had started to fall too. It was just a matter of time before it would collapse entirely, bringing the rest of the building with it. We'd be buried before we knew what was happening.

I tripped over something and fell against Valya. She shoved me upright with her usual rebuff of 'clumsy sod' and steadied me. Over my shoulder, I noticed the something was a severed arm, exposed, bloody, and alone. *Did it just twitch?* I nearly fell again, close to delirious.

We were close to the tunnel when Valya gave a startled cry and let go of my waist. She ran off, veering to the right.

30

Longrider

*I*nitially, I looked past him. He was garbed in a fluorescent-yellow technician jacket and propped up against a car door, one leg folded unnaturally underneath him, while the other extended in front and bent slightly at the knee. A nasty wound pulsed at his neck. A spike of metal protruded out of it, his right hand wrapped around it, weakly stemming the flow of blood. It trickled over his long, gloved fingers. The other hand rested on his lap, palm up almost meditatively. His grey eyes were open and glazed, and though he smiled wanly toward me, I was unsure if it was recognition.

My chest felt tight.

No, no, no!

I let go of Butcher's waist and sprinted to my father.

When I reached the car, I fell to my knees and I applied pressure to the wound with both hands, being careful to avoid the metal shard. His breathing was quick and shallow, his skin clammy and cold. Urgently, I turned around and implored, "Find a medic! Get help, *please*, Butcher!" Already, my sleeves and hands were scarlet. It was staining his clothes and pooling underneath him.

How can there be so much blood in one body?

Butcher's baritone voice bellowed for a medic. For several minutes it was the sole sound.

One of the remaining Springhavians called back from the far side of the lot. "There are no medics here. Henny's upstairs and the others are gone. We should do the same."

Sparing a glance, I checked over my shoulder. He was right. Most

Springhavians had fled to the tunnel and made their way to the desert while the remainder were in no state to attend to anything except their own wounds. Emitting a final resounding groan, the top section of the spiral staircase dropped to the floor, spraying more debris. It landed with a deafening clang, misting us all with a thin layer of dust.

"Valya." Father's voice came out as a gurgled croak. He took several deep breaths, his Adam's apple moving exaggeratedly. "My darling girl…"

"Please save your strength. We're going to find you a medic and then we can get out of here. Hold on." I took out the Medex Cube, it told me that hospital treatment was required immediately and gave him painkillers in the meantime. Frustrated, I threw it away.

"No time… so proud of you. Always… Muffin…" Again the half-smile.

"Please don't. Not yet." It sounded like a goodbye. Tears coursed down my cheeks and dripped from my chin. My vision wavered. "We'll get you a medic and they'll tend to your wounds, and then you'll be okay."

With his fading strength, he clasped my shoulder and pulled me closer. "I'm sorry I left so suddenly. The project was in danger… had to protect it… we're so close… to be able to leave the house without a mask. To smell fresh air… without the filter of a mask." His face twitched and he gritted his teeth.

"I don't understand."

"We just needed a few more days… Red… is a genius. Set up project… set up this facility… the medical advances we made. So many… First human immune…" The last few words were barely audible.

What was he saying? In confusion and dismay, my grip loosened. The blood seeped quickly through my fingers. I adjusted my grip and pressed down again.

"Father, please save your strength, we can talk about this later. We need to get out of here. The building is collapsing. Just hold on."

Butcher shuffle-jogged past us, broad shoulders pumping. He made his way quickly through the car slalom and disappeared down the short ramp to the parking lot's second section.

Is he abandoning us?

31

Landmine

The dark spots in my vision started to join. Briefly, I rested my forehead against a car bonnet until the dizziness passed, careful of the shard in my eye. When the waves subsided, I stood upright and continued at a slower pace. Coordination was tough. I walked drunkenly. At the far end of the room, I spotted several people disappearing into the darkness of an unlit tunnel. My mask identified it as the exit and the individuals as Springhavian.

"Oi! Wait a minute! We need help. Any of you medics?" I yelled after them and sped up. They either didn't hear or, more likely, ignored me. Damn. I would have too if I were them. I shouted after them again anyway.

Light-headed, I had to stop, or otherwise fall over. When the nausea waned, the others had gone. Honestly, we needed to get out as well, we'd wasted too much time here already.

I returned to Valya.

She was kneeling in the same position, her hands firmly pressed over her father's wound. The man's eyes looked fixed ahead, unblinking and his chest lay still. His mouth naturally curved upwards, faintly smiling, and a pitch-like liquid dripped from the corners and trickled down his chin. The ooze looked uncomfortably similar to a densified Shade. I don't think Valya noticed any of this because she continued pleading for help.

"Butcher! Please!"

Instead of resuming the search, I walked over and crouched beside her, put my hand on her shoulder, and squeezed. She bowed her head and her shoulders sloped. Her bloodied hands dropped to her lap.

"Michael…" she whispered, looking up at me.

I drew her closer and she buried her face in my shoulder. We didn't say anything. Shallow sobs racked her body and grew more intense as she tried to hold them back. Her body shook as much as the ground.

Our search was over.

After a moment, I clasped her arms and pulled her away. "Valya," I said quietly. "Let's get out of here?" Grief would have to wait.

She nodded sadly, but stayed where she was. Moving between them, I quickly stripped him of the noticeable jacket because it was hard to say how Springhavians would react if they saw us carrying a facility worker. I hoisted him over my left shoulder and straightened up, breathing heavily through the dizziness.

I nudged her with my boot. "Come on, get up! We can't go back the way we've come because the staircase has gone and the building is about to collapse on us. Let's get to the tunnel."

Taking her gun out of her holster, she clicked it on. She jumped to her feet.

"Right," she said, wiping her free hand under her mask and over her eyes, all practicality now. "Downwards and onwards then. I'll lead. You follow."

* * *

The emergency lights in the tunnel weren't working, so our masks' torches automatically switched on. The road's incline increased with every step. And there were obstacles scattered throughout the tunnel, bits of wall, ceiling, broken vehicles, and black energy spills. Feeling dizzy and disoriented, I mis-stepped more than a few times. Valya plodded close by, her hand rested on the small of my back for support. Her father's lifeless bulk lay heavy on my shoulders, harder to carry when the wooziness set in, but I agreed to find him and bring him back, and I'd be damned if I wasn't going to return him to Mayton.

The painkiller had worn off. My face throbbed and my mask was glued to my skin. I just wanted to pull out the bloody shrapnel.

"Not much further. Maybe another five hundred metres," Valya said encouragingly.

We hiked towards the glow in the distance. It got paler with every passing minute. I felt the breeze, finally. We pressed on.

251

What felt like hours later, we emerged from a hole in the desert floor beside a heap of artificially stacked boulders. Around us, starlight and the light from the crescent moons dimly outlined the flat plain and sinewy trees, and framed the mountains.

The remains of the base were nowhere in sight. A few exhausted Springhavians were propped against a couple of tanks nearby. A short way off, a larger crowd of about thirty people stood in a rough circle, warming themselves by several small fires. Another group had their guns trained on a small group of apparent hostages, keeping them in check.

Alvise and Seraphina stood outside the main group. Their voices were loud, arguing about something. Their faces were contorted, spit flying. I sighed. *Why aren't they wearing masks? Fucking idiots.*

I lowered Valya's father and sat him against the nearest vehicle.

As we approached, Seraphina slapped her brother. He growled angrily. His hands jerked out and grabbed hold of her arms, pulling her closer to shout directly in her face.

"I wonder what's going on," Valya mused without much enthusiasm as we passed by the arguing couple and walked towards the main group. "Can we get a medic here? My friend's injured."

When no one reacted, she barged through the formation and I followed closely. In the centre knelt five people in grubby and torn uniforms, another two in decontamination suits, and a last figure in a blood-splattered designer suit. Cable ties pinned their arms behind their backs. Again the Hunter in me flinched at the lack of goggles or anything to cover their faces.

"Red?" Valya exclaimed, stepping towards him. The people either side eyed us suspiciously. The man kneeling in the suit glanced up at Valya. She started to go to him, but the Springhavians shoved us back and reclosed the circle, muttering threats.

"Huh?" I asked.

Impatiently, she told me, "That's James Martin, ShadeCo's CEO. The man in the suit." Then more to herself than me, "Alvise was right... he's involved." She raked her fingers through her hair.

I shook my head. "Never met the guy."

She grew angry. She ducked down and went in between the Springhavians. "Red! What are you doing here?" she shouted accusatorily.

He opened his mouth to answer, but before he could, one of Alvise's troops hit him on the head with the stock of his gun. He ordered Red to shut up and Valya and me to keep out of it.

Valya was having none of it. She turned on her heels and strode towards Alvise and Seraphina. I smelt trouble. I reached for my rifle and staggered in the same direction, the barrel of my weapon pointing downwards. For now.

"What's going on?" she demanded through gritted teeth, her voice tight in annoyance. In my opinion, anger was better than tears. "And for crying out loud, why aren't you wearing masks? Are you stupid or insane — or both? Shades are harder to identify at night and we're prime targets with all this blood around. You'll be easy pickings."

The two of them got the message and put their masks back on sheepishly, then turned to us to continue their argument.

"Seraphina is adamant the hostages should have a fair trial in Maytonian law courts! As if they deserve such treatment! That we should show them mercy." He rounded on her. "When they should be hung. Or, even more fitting, they should be left out here for the Shades and then they can feast on each other." He sounded vengeful, on the verge of madness.

Seraphina argued back, slapping her fist into her palm. "They deserve to be tried like other criminals—"

"They'll buy their freedom and I won't get justice. They killed my family! And they've been experimenting on us for years! I don't care about *fairness*."

"Alvise, I am not sympathising with them. I am not. But I don't want to act rashly when we've put so much time, energy and resources into getting our people back and trying to be left alone so that no one else would be killed. I don't want to do something we might later regret or that may bring repercussions on Springhaven. I love you, Alvise, and I know how important it is, but it wouldn't be wise to simply murder them. Please don't descend to their level. We should hand them over to their authorities and let them deal with them in accordance with the laws."

"And let them get away with their experiments? After the losses we

253

suffered? They have to die, sister. There is no other way." His hand went to the handle of his gun. Seraphina grabbed his arm to prevent him from taking his gun from his holster. Valya shoved him back and I pointed my rifle at him. I sensed others taking aim at my back, though I didn't give them the satisfaction of looking around.

"We want answers, for fuck's sake! It's impossible to wrestle answers from corpses," Valya spat at him.

"If you kill them, their families will want justice too, and we will never be safe. For instance, that man alone," Seraphina said, pointing towards Red, "is considered a pillar of Mayton society and it will not do to kill him like this. There will be so many repercussions that all our efforts will be wasted."

"My wife and son were captured," he cried. "And that man was responsible. I petitioned to him, pleaded, begged. He covered it up and had them killed because of it."

Behind us, Red scoffed and denied it. One of Alvise's troops punched him, hard. He fell back and was silent again.

Seraphina placed her hand gently on her brother's chest. "The whole point of the raid was to end this, not to start a war. There is more than enough evidence from just the footage Michael sent us. Trust me, they will be suitably punished. If we take them to the authorities, we can wash our hands of this and move on with our lives. No aftermath, no cycle of violence. That is what they would have wanted for you, I know it. They would not want you filled with fury, unable to carry on." She reached out and took his arm.

"I don't know if I can."

He looked down at the gun in his hand uncertainly, his head and heart battling it out. After some time, he made up his mind. He exhaled deeply, apparently calm, and strode into the middle of the circle. The group stepped back. He approached Red and ordered him to get up.

Two men pulled Red up under his arms and he slouched between them. The side of his face was swollen, one eye closed. His whiskers were stained as red as his nickname from a slash on his cheek.

In a sudden motion, Alvise hit him across the jaw.

Red toppled sideways. The people flanking him straightened him back up.

"You're scum," he said with controlled hate, turning his gaze to each hostage in turn. "And you will be destroyed like the parasites you are." His fists clenched and unclenched.

A cheer sounded from the crowd. Seraphina darted into the circle, yelling, "No!"

He raised his gun.

It hung there.

Slowly, he aimed it at all of the captives in turn. Suddenly, he pulled the trigger, shooting the person beside Red in the stomach. People near me jumped at the noise. The hostage slumped forward into the dirt with a thud. Seraphina rushed towards her brother and pushed his arm down. He growled and shook her off and shoved her away. She fell, badly.

"Alvise! Don't!"

He moved closer to Red and rested the barrel against his forehead. The others did nothing except watch their leader.

Red never glanced away. He kept steady eye contact with Alvise. I was impressed, despite myself and despite what the man was mixed up in. He wasn't a coward.

I watched Alvise. He tightened his finger on the trigger. A hairbreadth more... I felt a spasm of nervous laughter grip my chest, and I pushed it down.

Seconds passed.

Minutes passed.

Alvise's aim lowered. He turned away.

"Seraphina, do what you wish," he stated dejectedly. The circle parted again to let him through.

He carried on walking into the desert. We watched him go until he was swallowed by the night.

32

Longrider

The cell was bright, almost unbearably so. A panel of thick glass in the centre of the room severed it in two and the table appeared to pass through it, though it was actually comprised of a couple of smaller neatly aligned desks and chairs. A grill in the centre of the glass allowed communication with the prisoner. MIDs are removed when a criminal is incarcerated.

In the reflection of the glass, I watched the guard waiting by the door behind me. His arms were folded and he stared at me warily as if I were the criminal and a dangerous one at that. My fingers drummed on the table's surface.

Where is he?

I felt a combustible mixture of anxiety and anger. The last few months had been bleak, the worst of my life. The trials of Red and several key ShadeCo staff, including his PA, were at the forefront of my mind all the time. Since the revelation, I had avoided ShadeCo and handed over my ore quota via an intermediary, though it is still business as usual from what I am told. The colonies still need energy and it was established that the project was a separate venture.

Was Red capable of such heartlessness? Were so many others? Did my father assist willingly or out of some skewed loyalty?

Despite evidence to the contrary, I could not reconcile the caring, dedicated professionals to the heartless individuals who sanctioned, and frequently assisted in, fatal experiments on people of all ages.

Red's trial took place at Mayton High Courts of Justice and, though I was a witness and should technically have left after both the prosecution and the defence interrogated me, I was permitted to remain in the courtroom. A key aspect of Red's trial was Michael's footage of artificially grown foetuses nourished by an 'Active-Shade' compound. Until then I did not know there was another state for a Shade, it was either live, in the adaptable and lethal mist form, or dead once condensed. These foetuses were planted inside host women to grow further and often neither mother nor child survived. And the things they did to the men were enough to turn your insides, inserting 'Active-Shade' into their testes supposedly to increase virility.

When Red stood up to testify, he did not discuss the experiments in detail, focusing only on the intended aim of the project — to cure Umbras, by any means necessary. Considering the visuals and witness testimonies, it was unsurprising that the jury rapidly found him guilty on all charges with evidence so overwhelming no defence lawyers on the planet could swing the verdict.

A week had elapsed since the trial ended and his sentence is due to be carried out tomorrow. In a last-ditch attempt, I understood his lawyers were working on an appeal to postpone the inevitable but I doubted they would succeed.

During the trial and the period since, I had tried to visit Red but he refused to see anyone apart from his immediate family. Then suddenly, in a last-minute change of heart, he agreed to speak to me today.

I have to find out what truly happened from him even if it sickens me to be here.

From the other side of the glass, the door slowly creaked open. One armed guard emerged and positioned himself by the entrance. Red shuffled in followed by another guard, who prodded him with the barrel of his weapon and forced him to sit when he reached the chair. The second guard told me we had thirty minutes.

Red looked awful, swollen faced, both eyes black and his slacks spotted with flecks of dried blood. No more than he deserved.

"Red," I stated in greeting.

"Valya, it's good to see you."

I sat forward and spat at the glass. If it had not been there, it would have hit his cheek. The froth slowly slid down.

"You know why I'm here, Red, I don't care to hear more of your bullshit. I heard enough of *that* at the trial."

Wearily, he said, "I suppose the media portrays me as a murderer."

"They're not portraying you — you *are* a murderer."

He sighed wearily. "Your view has changed so quickly. After all I have done for you and your family over the years, I didn't think you would turn against me so quickly. As a Hunter I hoped you would see the value in this project."

"I saw the output of this project, Red, and that's enough for anyone to hate you regardless of personal history. How could you sanction this? How the hell did this even happen?"

"Hard to say when we got involved. I suppose it started when an innovative team of medical research scientists approached me and my team to provide Shades to test on. They wanted to cure Umbras and I would've been mad to say no. I've witnessed first-hand the horrors of Umbras and, as a Hunter, was naturally drawn to their cause. Don't shake your head at me, Valya. I wasn't alone in feeling this way. We all were, including your father. For a few years my team and I supplied them with Shade infected animals alongside our usual ShadeCo hunting duties, slipping them a few here and there, without anyone being the wiser. But after a while, a number of executives were given tipoffs and they noticed the dip in our ore production rates, despite still being the best in the company. I was brought in front of the board and they confronted me but I was open at that point, and told them about the project, even tried to get their support.

"Unfortunately, we didn't see eye to eye. They considered our ideas too extreme. And in fact, a few actively tried to stop us assisting the researchers. And we learnt to be more cautious about approaching anyone else unless we knew they'd come on board."

"Who tried to stop you?"

"I suppose it doesn't matter if you know now…" He reeled off some names, "Richard Butcher, Vanna Khat, Jasna Milojevic." He murmured into the grill. The first two were former ShadeCo CEOs, the third CFO.

I gulped. "You got rid of them?

"Yes."

"My father was involved in that too?"

"Yes."

258

"Of his own free will?" I asked, desperately hoping his answer would be in the negative.

He paused briefly then nodded.

Stunned, I slowly sat back in my chair. If my legs would have worked at that point, I would have left, but I was too shocked to move.

I thought I had reached the lowest point but it keeps dropping. His team killed Michael's family.

Something smothered in the back of my memory resurfaced. Until now, I had buried it deep and tried to forget what I overheard. Yet, it was one of those rare memories from early childhood with distinct details. At the time, I must've been about seven or eight. I eavesdropped on Red and my father in the middle of a heated row and the details only now made sense to me with the additional context.

***

Little Valya tiptoed along the corridor and edged towards the main room. There was one creaking floorboard about five paces before the wall ended, she was accustomed to ninja stealth manoeuvres when her mother lapsed into one of her moods and well aware of its position. She hopped over it, crouched and waited and listened a moment before continuing. Another couple of paces, she lowered herself down and sat cross-legged on the carpet. At this proximity, their words were discernible.

"I never signed up for this, Red! You're a fucking liar!" This shocked her. Valya had never heard her father this angry, even when she misbehaved. "You said the volunteers would only have drug trials and now you're telling me they're infected too? How the hell does that happen? How does a Shade infect someone unless they've inhaled it? There's no fucking pill I've heard of that does that!"

Red's voice snapped. "It's exactly what I explained to you. Human testing had to be done at some point." He attempted to moderate his temper and was failing, badly. "Nothing was hidden from any of us. The scientists explained each stage of the project, what was to be done, and this was the next step. A few lives lost to the majority's benefit is acceptable and besides, their families won't care much anyway when they understand what we're trying to do. Medicines for other diseases progress to human testing and finding a cure for Umbras isn't any different."

"I'd love to be there when you tell them that. I really would. They've got every ground to sue us or worse, we'll be thrown in jail for who knows how long. It won't go away, Red, no matter how much money you throw at it and anyone with a modicum of sense would see that. Butcher was right, we should've left it well alone, and now we have his blood on our hands along with the others. How can I face my family knowing what I'm part of? What sort of role model am I to my daughter when—"

Red interjected massively. "Harald! It. Is. Too. Late! It's too late to extract yourself and you're not going to mess it up either. I won't allow it!" The threat was obvious. His voice sounded feral, more of a growl. "Am I making myself clear? The only way is to carry on forward with the experimentation, like we agreed, until we create a vaccine."

Harald groaned. "But, why do we have to test this on humans? Why not carry on using rodents or chickens, or maybe something else?

"Because human testing is necessary."

"Your lack of empathy disturbs me. It really does. It doesn't matter if they're from Springhaven. They're still people at the end of the day, they've human rights and we're violating those by infecting them with Umbras."

"Please spare me the preaching, Harald, and the sudden appearance of your conscience. You know why we need human testing. Our DNA reacts differently to the Shade menace than animals. To find a cure we need to have human trials to confirm it definitely works. You were there at the briefing too, so I'm not telling you anything new. Animals react differently, it would be a waste of resources to continue on that course…"

At that point, the girl decided to sneak back to her bedroom. If they found her here, she knew she would be in deep trouble.

***

For a moment, I must have zoned out, lost in the memory. Red said something I did not quite catch and I asked him to repeat it.

"We gave researchers Shade-infected animals as often as we could spare them. Then, on one occasion, they paid us a considerable sum to acquire two dozen in one hunt but it was more than our group could manage, so we enlisted the help of four other sympathetic teams. Sibilius Mount was and still is a nest of Shades, and if we succeeded, it would've been the biggest hunt on record. We brought along twenty animals and a couple of human bait — serial killers who'd have died in jail anyway, so if you really think about it, we saved the taxpayers money..."

I made a disgusted noise but let him continue.

"As you know, the rest is history. The hunt was a tragedy. We lost Yossi and Balendin that day, not to mention casualties from the other teams."

I never heard what actually happened before. Father kept silent on the subject and the other survivors only related the bare facts.

"These Shades didn't react as they normally do. They attacked in a coordinated way, not individually, but as a group in unison. None of us were prepared for that. They chose a victim, swamped him, pinned him down until one of the Shade group infected him and then moved to the next. I've never seen them act in such a sentient way, before or since. It was extraordinary. We killed a fair number of Shades but they overwhelmed us and in the end, we ran. Of the thirty-five who went out on the hunt that day only twelve returned." He paused, eyebrows knitted.

"It gave us greater incentive to find a cure for Umbras. We redoubled our efforts and pooled our resources to construct a facility in the wastelands. Initially we'd enough test subjects to utilise but they rapidly ran out — after all, there's not an endless supply of violent criminals without family connections. Or people willing to be exposed to Umbras for that matter."

"When did Springhaven come into it?"

"Springhaven was rumoured to have many inhabitants infected by Umbras with only minor symptoms. We watched the settlement for some time before picking a few choice subjects and they responded well to our tests, better than any from Mayton or Winsford. And from that moment onwards, they became our main source of test subjects, apart from criminals..."

"How many people knew about the project?"

"More than you think. Many denied knowledge of the project. I suppose it was to be expected. Politicians, police, ShadeCo staff, medical staff, and building contractors — it's amazing who'll be persuaded to help you if the price is right. And at least I coordinated the project with a noble aim in mind."

I scoffed. "Sure, noble aim with horrible means to achieve it."

"Valya, you need to look at the bigger picture. Umbras has already claimed hundreds of lives and will continue to do so. If a handful of people are sacrificed to the greater good—"

"It wasn't a handful. The records show over a hundred."

"Then it is forgivable. Human testing's a necessity. There's only so much you can do with animals, once you discovered how they respond to the treatment, you need to find out if it applies to humans too. Humans are more difficult to vaccinate."

"But even after all those years, you still didn't manage to make anyone immune."

"Are you certain of that?"

"What? Don't try to confuse me. None of the hostages were. We had doctors check them over after we rescued them from the facility."

"True. *That* group were not." He chuckled to himself. "However, we've one test subject that responded to the vaccine. Superbly so. It didn't kill her or damage her brain or musculature in any way and I am pleased to say that she's the first person immune from Umbras."

"Which one?"

"You think we'd leave our most valuable asset in the facility for the Springhavians to find and snatch away? She was the first to go. I went there personally to assure her safe passage."

"Where is she?"

"You won't find her. Not without me."

I ran through the list of main settlements trying to catch any of his tells, "Mayton. Winsford. Springhaven. San Cristobel." No reaction to any.

"Time's up." One of the guards strode over to Red and placed a hand on his shoulder. "Time to go, inmate."

"Wait! We haven't finished!" I shouted.

The guard my side of the divide said, "Sorry, Ms Ericksen, these are orders. Thirty minutes is all that's permitted."

I pleaded. "But he's just told me they've vaccinated someone against Umbras! Please, just give me ten more minutes."

"Sorry, Ms Ericksen, rules are rules. Condemned criminals tell you all manner of lies."

"You don't know it's a lie!"

On the other side, the guard had already escorted Red out of the room. As I watched the broad, retreating figure, I felt infuriated. My questions were not answered. In fact, they multiplied.

Could it be true? Is there someone immune or is he trying to confuse me? There is no way of knowing unless I can somehow speak to him again and probe him for more information.

My thoughts switched to Michael. If I confess the truth about his family, if he knew my father was involved, he would hate me. I knew it instinctively. And he is the only one keeping me sane right now. The only friend I have. I chewed my lip in indecision.

Intercepting Red tomorrow is the only option.

Epilogue

Longrider

As I looked at the dense crowd, I wondered how I could get to Red. It seemed like every Mayton citizen showed up to witness the sentencing, probably more. Representatives from other settlements came too and, though I had yet to spot the Springhavians, I knew they would be here. I stood with the convicts' families atop the city hall, elevated from the rest of the crowd ostensibly for protective purposes. Though my father died before he could be brought to trial, the public knew of his involvement and police advised me to stay here instead. The public were hostile towards anyone involved with the project and keen to see the sentences carried out.

Exile is the most severe punishment on Diomedia and a rare occurrence. There are only three previous cases on the planet. Yet, many felt exile too lenient and called for the introduction of capital punishment; hatred for the prisoners was intense. A line of droids ahead held the masses back, behind them stood armed police forming another barrier. The crowd wanted blood and would try for it, given half a chance. Many had lost friends and family over the years, people previously listed as missing, and their hopes were destroyed with the discovery of a large amount of human remains a mile south of the facility. They accounted for the majority of missing people. Only a relatively small number of captives were brought back and restored to their families. My Springhavian teammate, Emily, insisted her daughter was alive; the girl appeared neither with the rescued captives nor in the grave. Admittedly, Red's revelation yesterday suggested another facility somewhere holding the immune individual, so perhaps Emily was correct.

Once I left the prison, I notified the police. No doubt they interrogated Red. No doubt they encountered the silence he maintained during the trial because if he talked, surely the exile would be postponed until they had the information they needed to find the facility. His silence did not make sense. It was likely his sentence would be lightened by providing this information, so why withhold it.

The crowd whooped and a stickyfruit landed in our midst. It cracked open on the stone tiles and the cerulean seeds spilled out and seeped onto the grouting. I kicked it over the edge with disgust. Other projectiles, fruit and even chunks of meat, littered the rooftop and stunk in the heat. I checked that my mask remained secure; a Springhavian mask is so light it is easy to forget you are wearing it. Michael had modified it to efficiently track Shades like Maytonian masks.

Michael, as unreliable as ever, had not shown up yet. I checked my MID and it was very nearly midday. No messages. His tardiness irritated me.

A short way off, I noticed Sophie crying quietly with an older woman, presumably her mother. Both looked devastated and red eyed with grief. I went over to them and offered my condolences. Conversation fizzled out quickly, as there was little else to say, and I drifted back to my place by the balustrade.

In a wave, the crowd began to jeer. It started from the front and drifted backward until it reached the city hall. Preceded by two guards, four figures shuffled slowly on cuffed feet out of a building behind the droid line. Their luminescent overalls with black digits emblazoned on the chest identified them as prisoners. Several guards followed, guns trained in case of an attempt to escape. Red led the procession of prisoners, standing almost half a head taller than the others. I zoomed in on his face and saw his neutral expression as he tried to ignore the items hurled at him: animal blood, mud, water, fruit, and excrement, just to name a few. He seemed composed until an open bottle of urine smashed against his chest, spraying up and soaking his face and shirt. In disgust, he spat out the liquid that had gotten into his mouth and halted. He looked past the police and droids to find the person who'd thrown it, then crushed the bottle and threw it into the crowd. A couple of his guards thrust him forward again.

I discerned chants of 'murderers', 'scum', 'hang them up', and other variants of these curses.

As the prisoners trudged along the empty street and onto the raised platform, the crowd's roar grew again. When they took their positions behind the bundles of equipment, it was deafening. The guards stepped forward as a barrier. Suddenly the droids aimed their weapons at the crowd. Instantly, they quieted down and I observed a ripple of movement as they backed away from the platform.

We waited for the minister to arrive. She was simply coming to carry out the sentence.

After a while, we heard the rumble of Minister Irenka Gorski's swish car. The car's doors slid open and an aide rushed forward to assist her out of the vehicle. She was one of the most recognisable politicians in Mayton Hill and a prominent member of the president's cabinet, one of her closest confidents. Today, she wore her trademark pinstripe suit and passwa hat, which gave her an extra foot in height despite being tall already and sent messages to the minds of people within two hundred metres of her.

Instead of going to the podium straight away, she walked along the crowd, stopping to talk to people and shake hands. Even in this horrible situation she did not miss the opportunity to campaign.

Only once she had completed her rounds did she approach the podium. The noise of the crowd dropped to a barely audible murmur in anticipation and by the time she climbed up the podium's steps and reached the lectern, you could have heard a Shade move.

"Ladies and gentlemen," she began in a clipped and eloquent voice. "We are gathered here today to bear witness to the exile of James Reginald Martin, Jennifer Laurinda Frost, Yosef Ben Arbia and Anton Shirakov to ensure the sentence is correctly carried out according to the laws of Diomedia.

"Never in our history have we witnessed the barbarity and horror associated with their crimes. We assumed such atrocious acts were inhumanities left on Earth and we would have a fresh start on Diomedia. But four months ago, our society uncovered an evil, the very worst of human nature, down in that facility. Our sincerest thanks go to those who brought these disturbing truths to light to expose and finally end these hideous experiments that occurred over the last two decades. Like a tumour infesting our society, we will operate on it and excise it, leaving our society healthy once more."

A few people from the crowd shouted 'Hear, hear'. I distinctly heard someone nearby shriek, "Kill them!"

The minister ignored them and continued. She shifted on the pulpit towards Red, the nearest prisoner. "James Reginald Martin. I have been voted to speak on behalf of the people of Mayton. You have been judged and condemned for architecting the project, for the lives that it destroyed, and for their families that suffered too. For all of the innocents experimented on for profit, and it was profit, no matter what higher purpose you cited, we are no closer to finding a cure for Umbras."

She paused here. The last few words echoed across the square, over the heads of the people in the silent crowd.

"You are hereby stripped of your property and assets, all of which have gone to the state. All ties to your family and friends and acquaintances are severed and if they assist you, they risk bringing your sentence upon themselves as well. From this moment onwards, you are a stranger. We do not know you. You are no longer welcome within the walls of Mayton Hill, Winsford Lake, Springhaven, Mizuki, or San Cristobel. And may this be a warning to all present here today. Anyone who tries to harbour these criminals will be punished severely. You are hereby banished."

The crowd jeered. More items flew through the air before thudding on the platform and splashing against him. Again, the droids aimed their weapons at the crowd to subdue them. Another guard came forward holding a backpack and placed it at Red's feet before re-joining the line.

When she was satisfied order was restored and everyone was listening, the minister carried on. "We will allow you a small mercy, as it is inhumane to cast you out into the desert without means of protection. Placed before you is a Shade-effective gun along with ten rounds of ammunition, one gas mask, and a day's ration of food and water."

Red stooped and picked up the gas mask and secured it before he clipped the munitions belt over his shoulder. He lifted up the bag and old-fashioned Shade-hunting rifle then resumed his place in the line, holding his straight and composed bearing.

Meanwhile, Frosty was dragged forward and was addressed by the

267

minister. She openly wept. I drew my eyes back to Red. I watched him load the rifle with one of the cartridges.

"Jennifer Laurinda Frost, for the lives you have ruined beyond repair, for all of the innocents who have been tortured for profit—"

Abruptly the minister stopped speaking and leaned forward. Her mouth gaped for air, opening and closing. When she found her voice again, it was a piercing scream. We clamped our hands over our ears ineffectively because the noise was already inside our heads. People fell to their knees. Her arms flailed wildly and she frantically clutched at her face, falling backwards off the podium in her panic.

From the depths of the crowd, I distinctly heard Michael roar, "Shades! Get inside!"

Immediately, the mood of the crowd changed from anger to panic as his warning sunk in. A lot of people felt overly safe inside the city walls and neglected to wear gas masks or even respirators leaving them entirely vulnerable to the Shade menace. Belatedly, the wall guards kicked into action as a siren blared, adding to the confusion. The minister's screaming stopped. People started to run, turning into a stampede.

I darted downstairs, shoving people out of the way.

When I reached the ground floor, I fought my way out of the city hall against the people trying to get in. Outside was chaos. I pushed through the crowd towards the platform. One step forward, two steps back, three steps forward. I was like a small fish trapped in a frightened school, and heading for the shark, for the predator. They shoved me back for protection, someone even spun me around to face the way I had come. I turned around and kept going.

As I neared the droid line, the crowd eased. The droids lay crumpled on the ground, de-activated. I leapt over and ran to the platform. Fresh Shade matter was splattered across the platform steps and beside the podium. At the foot of the podium lay the distorted body of the minister. The back of her head was gone from a bullet's exit. I nudged her with my foot.

She did not move.

With great care, I crouched down and turned her over by the shoulder for a better look… *definitely dead*. I let go.

Further along the platform, Michael wrestled with a guard. Even through the tangle of limbs, I knew the guard had Umbras and already undergone the change; the unnatural, feline curve of his spine, the incredibly sharp nails and teeth gave it away. The man's mask hung ineffectually around his face and veins on his forehead pulsed with the effort to get at him. Michael had a firm grip on his neck and forced his head back, inch by inch; his muscles bulged with the strenuous effort. They were too intermingled. I could not get a clear shot.

Remembering the knife in my holster, I snatched it out and sprung forward and plunged it into the infected's eye. He let out a bloodcurdling cry, a mix of fury and fear. Feral.

He stopped resisting Michael. With another burst of strength, Michael yanked his head all the way back, snapping his neck with an audible crack. Shuffling away from the body, he rolled back and rested on his haunches, slapping his hands on his thighs. He caught his breath and fixed me with a stare with his real eye, while the artificial one seemed to look past me and into the distance.

I took the safety off of my Shade-effective gun and approached the broken body to wait.

No more than thirty seconds passed before the misty form of the Shade emerged from the guard's open mouth. Its black tendrils barely had time to reunite before I shot it with two rounds. The creature projected across Michael's torso.

"Thank you," he stated dryly, pulling at the gloopy mess on his clothes and flicking it onto the ground in disgust.

"That was for sleeping in when I told you to be here on time."

"I arrived for the important part."

"Please spare the crap. Are there any more around here?"

"No — that was the last one I identified in the area. I've neutralised the others and the minister."

"When you say area, what do you mean specifically?"

"About half a mile radius from where we stand."

"But that's not the whole city."

"She's a quick one this one," he stated sarcastically.

I punched him in the arm. "How much ammo do you have left?"

"Not much, two or three rounds. While you were faffing in the crowd I was actually working. In all seriousness though, Valya, these Shades acted strange. They worked together and moved from one victim to

269

another. It's bloody horrifying."

The hackles on my neck went up. It sounded similar to Sibilius Mount.

"Did you see which way Red went?" I demanded.

"No. Why?"

"He's the key to this."

My MID lit up. It was the wall guard. I answered and they requested that I go to assist at the north-west gate. I agreed and hung up.

As I turned to leave, I said, "Michael, there're more Shades inside Mayton and I'm obliged to attend to them. In the meantime, look for Red and the other prisoners. Please? They mustn't have gone far."

"And do what if I find them?"

"Stop them leaving the city. Shoot them in the kneecaps if you have to."

***

Once the threat on the north-west gate was neutralised and there were no further Shade alerts, I returned to the sentencing area. Already the street cleaners cleared the debris, they placed bodies in black bags and carried them away. Soon it will seem like it never happened.

I spotted Michael standing on the walls and went up to join him. I stood beside him and rested my arms on the battlements.

"Could you find them?"

"No. They hightailed it outta' here pretty fast."

"Well, they might've fled but there's one thing they didn't count on."

"What's that?"

"We're going to track them."

"And then what?"

I grinned at him and he chuckled.

He shook his head, "You're persistent, I'll give you that."

My good mood faded and was replaced by an uneasy feeling as I wondered if this was planned. If Red knew all along the Shades would launch a coordinated attack and they could escape in the ensuing chaos. Did he somehow control the Shades? I dismissed the idea. It was impossible. But then, they said it was impossible to immunise against Umbras and Red claimed that they managed it. Where is that person now?

We both turned to look beyond the walls. In the distance stood the observatory mountain, faded and hazy against the skyline, apart from the patchwork of farmed fields near the city and the orchards, the rest was flat plains with a few spindly trees and boulders. Not a human in sight. A group of gi' mont lizards traipsed towards the tree with the largest bough and a smattering of foliage. Their lows echoed across the desert, the only sound to be heard.